Death strikes down a man on the eve of his wedding to a lovely girl. The verdict is suicide, but the girl is certain it is murder—certain because of a closing door. Inspector McKee wonders, too, and soon both he and the girl have their hands full trying to catch up with an ingenious murderer who leaves a corpse-dotted trail.

Persons in the *Mystery* "Staircase 4"—

GABRIELLE CONANT,
a slim, lovely brunette, has given up her job in an advertising agency to marry Mark Middleton. She has pushed the date ahead to assure him—and herself?—that it is love rather than pity that is making her go ahead with the wedding.

MARK MIDDLETON,
wealthy, genial, worldly, has been reduced in three months from a strong man to a cripple, and for that reason has offered Gabrielle her freedom. Big, direct, generous, Mark is a man to whom right is right and wrong is wrong—nothing halfway for him.

JOHN MUIR,
long a close friend of Mark and Gabrielle, is handsome and competent. Too late to do anything about it, Gabrielle discovers that she loves John. And John comes to her on her wedding eve with a strange warning not to marry Mark.

THE ROUND MAN,
whom almost everyone becomes convinced is a vagary of Gabrielle's imagination, is said by the girl to have had secret doings with the victim shortly before the murder.

SUSAN VAN NESS,
Gabrielle's cousin, of whom she is very fond, is uncomplicated and domestic, and still in love with her husband in spite of what he has been doing to her and the children in the last five years.

TONY VAN NESS,
Susan's charming, unscrupulous, irresponsible husband, is a highly paid illustrator, but much good it does him—or his family—since he rarely fails to gamble away his checks.

TYRELL AMORY,
clever and scholarly, is another of Mark's close friends.

(Continued on next page)

Persons in the *Mystery* "Staircase 4"—

(Continued from preceding page)

ALICE AMORY,
Tyrell's small, dark, elegant wife, has ordinarily a sweet temper, but something seems to be putting a feverish edge to it.

JOANNA MIDDLETON,
Mark's sister-in-law, disapproves of Mark's marrying Gabrielle, and makes that disapproval subtly plain.

CLAIRE MIDDLETON,
Joana's tall, shy daughter, stands to inherit her Uncle Mark's fortune if he doesn't marry—and for that reason her dislike of Gabrielle is burningly violent.

BLAKE EVANS,
Claire's fiance, is easy, debonaire, and strikingly handsome. His almost feminine gentleness makes him popular with everyone.

BRENDA HOLMES,
whose name has often been linked with John Muir's, is 31, beautiful, and an opportunist. She has never married, although she is made for love and has been groomed for marriage since infancy.

PHIL BOND,
Mark's lawyer, is big, jovial, and not exactly a miracle of tact.

E. P. GLASS,
taxi driver who turns up suddenly in place of the regular driver, is a surly brute with a bullet-shaped head.

FLORENCE NELSON,
thin and badly dressed, is a possible clue to the round man.

JUDGE SILVERBRIDGE,
distinguished, well-liked, has been on the bench for 19 years, during which time no breath of rumor has touched his name.

CHRISTOPHER McKEE,
brilliant chief of the Manhattan homicide squad, is very tall, with a thin clever face, a courteous manner, and a reputation for solving extremely baffling murder cases.

AN INSPECTOR McKEE MURDER MYSTERY
••

STAIRCASE 4

By HELEN REILLY

Author of
"The Farmhouse"
"The Silver Leopard"
"The One That Got Away"

WILDSIDE PRESS

This story was published serially in
The Woman's Home Companion
under the title "Remember Every Word."

All the characters and incidents in this novel are entirely fictional.

STAIRCASE 4

List of *Exciting* Chapters—

Staircase 4

Chapter One: THE ROUND MAN

GABRIELLE CONANT SAW THE ROUND MAN for the first time
on the twenty-fifth of June. She was lunching that day
with Mark Middleton, the man she was going to marry,
in Mark's apartment on Central Park West. The round
man came to see Mark. He arrived with the sweet. It was
being placed on the table when the front doorbell rang.
To Gabrielle's surprise Mark answered the ring himself.
He said to his housekeeper, Mrs. Pendleton, who was
serving, "I'll go, Etta," and pushed back his chair.

Phil Bond, Mark's lawyer, and Phil's wife, Julie, were
there. They both protested. "Mark, must you?" "Look
here, old man, let me—" They knew Mark well.

Gabrielle knew him better. She said nothing. Three
months earlier, out of a clear sky, Mark had been stricken
with polio. It was a vicious attack. He recovered, he was
very strong, but the disease had left him with damaged
knees. The doctors told him that he was remarkably lucky
to have got off so easily and that in time, with the proper
treatments, his condition would improve. They couldn't
promise that he could play tennis or golf or ride again,
at least not for a long while. Mark had always been active
physically, was fond of sports, had been a runner-up for
the amateur golf championship in '46. The affliction was
a bitter blow.

He had offered to release Gabrielle from her engagement as soon as he was out of the woods. Gabrielle had
smiled, tapping his cheek with slim fingers. "Trying
to jilt me, are you? Very well, I'll sue for breach of

promise." She had advanced the date. They were to be married on the twenty-third of August.

That day in the dining-room, Mark said to Phil Bond, "Stay where you are, Phil, I won't be a moment," and picked up his canes.

All three of them, Phil and Julie and Gabrielle, watched him make his difficult way from the table to the door, big body twisting from side to side, one shoulder higher than the other. His limping progress was heart-rending. He opened the door and went out. As he did so Gabrielle, and Gabrielle alone from her position, caught sight of his visitor.

The living-room adjoined the dining-room. The foyer was at the far end of the living-room. The round man stood on the threshold of the foyer. Hot August sunlight striking through the west windows was full on him. He wore a gray suit and a gray soft hat and carried a brief-case under his arm. He was of middle height or slightly under and everything about him was round, his head, his face, his plump shoulders, his arms, his legs, his body, the thick-lensed glasses hiding his eyes so that he didn't appear to have any. A seal dressed in male clothing would have had the same sloping contours. The door closed then, cutting off Gabrielle's view.

Mark wasn't long, he came back in a moment or two. Gabrielle looked her interrogation but Mark said nothing informative. He picked up the thread of the argument he was having with Phil Bond about flight records when the interruption came, and she forgot about the round man for the time being.

She saw him again eight weeks later to the day.

It was on Wednesday, August the twentieth, and she and Mark were to be married on Saturday. They were to have met at the Devon for lunch at one-thirty but Gabrielle was late. A disturbing telephone call had detained her just as she was leaving home. The trouble wasn't new. Susan's husband, Tony Van Ness, a magazine illustrator, was on the rampage again.

Susan was Gabrielle's cousin and the two girls had been brought up together. There ought to be a law against men like Tony Van Ness, Gabrielle thought vindictively, driving south. It was too bad the stocks weren't still in existence—that was where Tony Van Ness ought to be made to take up permanent residence. For one thing he was an inveterate gambler and nothing would ever change him. For another he was completely undependable. All his magnetism, his good-humored gaiety and charm, couldn't wipe out what he had done to Susan and the children, taking the roof from over their heads, the food out of their mouths with his debts, not once, but again and again. When he had completed a commission and had money he spent it, or gambled it away. Then there would be another period of poverty.

Susan had said over the phone, "Tony didn't come back from New York last night with his check. He got it yesterday. No, Gabrielle darling, there's nothing you can do—except if you see him don't give him any money."

Gabrielle had no intention of giving Tony Van Ness a penny. She had already underwritten one of his major indiscretions with a considerable sum, the bulk of her backlog. Susan didn't know about it. She was independent, proud, and it would kill her to know, Gabrielle thought, as she entered the lobby of the Devon.

Mark was there, off to one side, leaning on his canes, big and wide-shouldered but too thin for his height, and with the pallor of illness still bleaching the tranquil planes of his face and making the shining green-brown eyes under straight brows seem too large for it. A little rush of tenderness went through Gabrielle at the sight of him. How brave he was—and how right she had been.

She started toward him.

Mark was facing in her direction but he wasn't look-ing at her. He was gazing fixedly past her shoulder at someone or something beyond her. Gabrielle turned, looked where Mark was looking—and saw the round man, in the same gray suit and gray hat, trotting busily through the revolving doors and across the pavement to the curb. There was a car drawn up there. The round man got into it and it slipped into streaming traffic.

Gabrielle turned back. Mark had hobbled across the lobby. His expression shocked her. He didn't often lose control. When he did he grew cold instead of hot. White and coldly staring, utterly still, his face was a death mask of itself. He was pale with fury.

The mask stirred. His lips parted. "So that was it," he said in a low voice, *"that* was it."

Oblivious of where he was, of the hotel lobby with people passing to and fro, Mark was talking to himself. "Mark!" Gabrielle laid a q ick hand on his arm. She had to speak twice before . fark heard her. He with-drew his gaze from the street slowly, looked down at her as though she were a stranger. Then his face cleared.

"Gabrielle . . . I didn't see you."

She said, "I know you didn't. Mark, what is it? What's wrong? Why were you so angry? Who is that round man?"

"Round man?" Mark was puzzled.

"The man who came to the apartment in June—the man in the gray suit who just went out."

Mark looked down at her. For a moment, rather a long moment, Gabrielle thought he was going to explain. If he was, he changed his mind. Straightening his shoul-ders, shifting a cane, he took her arm. "I'm not angry now. I'm hungry. That fellow is of no importance, none whatever. Come on, let's get something to eat."

During lunch in the big cool dining-room with the

fountain in the middle and bright birds hopping around in silver-gilt cages he was himself again, calm, cheerful, asking her whether she had had a good sleep, what she had been doing, describing his morning with the doctors. "I think they do it with mirrors, at a price. Oh, well, let the boys have their fun. Anyhow, my knees are much better. Dollars to doughnuts I'll be beating you at tennis out in Phoenix before Christmas arrives. I wish that we could have gotten away sooner, though." He was regretful.

They were to spend their honeymoon in New York so that he could go on with his treatments for another two months. After that they were to go to the Southwest for an indefinite period.

"Nonsense," Gabrielle said. "I like New York. And I'd rather have my cake and not eat it. We'll have the West to look forward to. As long as you're getting better steadily, and we're together—"

Mark glanced down at the canes leaning against his chair and then across the table directly into her eyes. "You're sure, Gabrielle?" His voice was deeper.

Gabrielle didn't have to steel herself to bear his glance. All that was gone, over and done with. It had been burned away, purged out, when Mark was ill and fighting for his life. Nevertheless, she was glad John Muir wasn't in New York. It had made things easier. She said, smiling at Mark, "I absolutely refuse to answer foolish questions," and put out her hand. Mark covered it with his.

After that they talked plans. The wedding was to be very simple, a short church ceremony followed by luncheon at Sherry's for their few relatives and one or two close friends. Mark said his sister-in-law, Joanna Middleton, and his niece, Claire, were in town. They had come down from the country that morning, were at the Waldorf. "Joanna wants us for dinner tonight.

Get there as early as you can, will you, dear? I may be detained."

There was nothing Gabrielle craved less than a tête-à-tête with Joanna Middleton. Joanna didn't like her, didn't approve of Mark's marriage, had made her disapproval subtly plain. Mark knew nothing about it. There was no reason why he should. Joanna Middleton's likes or dislikes were of no importance.

"Detained?" Gabrielle asked. "But you *will* be there?"

Mark shrugged. "Probably. If I can't make it, I'll call. I've still got a lot of odds and ends to attend to."

It struck her suddenly that he was tired, that his face had a closed, white look to it. The doctors had warned him not to overtax his strength. "Don't try to do too much," she pleaded.

He laughed. "I'm not likely to—loafing's my meat."

There was a faint undertone of bitterness in him she didn't understand. At thirty-eight Mark was a vice-president of the firm in which he owned a large block of shares. He was taking a year's leave of absence which, he said himself, was merely a formal gesture, as he seldom had anything to do except to sit at a big desk and twiddle his thumbs. But his mother had been a very wealthy woman and he was accustomed to leisure. Early in life he had learned to play and enjoy it. Inherited wealth hadn't made him selfish. His charities were personal and extensive and he was always ready to help a friend out of a jam, sunnily and without ostentation. He wasn't sunny now.

Gabrielle studied him. Something was worrying him that he didn't want to talk about. "Mark," she said on impulse, "take the afternoon off. Let's drive out into the country somewhere—get away from New York. Let's—"

He shook his head. "I wish I could, dear. I can't. There are certain things I've got to wind up. Then I can rest—and forget about them."

The shadow was back in him again. It was more than a shadow, it was a terseness, a hard, cold, cutting edge with which she was totally unfamiliar. For a moment he looked like a different man. What *was* he worrying about? She didn't insist. The waiter brought the check.

Outside, in front of the cloakroom, Mark gave her the pearls.

It had rained earlier and Mark had a raincoat with him—even in the warmest weather he had to be careful. The attendant handled his coat clumsily and the box fell to the floor. Mark's canes handicapped him. He made a move but Gabrielle picked up the box. It was of green leather, beautifully tooled. She extended it to Mark. He sprang the lid, and Gabrielle looked at palely shining bubbles against ivory satin. It was a string of pearls. The pearls weren't large but they were exquisitely matched. She said, "Oh, Mark, you shouldn't have—"

He said, "Nonsense. Bought them for you this morning—but I didn't give them to you because the catch is defective. I'll have it fixed. I thought you might like to wear them Saturday."

Saturday. The day they were going to be married. In less than seventy-two hours she and Mark would be man and wife. It would be a relief to get it over with. Not that she had any last-minute doubts. If her own misdirected and undisciplined nature had led her into devious bypaths, she was back on a straight road.

They left the restaurant, parted on the pavement outside at a few minutes after three. Mark was going down to his office, Gabrielle was going home to do some packing. "Don't forget," Mark said, "dinner with Joanna and Claire at seven. I may be late."

"Don't be," Gabrielle begged. "What could possibly keep you so long?"

He said vaguely, "Oh, this and that," kissed the tip
of her nose, put her into the waiting cab, closed the
door, and waved good-by to her with a cane.

Ten blocks to the north Gabrielle stopped her cab
and got out. She felt the need of exercise. She was too
tense. Midafternoon light, syrupy and straw-colored and
uninspiring, filled the streets. There was a dreamlike
drowsing quality to the day, like a slow-paced half-
hearted dance. She had always disliked August, the
month without drama, the turn of the year, with summer fading and autumn not yet ready to take its place.
The pavements were hot underfoot, the city heat-
blanched and stickily depressing.

At Thirty-eighth Street she turned east into the Murray Hill section. How delighted she had been to get an
apartment there when Susan was married five years ago.
Now she was glad she was leaving it. Mark's huge duplex
on Central Park West with the trees a vast green lake
below was infinitely nicer. There was space there, and
you could breathe. She was to have her own sitting-room
on the second floor. When Mark had had the room done
over for her, he said, "I know you'll want to be alone
sometimes. You can have your books and pictures and
close the door whenever you like and no one will disturb you." How understanding he was! She had lived
an individual life for so long that occasional solitude
was a necessity to her. Yes, it would be pleasant to make
the change. And Mark's apartment held no memories.

Involuntarily, her thoughts went to where she seldom
permitted them to go these days, to John Muir. She had
known John for years. He had been a close friend of her
dead brother's, he was one of Mark's oldest and closest
friends. There was nothing new or strange about him.
She had always liked being with him, in his company,
without giving the matter much thought. And then, on
a night in May, in her crowded living-room, between

moment and moment, while John was standing above her looking down and she was looking up at him, it happened. She thought with a feeling of intense surprise, *Why—I love this man.*

The acknowledgment of it must have been in her eyes. John's gray ones fastened on hers had widened and darkened, then narrowed. His humor, his irony, the near-violence of his keen, casual, and cutting judgments, had fallen away. He put out a hand and she rose without a word and they went out on the terrace together. Standing there in coolness, beyond the rim of light from the windows, she reached up and touched his face with her fingers. His hands were on her shoulders. He started to draw her toward him, and stopped. The screen door opened and someone—Alice Amory—came out calling her name. That was the closest, physically, that they had ever come.

For a brief space—looking back, it was hard to measure time—she had been filled with a deep and undemanding content. John Muir existed. He was. It was all she needed to know. That particular stage didn't last long. Her desire to be near him, with him, grew by leaps and bounds. With it came realization, and pain.

John Muir had said nothing to her after that night on the terrace. They saw each other occasionally but never alone. He created no opportunity to see her alone. Presently she became conscious that she had made a horrible mistake. She was engaged to Mark. Mark loved her and she had thought all along that she loved him. She did, in a different way, a better way, perhaps. But could she marry Mark, feeling as she felt, doing what she had done? He would have to be the judge. On the eve of telling him, he had come down with polio. And then she couldn't tell him. She knew, without the doctors saying so, that she was the person who had kept Mark alive during those first dreadful days. His offer to release her from her engagement had been genuine. To have accepted it would have been like picking up an ax and striking him with the naked blade.

She had said, "The sooner we're married the better pleased I'll be," and had meant it. Her infatuation for John Muir was a poisonous growth that could lead to nothing but destruction, had to be rooted out.

Circumstances had made her fight with herself easier. As soon as Mark was out of danger John Muir had gone to South America on business. He was to be there six months. By the time he got back she and Mark would be in the West, where they intended to stay for perhaps a year, moving about as it suited them.

Gabrielle went around a sun-drenched corner. Midway along the block the tall, red-brick house in which she had an apartment drowsed in the heat. She inserted her key in the inner vestibule door and mounted the stairs. The shadowy coolness swung around her like a cloak, was refreshing after the glare outside. Call Susan and find out if Tony had gotten home, how bad things were. She reached the top of the stairs and turned. Her door was at the end of the hall. Fifteen feet short of it she came to a standstill. The man she had thought of as thousands of miles away was there, in shadow, leaning against the wall to the right of the door.

Chapter Two: WARNING FROM AN OLD LOVE

GABRIELLE CAUGHT HER PURSE IN TIGHT FINGERS as though it were a post and she could steady herself by clinging to it.

"Hello, Gabrielle."

Tall and hard, John Muir moved his shoulders away from the wall and stood erect. He looked at the girl in front of him, at her braced figure, slender in blue linen, at her face, matte-white against waves of dark hair framed by a huge circle of leghorn, at the tilted eyes staring at him between rims of dark lash. Only her lips— she had a lovely mouth—had any color. What he had to say to her couldn't be said here.

"Surprised to see me?" he asked. "I've been ringing your bell for the last five minutes."

His tone was careless, almost curt. It was the tone he used when he was bored, uninterested. It steadied Gabrielle.

"The bell doesn't work, John. When did you get into New York? Mark doesn't know you're here. I just left him."

Finding it curiously difficult to move, Gabrielle advanced to her door and unlocked it. Inside the shaded living-room she pulled off her hat, lowered the Venetian blinds another foot, and began to talk into the silence behind her a little feverishly. "Mark will be awfully glad to see you. So will Alice and Tyrell Amory. Now you're up you'll stay for our wedding, of course. It's to be on Saturday at noon."

John Muir spoke then. "Gabrielle, don't turn your back. Turn around. Look at me. Don't be afraid."

Gabrielle swung. She was shaking, and appalled. "What gave you the idea that I was afraid, John? You're being a little ridiculous, aren't you?"

She looked at him straightly, at his fine head, at the face she knew so well, green-speckled gray eyes under flying brows, wide and well-shaped mouth.

He said easily, "I don't think I'm being ridiculous, or I wouldn't be here. I didn't come up on business connected with the firm. I came up to talk to you about Mark. I'm going back with the plane that leaves La-Guardia at five-thirty." He glanced at a watch strapped to a lean wrist. "Which doesn't give me much time."

He dropped down on the arm of the wing chair beside the bookcase, linked brown fingers around a crossed

knee. "I never dreamed you were going through with it—
that Mark would let you. You don't love him, Gabrielle.
And he— It won't work."

Gabrielle stared at a sheaf of zinnias and bachelor's
buttons brilliant against a stretch of dove-gray wall. She
was dazed at John Muir's onslaught at the last minute,
after months of silence. What right had he to come here
and talk to her like this? Was it, she thought bitterly,
because he considered that she had given him the right?
She was the one who had made the move, here in this
room four months ago—she was the attacker, John Muir
the attacked. A kiss in the dark, an interrupted kiss,
snatched at a party. Was that how he saw it, saw her,
as light, devious, tricky, promiscuous, willing to play
around off the reservation as a pastime, not fit to marry
a decent man?

She took a cigarette out of her purse, flicked the
jeweled lighter Mark had given her, fought for control,
and achieved it. "Who says I don't love Mark?"

John Muir studied her. "I say so. Oh, you love Mark,
sure, we all do. But you're not in love with him. And
fondness, affection, pity—aren't enough, not with a man
like Mark. No matter how hard you try, you're not
going to be able to fool him, not indefinitely, anyhow."

Fool him, fool Mark. So that was what John Muir had
decided, that she was marrying Mark for her own selfish
purposes, for money, perhaps.

"Listen, Gabrielle—"

But Gabrielle wouldn't listen. She was too angry. She
touched Mark's ring, moved it so that it caught the light,
and said sweetly. "I like you, John. You'd be quite a nice
person if you weren't such a profound egotist, so completely wrapped up in yourself, so sure that you're in-
variably right. Everybody's out of step but Johnny—
splendid. Only it just doesn't happen to be that way. I
don't know what made you think so, unless"—she

paused, frowned at the tip of her cigarette, and then smiled gently—"could it be—could it be, John, that you got the idea into your head that I had conceived a hankering for you on the night here that I had too much Swedish punch?" Her heart was beating like a trip hammer, in, out, in, out. She couldn't stand much more of it. She stopped smiling and crushed out her cigarette, so furious that speech was troublesome. "I've had about enough. Will you go now, please?"

John didn't move. He remained where he was, fingering the strap on his wrist and looking at her from under dark brows, his sharply focused gaze inscrutable. "Don't marry Mark, Gabrielle. I'm warning you."

His voice wasn't rough or loud, it was low, even. There was sadness in it, and an odd sort of finality. Coldness played up and down Gabrielle's spine. John hadn't answered her gibe, had let it go past him as though she hadn't spoken. She said calmly, "I'm marrying Mark at noon on Saturday."

John Muir uncoiled his length in a single lithe motion, was on his feet. "You've made up your mind?"

"I never unmade it. I—"

He didn't wait for her to finish. He swung, opened the door, closed it behind him, and was gone.

Gabrielle's knees would no longer support her. She sank into the nearest chair. The pain was frightful.

At half-past five that afternoon Gabrielle entered the Finsbury, the apartment hotel on Central Park West where Mark lived, took the elevator to the fourteenth floor, got out the little key on the gold key ring Mark had had made for her, and opened the front door. It was a massive affair, with iron strap hinges. One of the hinges creaked. The reason she didn't ring was that Mark's housekeeper, Mrs. Pendleton, generally took a nap in the afternoon and didn't care to be disturbed.

Gabrielle carried her bags inside, put them down in the foyer, and listened.

Rain spattered suddenly against the tall windows in the living-room beyond. The wind was rising. It was twenty-eight minutes of six. John Muir's plane had already left LaGuardia Field, but if Mark was here and he had found out by some chance that John Muir had been in New York that afternoon, what was she to say to him? At best it would look odd that John Muir had flown up without letting Mark know, and that once here he hadn't gotten in touch with him directly. Certainly the subject matter of their talk wasn't intended to be known, that was implicit in what he had said to her. But John Muir was unpredictable. He might have phoned Mark before he left for the airport, might have mentioned his visit to her. If so, and if she said nothing about seeing him, it would seem peculiar. He had been away for three months, expected to be away another three. His return to New York would be important, an event, to his friends.

How cold and withdrawn he had been at the end, how unlike the man she had thought she knew. . . . She put his image resolutely aside. What she could see of the immense living-room, running two stories to a beamed ceiling, was empty. But Mark could be in his study off on the left. He wasn't. The door was open. She mounted the little winding staircase to the upper floor, feeling like a thief, went along the gallery to the room above the dining-room that Mark had had redone for her. A fuller view of the living-room and Mark's study showed them both untenanted. All right, where did that get her? It was simply putting off the evil day. In an hour, an hour and a half at the most, she would be at the Waldorf with Joanna Middleton and Mark would come and she would have to say something about John Muir's being in New York and his visit to her—

or not say it.

Be guided by circumstances, she thought, tiredly, shutting the white door on the vista below, a heavy-handed mixture of Gothic and baroque. John had laughed when he first saw it. Mark had asked why and John had said, "It's rather overpowering, but the baronial atmosphere suits you." It was true. There was a bigness about Mark, a generosity and sweetness that made him seem like a denizen of more spacious times.

Except for Mrs. Pendleton, drowsing somewhere in her lair, she was alone. Gabrielle opened her bags and began to unpack. Cream-colored walls; hand-blocked linen, yellow, orange, blue, and scarlet, at the windows; built-in bookcases; low, soft chairs; tables; lamps; most of her pictures had been transferred a week ago. It had grown darker out. Lightning flashed briefly. She hung the red chalk above the desk, put her blue Wedgwood pitcher under it, rearranged the chairs and shifted some of the lamps. She and Mark would be here for only two months now, but Mark had a three-year lease on the apartment and both of them wanted something approximating a home to return to.

Her pleasure in the pretty room was gone. She was bruised and sore and shaken. Forget about John Muir and what he thought of her, she told herself curtly, and went on unpacking small personal objects, paused to switch on the lights, and continued with her work.

It was almost half-past six when she finished. The storm had begun in earnest, filled the room with the slash of rain and the dull boom of distant thunder. The lights of the city were cobwebbed and golden in the wet lavender dusk. Nothing to do now but put on powder and fresh lipstick and go. She dawdled, acknowledging frankly to herself that she was afraid of Joanna Middleton's sharp eyes, her tongue, not for herself but for Mark. She could imagine Joanna saying, *John Muir flew up here to New York and didn't let any of us—let Mark know? You were the only one he saw? But—how odd!* Mark was the last person in the world to be suspicious, but he was peculiarly sensitive, and his friends meant a lot to him.

Put Joanna off, Gabrielle decided suddenly. Ring up and say she wasn't feeling well and thought it better to go straight to bed. She crossed to the desk. There was no book in the room. Call Information for the Waldorf's number; she lifted the receiver. Someone, Mrs. Pendleton, was using the phone downstairs. The dial was clicking. Gabrielle dropped the instrument into its cradle. It wouldn't take her long to get home and she could phone Joanna from there just as well.

Gabrielle put on her hat. She was picking up her purse and gloves when she heard the explosion, a short, sharp, staccato bark that sounded like a shot. She jumped nervously, relaxed. It was a car backfiring in the street or one of those unexplained noises you constantly heard in New York. Nevertheless she held herself tightly as she walked to the door, opened it, switched off the lamps, and closed the door behind her. The gallery was dim. The living-room below was illuminated. Mrs. Pendleton must have turned on the lights.

Gabrielle started along the gallery, her heels clicking in the stillness. She had traversed less than half its length when she heard a second sound. It wasn't violent like the first, it was high and thin, a musical note off key. It was the front door opening or closing.

Gabrielle stood still. She gripped the railing with her hand. The odor that assailed her nostrils was cordite. The explosion that had made her jump while she was shut up in her room wasn't a backfire. It was a shot and the shot had been fired somewhere within these walls.

She flew along the gallery and down the steps into the foyer. The front door was closed. Silence, emptiness, a faint moan somewhere? She stumbled into the living-room, turned her head, and saw Mark. He was lying on the floor of the study, almost in the middle of the floor, in an awkward twisted position, one leg at a sharp angle, his arms flung out. He was hurt, wounded. There was blood welling over the front of his suit high up near his chin. His eyes were open. He was staring at her, didn't seem to see her.

"Mark—" She rushed to him, knelt. Mark didn't speak. He was unconscious. A doctor—there were doctors in the building—help. Gabrielle got to her feet and ran. She was through the front door. Someone was coming toward her along the hall. It was Joanna Middleton. She cried to Joanna out of a strangled throat, and ran on, was ringing the elevator bell, keeping her finger on it. At the end of uncounted eons help came. The elevator man first, and then other people, a doctor among them. After that a stretcher appeared and two men in white, interns. Mark was lifted, placed on the stretcher, and carried out. It was the last Gabrielle saw of him, alive. Mark died on the way to the hospital without recovering consciousness.

Chapter Three: UP AGAINST A STONE WALL

"MARK—MR. MIDDLETON—DID NOT KILL HIMSELF."

Gabrielle spoke slowly, careful to keep her voice at an even pitch. The slightest hint of hysteria would ruin whatever chances he had. The room in which she sat was the Commissioner's office on the second floor of Police Headquarters on Centre Street, a big room, heavily carpeted, with long windows at one end looking out on changing foliage in thin sunlight. Behind his desk Commissioner Carey remained silent, as did the half-dozen other officials present.

Gabrielle's closest friends, Tyrell and Alice Amory, flanked her on either side. They had been Mark's friends, too. They had refused to let her come alone. Tyrell Amory was the first one she had called on that dreadful night in August. Next to John Muir, he had been the nearest to Mark. She looked at Tyrell for support.

Tyrell wasn't looking at her, he was looking moodily at the floor. His brush of fair hair was almost white in the gloom, his clever scholarly face was worried. He kept stroking his hair with a thin hand. He had left his work at the laboratory, important work in which he was engrossed, to come here with her and do what he could to help. It was an empty gesture. He no longer agreed with her. Bit by bit, during the seven weeks since Mark's death, he had been won over.

Gabrielle glanced at Alice Amory, slight and dark and elegant, playing nervously with the alligator bag in her lap. Alice too had been sympathetic in the beginning. Now she was simply playing along with a lip service that no longer had any conviction behind it. These friends of Mark's, and of her own too, of course, had believed her at first. They didn't now. They agreed with the police that Mark's death was suicide. Gabrielle knew it was murder.

Late afternoon light beat pitilessly on her eyelids, became part of the blind pattern of skepticism and unbelief that surrounded her. She moved in an aura of darkness. She repeated her assertion, speaking to no one directly, but to all of them. "Mark did not kill himself. Why should he? We were going to be married in three days. He was happy, he was full of plans. He wasn't the sort of man who would do a thing like that. Don't you see?" Her eyes went from face to face, all closed, all unresponsive. There was a despairing fall to her voice. It faded out.

The Commissioner drummed noiseless fingers on the blotter in front of him. The Borough Commander and the Chief of the Detective Division exchanged glances. A precinct man shuffled his feet. There was nothing to say. The inquiry into Mark Middleton's death had been very thorough. Members of the family never liked suicide, but the facts were all there. Incentive and opportunity had been established. They were borne out by the evidence. Mark Middlton was an invalid. He had been reduced from a strong man to a cripple in the space of three months. He was engaged to marry a young and beautiful woman. His physical condition preyed on his mind. He hadn't been able to face marriage, had put an end to its possibility with a bullet. According to his sister-in-law, Joanna Middleton, he had alluded to himself bitterly as a cripple many times. It was the girl herself who had insisted on going on with the marriage.

Everything about the dead man underscored this reconstruction. He had no enemies, no financial troubles; he was a wealthy man. He had lunched with his fiancée the day he died. It was a farewell luncheon. He had already provided for her financially. Very early in the game a suggestion had been made that his fiancée might have killed him, but there was absolutely nothing against her, and she had no motive. She was unaware of the disposition of the estate, and the relationship between them, her background, reputation, negatived the idea in the light of the general setup. Gabrielle Conant didn't know Mark Middleton was in the apartment when he killed himself. He didn't know she was there; he thought he was alone, had arranged to be alone. He had sent his housekeeper out on an errand and then pulled the trigger of the gun, which was his own.

There wasn't a scintilla of evidence to bolster Miss

Conant's assertion of murder. She thought she had heard the front door close. It was possible; a great many things were possible. They were of no importance unless they were back to back with proof. And there was absolutely no proof of the presence of a third person in the Middleton apartment when the bullet that killed him entered Mark Middleton's body. For the rest, the girl's vague charges against—peculiar verbiage—"a round man in a gray suit" who had called on Middleton eight weeks before he died and whom Middleton had stared after angrily in the Hotel Devon on the day of his death, didn't amount to a hill of beans.

Sitting there in frost-edged, sparkling October sunlight, her eyes shadowed, clasped hands tight in her lap, Gabrielle felt the atmosphere of disbelief. It beat against her in waves. *Why wouldn't they see?* she thought despairingly. There was only one thing that could possibly have made Mark kill himself, just possibly, and even that she doubted. If he had found out about herself and John Muir, how she had once felt about John Muir, he might have done it. But he hadn't found out. No one knew that John Muir had been in New York on the day it happened. Cables informing him of Mark's death had reached São Paulo too late for him to come back for the funeral. No. Mark had been shot down in cold blood, without a chance to defend himself, by an unknown assailant.

She went back doggedly to the round man, fighting a tight throat. "That man, the round man, had something to do with Mark's death, Commissioner. I know it. Mark tried to get in touch with his lawyer, Phil Bond, that afternoon, and couldn't. I think he meant to tell Phil Bond something—something important that he found out. I think he sent for the round man too, and that the round man came—and killed him."

Gabrielle stopped talking. She felt exhausted, spent.

The silence was heavy. It remained unbroken. The police officials sat with folded arms, except for the Commissioner, who continued to drum soundlessly on his desk. Tyrell had turned and was looking at him. Alice was looking at fading leaves beyond the window, a handkerchief pressed to her lips.

There was one exception to the general attitude of negation that Gabrielle didn't see. A small mousy man in a corner, a little wisp of a man completely nondescript in appearance, had listened intently, his ears wide open. His name was Todhunter and he was a detective attached to the Manhattan Homicide Squad. He was there because Christopher McKee, who headed the Homicide Squad, was out of town. Todhunter also looked at the Commissioner, and reached unobtrusively for his hat. The girl was about to be given the official brush-off.

Commissioner Carey was on his feet. "I'm sorry, Miss Conant, but we've done everything we could, and, as things are now, I'm afraid the verdict must stand. Of course, later, if anything should develop—"

The blow fell crashingly on Gabrielle's bent head. She had hoped for so much from this personal interview with Commissioner Carey, had heard that he was different—perceptive, understanding, clever, that the obvious meant little to him, that he could see where blunter and more forthright officials were blind. She was mistaken. He hadn't seen. She got up a little unsteadily. This was the end of the road.

Chapter Four: A GHOST OF A CASE

THE RADIATOR HISSED, wind blew, a siren wailed, the distant clamor of traffic rose and fell, the clock on the mantel ticked. It was a ghost of a tick, constant and inexorable behind the outer sounds. Gabrielle put the book she was holding face down on the coffee table in front of her with a small slam. She sat up, swung her feet to the floor.

It was ten minutes after eight on the night of November the twelfth. A little over a month had passed since the interview in the Commissioner's office put the official stamp of suicide on Mark's death. She had spent most of the intervening weeks alone, shutting herself away from her cousin Susan and Tony and Alice and Tyrell Amory, from all her associates and friends—they meant to be kind but their solicitude merely succeeded in rubbing her raw. Belief was what she wanted, belief that Mark had been killed, and that she had heard his murderer fleeing from the apartment. No one believed her.

She left the lighted emptiness of the living-room, went into the bedroom, and threw off her housecoat. It was Tyrell Amory's birthday and Alice was giving a party for him. She had asked Gabrielle to go but Gabrielle had refused. What had happened that afternoon, because she couldn't get rid of it, shake it off, made her change her mind.

She had been fighting it ever since she got in at four o'clock. The fight was lost. For the first time she was afraid, not of anyone else, but of herself. Perhaps the doctor to whom Alice had insisted on taking her was right. He had said, "It won't do, Miss Conant. If people don't bend, they break. I wouldn't want to answer for your condition if you continue to remain alone and brood." There were the others, too, Tyrell and Alice and the Bonds and Susan and even Tony Van Ness; they no longer said, "Mark may not have committed suicide, he may have been killed—but how are you going to prove it?" They said, "Yes, dear, yes," and turned the subject to what she'd like to do, where she'd like to go.

The incident of that afternoon was an accident, of course. A crowded subway platform, gloom, murk, dripping umbrellas, bodies pressed close together in a wedged mass, a mass that eddied and shifted under the impact of additions from the locals, the stairs; she was standing near the southern end of the northbound platform and an express was coming in fast when someone gave her a violent shove. She had almost fallen to the tracks, had missed falling by a hair, and by the edge of the guard rail with which her shoulder collided. The people milling around her hadn't noticed, except for a stout red-faced man with an umbrella, who had said, "Here, Miss, here," and had hauled her back a foot or two, with a suspicious glance, hurrying off as the train came to a grinding stop. The red-faced man was evidently convinced that she had attempted suicide and wanted nothing more to do with her. Certainly the shove was accidental. There was no question about that. It was the thought flashing through her mind: *Someone is trying to kill me,* that frightened her. Not because she believed anyone really was, but because of the idea itself. That way madness lay, a budding persecution complex, the beginnings of dementia.

Her wild surmise was the warning signal, unless someone *had* tried to— *Oh, stop it,* she told herself angrily. When the case was at an end as far as the police were concerned, why should anyone want her dead? She had told everything she knew, to no avail. She had nothing more to add.

She did her hair, hoping that there wouldn't be a crowd at the Amorys'. Alice attracted people in droves with her quick tongue, her warmth, and her vivid, and fleeting, enthusiasms. Gabrielle smiled at the thought of some of them. She reflected that if Alice hadn't been born with money she would have been an artist, a painter, probably. She only dabbled with painting now,

as she did with sculpture and music. Tyrell was perfect
for her flamelike ardor, her restlessness. He was as
steady as a rock, gave Alice something solid to tie to.
It was a pity they had no children.

At the closet Gabrielle replaced the black crepe she
had instinctively reached for. She hadn't gone into
mourning for Mark, mourning was an outmoded sym-
bol, it was simply that she hadn't felt like colors. Instead
of the black crepe she took out a plain white sheath. of
heavy silk with long bishop sleeves, slid it over her head,
threw a sling of gold coins around her throat, and did
her mouth. Looking at her reflection in the mirror as
though she were another person, she thought disinter-
estedly that the effect was good. The dress accentuated
her slenderness, the darkness of her upswept hair. White
skin, gray eyes at a tilt under long brows—good, yes—
but good for what? She turned aside, got into a cape,
and picked up purse and gloves.

Twenty minutes later she entered the Amorys' apartment in the East Sixties, and received a severe shock.
She heard a voice beyond the green taffeta curtains
(new, they had been yellow satin two weeks ago). It
was a voice she would have known if she heard it in a
sandstorm in the middle of the Sahara. John Muir
wasn't in São Paulo, he was in the Amory living-room.

Alice came into the foyer. "Gabrielle, darling!" She
was surprised and pleased. "It was sweet of you to come
—but why couldn't you make it for dinner? We had a
perfectly marvelous Smithfield ham." She linked an arm
through Gabrielle's and they went between the curtains together. The living-room, a long room stretching to a
solid sheet of glass at the far end that overlooked the
laboratory where Tyrell worked, had been completely
done over. The dim gilt and tapestries were gone. Light
was flung back from apricot walls on vivid greens and
yellows and blues and reds.

"Like it?" Alice asked anxiously and Gabrielle said it was lovely. Alice was uncertain. "I don't know. I saw a stunning zebra today—no, no, not a live one. China. In a place on Sixth Avenue. Stripes might have been better."

There were a lot of people. The Bonds were there and Alice's cousin, Sylvia Medford, and three or four strange men and the very rich and very boring Larks— and Joanna Middleton and her daughter Claire. Gabrielle hadn't seen Joanna since Mark's funeral. She was in black. It made her skin sallow.

At Gabrielle's entrance there was the slightest of pauses. It was as though a performing tiger had suddenly appeared. Conversations were immediately resumed and curious glances averted, but the break had been there. They all knew the stand she had taken about Mark's death, probably all thought her slightly mad. Let them, she thought coldly.

Across the width of the room Joanna nodded to Gabrielle without smiling. The nod was brief. Her gaze lingered on Gabrielle's dress, on the glitter of coins around her throat, appraisingly and without expression. Tyrell blanked Joanna out. "Gabrielle!" Like Alice he was pleased that she had come. She wished him many happy returns and he said nobody over thirty-five should have a birthday, that it tended to humiliate and degrade: then: "Guess who's here. John—he just got in."

John Muir was coming toward them. Gabrielle gathered herself together, turned. Her mouth felt stiff. "John —hello."

Change had been so much a part of her life for the last two months that she had expected him to be different. He was exactly the same, tall and commandingly casual and at ease, except for his taut skin burned brown by warmer suns. She looked up into his face, and was filled with a sort of dull wonder and relief.

Mark's death must have cauterized some essential nerve. She felt absolutely nothing.

John took her hand. His eyes studied her. "How are you, Gabrielle? Better? I hear you haven't been well," and then in a different, lower tone: "I wish_I had been in New York when Mark died. I might have been able to—help."

Gabrielle's pulse quickened. What did he mean by that? "Mark didn't kill himself, you know." She had to say it, aware as she spoke of the swift exasperation in Alice, of Tyrell's sigh.

John said, "Tyrell's been telling me how you feel about—Mark's death. I'd like to hear what you think. Let's go into the other room, shall we?"

Alice rounded on him, a darting firefly. "John! It's Tyrell's birthday. . . ." She sent out sparks, her mouth down-curving with annoyance.

Gabrielle didn't blame her. It must be tiresome to hear the same story over and over again, a story you didn't believe. "I won't keep her long," John promised. Again the glances, covert and observing, as she walked down the room beside him.

"Gabrielle—" Susan's husband, Tony Van Ness, tall and buccaneering and haggardly handsome, detached himself from a group around the piano.

Gabrielle said hello, and looked at Tony more closely. What was he doing in New York? He was supposed to be working. Excessive drinking wasn't one of Tony's vices, but he had definitely had a number of drinks. There were patches of color on his high cheekbones and his eyes were suspiciously bright. "I didn't see you come in," he complained, and, to John Muir: "She's been cutting us, Muir, there's no getting *at* her, she won't have a thing to do with us."

Tony's anxiety for her company amused Gabrielle. They weren't on those terms. An armed truce about summed it up. Under other circumstances she might have liked him, as Susan's husband he was impossible. He was a painter and a good one, could have all the work he wanted, if he would only buckle down. She said, "I didn't know you were in New York, Tony. Susan told me over the phone this morning that you were doing a cover for Drake's."

"Finished it, Gorgeous. Let's sit down and have a drink." He put a hand on her arm.

She drew away. "Not now, Tony."

"Oh, come on, honey."

"Honey"—he must be drunk.

John Muir said good-humoredly, "Gangway, Van Ness, your turn will come later," and they moved on.

Sitting erect in the corner of a red-leather couch in front of the fire in Tyrell's study, Gabrielle retold the story she had told so often before, giving John the salient points and keeping it brief. People didn't want to be bored.

As she talked she thought with part of her mind, *How amazing! What delusions we build for ourselves! I was madly in love with this man once, and now he means nothing to me.* Dark-brown hair, squarish brow, finely cut mouth, penetrating eyes, an air of power, of complete competence in anything he might undertake; she didn't need to glance at him to see how he looked.

She finished her tale. There was a pause. The silky yellow-apricot fire muttered. Everything else in the room was still. Gabrielle waited. John Muir was not a person to her then. He was a door on which she knocked, desperately seeking shelter, as she had knocked on so many others, to find them closed, gently, inexorably, in her face. "Rest, dear—rest. Don't think of it any more." Drink this, take that, powders, pills—and deaf ears. When murder had been committed, when Mark had been killed, shot down cruelly on the instant—and his

death made to look like suicide. She hadn't expected to
meet John Muir. If she had known he was going to be
here she would have stayed home. Now he had become
her last chance. She had exhausted the list of everyone
to whom she could conceivably go.

John spoke, and warmth rushed into the vacuum of
her coldness. He wasn't going to brush her away, at
once, anyhow. He said slowly, "If only I'd stayed in
New York that night. . . . I didn't get the cable telling
me about Mark until I was back in São Paulo." He took
an envelope and a pencil from a pocket. "Now . . ."

Dates. A description of the round man. The steps
that had already been taken to locate him. Gabrielle
described her visit to Mark's office to look over the
personnel, her visit to the Identification Bureau at Police Headquarters, the advertisements in the personal
columns of the papers asking for information from or
concerning the man who had called on Mark on the
afternoon of June the twenty-fifth at 2 p.m.

"What about the car the fellow drove away from the
Devon in?" John wanted to know.

Gabrielle shook her head. "The police asked me that.
I didn't see the license number. I don't know what sort
of car it was except that"—she thought back reachingly—
"it wasn't a new model. It had a gray top, I think, and—
it was long and low." A more precise image flickered
at the back of her memory, retreated, dissolved. She
shrugged.

"Never mind," John said. "Was there anyone else in
the car?"

Gabrielle gazed at spirals of smoke rising from her
cigarette and tried to concentrate. Hazy summer sunlight, the round man crossing the pavement with his
bouncy walk; the car was facing north and he had
stepped into it from the curb. His face visible through
the open window—another face beyond his? It was be-

ginning to come back.

She sat up sharply. "Yes. There was a woman in the car with him. The woman was behind the wheel. It must have been the woman who drove the car away."

She was excited. She looked at John.

John wasn't looking at her. They sat facing each other with the length of the couch between them. The couch was close to the hearth and the bulk of the room was behind it, shadowy in low light. They both saw it at the same moment, from different angles. Gabrielle saw it in the reducing mirror above the mantel out of the tail of her eye, a long black slit where there should have been unbroken whiteness—the door on the far side of the room was a little open.

John rose to his feet. His movement distracted her. He went round the end of the sofa and crossed violet broadloom, fast and noiselessly. Gabrielle looked into the mirror again and then over her shoulder. There had been no slightest sound, but long before John reached the study door it was tight in its frame.

He opened the door, looked out, closed it, and came back to the hearth. He threw an arm along the mantel and looked down at Gabrielle. His eyes were brilliant between half-drawn lids. Lines etched themselves from mouth corners to nose.

"Who was it?" Gabrielle asked on a breathless note, and thought of Tony Van Ness's effort to keep her from coming in here with John, of Joanna Middleton's cold glance, of the general air of watchfulness in the living-room.

John deflated her tenseness. His face had smoothed out. "What? . . . Oh, one of the maids, I think. But we can't talk here. Other people will be barging in. What are you doing when you leave? Any date?"

A date—how amusing! Such things existed in another world from which she was far removed. She said no.

John Muir said, "What about Blake Evans? He's a friend of yours, isn't he? He was here for dinner tonight, was talking about you."

Blake Evans, with whom she had gone to school, who had squired Susan around—Gabrielle laughed. "Yes, Blake's a friend of mine, an old friend. I went to high school with him. He's going to marry Mark's niece, Claire Middleton, I think—and hope. He's nice, and Claire's a lamb—in spite of her mother. No, I'm not going anyplace. When I leave here I'm going straight home."

"Good," John said. "I'll come over to your apartment later on, as soon as I can get away, and we can talk there in peace. This woman who was in the car with the round man may be important." He moved toward Gabrielle, took her hands, drew her to her feet, dropped her hands, and stood back and looked at her thoughtfully. "You know, if I were you I'd keep this woman who was in the car with your round man to myself for the moment."

Again Gabrielle's nerves edged. Was it possible that here, at Alice and Tyrell's, someone had deliberately tried to eavesdrop on what she had to say to John Muir? Of course it was possible, physically anyhow. The hall outside had a powder room at one end, angled round a turn at the other. Someone could easily have slipped out into the hall from the living-room. But why do such a thing? She hadn't attempted to conceal knowledge. On the contrary she had bombarded everyone who would listen with what she knew.

John was waiting for her assent. His face was closed, uncommunicative. She said, "All right. I won't say anything to anyone," and they left Tyrell's study and went back into the living-room.

Voices, laughter, raised glasses, the room was still full of people. Tony Van Ness had gone, home, Gabrielle hoped, thinking apprehensively of Drake's check in his pocket. Joanna Middleton and Claire were going. Tyrell was saying good-by to them in the foyer, but there were half a dozen new arrivals. Brenda Holmes was among them.

Brenda, in whispering gray-green taffeta that left her lovely shoulders bare, stood beside the piano talking to Phil Bond, one white elbow propped on the darkly shining wood. Brenda was as beautiful as ever. She was, Gabrielle thought back, thirty—no, thirty-one—but time seemed to pass over her without leaving a mark on her ivory skin, the lovely oval of her face, the gleaming fair hair fastened tight to her head and gathered into a knot at the nape of her neck. Brenda's one bad feature was her forehead. It was high and convex. She never permitted it to be seen in public, covered it with a soft fringe that effectively brought out the sea blue of her large eyes.

Odd that Brenda Holmes had never married, Gabrielle reflected, when it was what she had been trained for from infancy. Perhaps she had set her sights too high. Gabrielle neither liked nor disliked Brenda, she was curious about her. Part of the curiosity was due to the fact that among their friends Brenda's name had often been linked with John Muir's.

John caught sight of her. He left Gabrielle rather unceremoniously, with a murmured: "See you later, then," and crossed the room. Accepting a drink from a maid circulating with a fresh tray, Gabrielle watched them meet. A welcoming smile from Brenda, a widening of the large blue eyes; she and John Muir moved away together in the direction of the dining-room.

Gabrielle left a few minutes later, over Alice's protest and quick reversal. "My face is frozen into a permanent grin. I'm dying on my feet. I wish they'd all go. So many bores—we do seem to accumulate them." She looked tired and out of temper, which was unusual for her at a party. Gabrielle was back in her apartment with the door locked against chance droppers-in before ten. She wanted to be alone when John Muir got there. He had said elevenish.

It was at exactly five minutes of eleven that the call came. Gabrielle picked up the phone and said, "Yes?" A man's voice answered. It was a strange voice. She had never heard it before. At the first words Gabrielle stiffened. She leaned back hard against the little chair. The wooden slat cut into her shoulder. She didn't feel it. She said, her mouth dry, "Yes, yes, I am," and went on listening avidly.

At about the same time, in the offices of the Homicide Squad a mile to the south and west, another call was coming in over the long-distance wires. Lieutenant Quigley said, "For you, Todhunter," and the little detective lifted the instrument on his desk. It was the Inspector at last.

Inspector McKee was talking from Denver. He said, "I've been out all evening, just got your message. What is it?"

The Scotsman had left Todhunter in charge of a case that wasn't a case at all but merely the ghost of a suggestion of one. On the night Mark Middleton died, at almost the moment the shot that killed him was fired, McKee's private telephone had rung. He wasn't in and Todhunter had answered. When Todhunter picked up the phone there was no one on the line, there was nothing but a click as the instrument on the calling end was replaced.

McKee knew Mark Middleton well. They had been meeting for years at sports events and around town generally. It was a pleasant acquaintanceship. He had told Middleton once that if he ever needed help to come to him, and had given Middleton his unlisted number.

In spite of the verdict of suicide, it was Todhunter's contention that Mark Middleton had called on McKee for help, that the call for help had precipitated his death, and that it was the perpetrator who had replaced the instrument in Middleton's apartment the evening Middleton was shot. Todhunter based his contention on the fact that the instrument in Mark Middleton's study had been wiped clean of fingerprints. Middleton had been at home for almost half an hour before he died. He was known to have made at least one telephone call, a call to his lawyer, Philip Bond. Bond wasn't at home but his wife had answered.

A telephone call that had never been received wasn't much to go on where everything else pointed to suicide, but Todhunter's theory interested the Scotsman and he had given the little detective his head. "Got something?" he asked.

"Looks kind of like it, Inspector."

"The girl?"

"I don't believe so," Todhunter said. "I'm not sure, but I think someone tried to push her under a subway train this afternoon."

"*What!*"

"Yes," Todhunter said murmuringly, and went on to explain that he had been in Union Square at around four o'clock on other business when he caught sight of Miss Conant. He had been wanting a word with her anyhow, and he followed her into the subway. But the crowd was heavy and he lost sight of her momentarily. Then, from the ramp above he saw her again, saw . . . He started to describe the incident in detail.

McKee didn't let him finish. Flat and unaccented, his voice burned up the wire along which it traveled. "Better get over to the girl as fast as you can. She may know something. After you've seen her, call me back."

"Yes, Inspector." Todhunter replaced the instrument. Seven minutes later he was at the door of Gabrielle's apartment with his finger on the bell. He was too late. The bell rang on emptily in the empty apartment. Gabrielle Conant was not there.

Chapter Five: DEATH BY INVITATION?

"ALL RIGHT, DRIVER, this will do, thanks."

The cab pulled up. Gabrielle looked at the meter, paid the man, and got out. The light on a stanchion farther along gave very little illumination. There was a stationer's on the south side of the street. In front of it a man with a brace of spaniels was talking to a woman with a Sealyham. A few pedestrians, a dingy drugstore, a tall dark office building; beyond it a sign in red neon light above a big plate-glass window said: *Jordon's.*

It was to Jordon's here that she had been directed to come. There were Jordon's scattered all over the city, clean, antiseptic restaurants that dispensed short orders and orange juice and coffee. There was an innocuousness about a Jordon's that made Gabrielle consent to one as a meeting-place. She put her purse under her arm, brushed blowing hair from her forehead, and crossed an uneven stretch of pavement.

Warm air hit her. It smelled of vanilla and cigarette smoke and sizzling ham. There was a counter down the left-hand side of the big oblong interior. Indirect lighting beat back from the white ceiling, the white tiled floor, the white tiled walls. The place was sparsely filled; a few couples were eating and drinking in booths against the walls; three men and a dog were at the near end of the counter, a stout woman in purple in the middle of it. Gabrielle had been told to sit at the counter. She went past the woman in purple, mounted a stool at the far end, and put down her gloves and purse.

The counterman finished a remark about the Chicago Bears to a heavy man in a gray sweater and drifted toward her, cloth in hand. He gave the white enamel a swipe. Gabrielle said, "A cup of coffee, black, please." The man drew it, pushed it across to her. She paid him. The cash register rang.

No one of the three men farther along did more than glance at her; no one got up out of a booth. Gabrielle turned a little on the stool so that she could watch the door. Who was going to come through it and up to her? A man, certainly; it had been a man to whom she had talked over the telephone half an hour earlier. She went laboriously back over the brief conversation, dwelling on every word of it, every intonation. The man had said, "You the party that's trying to find the man who went to see a Mr. Middleton on the twenty-fifth of last June? Well, I can give you some dope on him, if you want it."

Gabrielle wanted it more than she wanted anything else in the world. The price could be too high. She was by no means blind to the danger she ran. An investigation into murder should be undertaken by the police and not by amateurs. But if the police closed their eyes and refused to do anything— She had said, "I do want information." The man then told her where to meet him. "And don't bring anyone with you. I'm not talking to a crowd." His voice was neither educated nor the reverse. It was without a recognizable accent. He had spoken quickly and in rather a low tone, as though he didn't want to be overheard. He had added, "I hope there'll be something in it for me."

Gabrielle had no cash beyond a ten-dollar bill, a few singles, and some change. But her checkbook was in her purse. Her balance was still a little over a thousand. It was all she had. If the man she was going to meet

demanded more than that she could get the money from
Tyrell or from Phil Bond; Phil had told her to come to
him if she needed any. It would be Mark's money, but
what better use could she put it to than to track down
his murderer?

The door opened. Cold air swept in in a refreshing
shaft. A thin blond man in his forties sauntered in with
it. He took a stool three down, ordered a Coke, and
began to talk about his arthritis to the counterman. The
blond man kept looking at Gabrielle in the mirror. He
made no attempt to approach her. He looked at her
as the men farther along had looked at her, curiously,
evidently wondering what she was doing in a place like
that alone at that hour of the night. Gabrielle had
changed hastily. She was conscious of hatless head, the
ribbon in her hair. She rearranged folds of her polo coat,
propped an elbow on the counter, and lit a cigarette.
Her cheeks began to burn. She was embarrassed, uneasy.
It was almost half-past eleven, and the man on the
telephone had said a quarter past. Where was he? Why
didn't he come? She wasn't afraid. The place was too
open, too brightly lighted, for it to be any sort of trap.
That was why she had agreed to it as a meeting-place.

There weren't too many women, most of the cus-
tomers were men. She was sorry when the woman in
purple got up and went out. That left a blond girl in a
booth, a dark girl wearing a scarf at a table near the
kitchen, and a heavy gray-haired woman in a battered
hat on her way to or from her cleaning chores in a
neighboring office building. Someone put a coin in the
juke box and the blonde beat time to the music and
began to sing in a low voice. Above the coffee urn the
minute hand on the electric clock moved in tiny leaps
like an insect jumping from stone to stone. The girl in
the scarf went. The man with the dog went. Three quiet,
well-behaved sailors came in and ordered steaks and

French fries and coffee. Gabrielle got another cup of coffee for herself. It was twenty-five minutes of twelve; it was a quarter of. Moisture that was fatigue and nervous excitement and mounting rage stung her eyes.

On the stroke of midnight, three-quarters of an hour after she had entered Jordon's, Gabrielle climbed down from her stool. She walked steadily to the door, opened it, and closed it behind her.

Warmth vanished abruptly and coldness struck at her. The wind was knife-edged. The stationer's was closed now, so was the drugstore. The man with the spaniels and the woman with the Sealyham were gone; there were no pedestrians in view at all. And no traffic. There was darkness everywhere except for the distant slit of Thirty-fourth burning redly to the north, and the light in which she stood, thrown out and down through the big plate-glass window at her back.

The light in which she stood . . . Gabrielle started to draw a breath, held it. It came to her then, sharp and clear, out of the darkness of the deserted streets, the murk, the obscurity, the emptiness—the awareness of danger. This was it. This was the plot, the plan. Get her to a certain spot, pin her there, and strike, with a bullet flashing from a car rushing at her out of blackness, or fired from some dark doorway. She tasted the danger, smelled it, felt the bite of it in her bones—and moved, darting, scarcely conscious that she did so, out of the light, out of the prominence, into obscurity off on the left. Her nerves stretched taut. She held herself tightly, lightly, ready to run, to leap back, leap forward, throw herself to one side. The danger was somewhere near, poised and waiting. She was sure of it.

Wind beat at her. Her eyes stabbed at the surrounding darkness, picking up shades and gradations. Factories, warehouses, closed shops, in the next block an apartment house, rectangled with dim lights high above;

no moon or stars. The sound of a shot—a backfire in the street. No one would raise a shade, open a window, or bother to look out. It happened every day, and got three lines in the papers, a man shot down in Brooklyn by an unknown assailant, a woman killed by a bullet on the West Side.

Gabrielle clenched her hands inside her gloves. She couldn't stand there indefinitely. She had to move. But which way? She was about a third of the distance along the block between Twenty-sixth and Twenty-seventh on Ninth Avenue. The street lamp at the corner of Twenty-sixth was a mere glimmer. There were no cabs here. She would have to go east. But if she went toward Twenty-sixth and then across she would have to pass the full glare of Jordon's window, streaming brilliantly out on the pavement. She turned north, putting one foot in front of the other softly, careful of heel taps. Luckily she had changed into sandals.

The street was still and hung with shadows, there was a cold scrap of a wind that flung dust in her face. The intensity of the gloom was defeating. Darkness walled it. The distant figure of a man walking hurriedly, shoulders hunched, in the canyon ahead, sparse traffic on Thirty-fourth, a million miles out in front— her eyes were fastened so intently on the safety of Thirty-fourth Street, her ears were so concentrated on the threat of approaching sound aimed at her, that she collided abruptly with a bulky object directly in her path.

It was a barrel. The barrel was at the edge of the curb. The faintest of rosy glows came up from beyond it. The glow was a red lantern. There was construction going on there. Straight ahead of her a boarded tunnel opened up. People went through the tunnel in the daytime, men carrying bricks and mortar to and fro. She wasn't going through it. The blackness filling it was impenetrable. Go out into the middle of the street.

Gabrielle started to swivel, didn't complete her turn. An arm came out of the blackness and she was pulled into it with a rough sweeping movement. She threw herself back. Her lips parted. The cry crowding her throat stayed there. A voice spoke. The voice was John Muir's. He said very low, "Don't scream."

Gabrielle rocked in nightmare. Faint redness from the lantern made John Muir a shadow on shadows. Boarding was rough under her feet. His arm was a vise around her shoulders. There was a smell of damp cement, of upturned earth, of brick dust. She got back the use of her muscles, freed herself. "John! What are you doing here?"

"Sshh," he said, "not so loud. Look over there." He pointed.

Gabrielle stared through an opening in the planks at the opposite side of the street. She could see nothing but unlighted building fronts, broken by an occasional darker rectangle, a dark gleam of glass.

John said in her ear, "There's a man over there in the door of that tailor shop. He trailed you here from your apartment. He was doing sentry duty up and down in front of Jordon's. When you came out he took cover."

"He—followed me?"

"Yes."

The icy wind whipped Gabrielle's hair across her forehead. She pushed it back, shrugged deeper into her coat. Could the man across the street be the man who had telephoned to her over an hour ago? He could have called her from the drugstore on the corner of her own street and waited outside her apartment to see if she was going to do as she had been told. But why? Why bring her over here when they could have talked just as easily uptown? Was he the threat, the danger she had felt so insistently, so warningly, the moment she stepped outside Jordon's? She could come to no decision.

John Muir was a formless figure beside her. She repeated her question. "What are you doing here, John? How did you come to—?"

John said patiently, "I told you. When I got to your apartment you had already left. You were on the corner getting into a cab. I was about to yell to you when I saw this guy"—he waved a hand—"at your heels. He got into another cab. He was obviously tailing you. My cab was still waiting for the light to change. That fellow over there followed you and I followed him. I would have joined you inside that joint but I wanted to see what your pussyfooting friend was up to."

Gabrielle's bewilderment refused to go away. If the telephone call offering her information about the round man was genuine, on the level, and if the man hidden in the doorway of the tailor shop was the man who made it, why hadn't he met her as agreed? If he wasn't the man who had telephoned her, who was he? She narrowed her eyes peeringly. All she could really see was the swinging sign of the tailor shop. She took a step away from John. She said, "Suppose we go over there and see who that man is."

John pulled her back. "Gabrielle, don't be a fool! This is no place to go looking for trouble. It's not exactly a healthy spot at this time of night. Come on. We're getting out of here. Let our friend across the street keep on enjoying the nice frosty air by himself. Watch your step, the going will be rough." He swung Gabrielle around.

She was too cold, too confused, to argue. She let John lead her over planking, between piles of brick, through a clutter of wheelbarrows and ladders and heaped debris, into the depths of the building and finally out of it into the side street. More darkness, but at least the sky was overhead, and here and there lighted windows began to appear and an occasional pedestrian and one or two trucks. Walking her fast to Eighth Avenue, John kept looking back over his shoulder. There were no cabs on Eighth. Across to Seventh and then to Sixth —it was a long trek. Gabrielle was breathless when he halted her just short of the corner. "Wait here, I'll get a cab."

He went to the curb. The wind had fallen, so had the thermometer. That part of the city was darkened, empty. Gabrielle was tired and depressed. The evening had promised so much; it had produced so little. The elusive round man was a fattish will-o'-the-wisp she might have dreamed up in a nightmare. She was leaning against iron railings, huddled down in her coat, her eyes vacant on private cars going north and south at intervals, when she straightened hurriedly. The signal was red. A cab had pulled up for it twenty feet out in front and sufficiently to the left so that she could see into the dim interior. The woman in the back seat of the cab was Alice Amory.

Gabrielle started forward. As she did so the signal flashed green and the cab went on. She stood still, staring after it, rubbing her cheek with her glove. She was mistaken. The woman in the disappearing cab wasn't Alice, it was a stranger. She had been saved from making a fool of herself by the turning light. John hailed her then. A taxi at last—he was holding the door open. She got in. He got in beside her, gave the driver her address, and said, "What was it—why were you staring after that other cab?"

"I thought the woman in it was Alice," Gabrielle said. "It wasn't. Besides—what would Alice be doing down here at this time of night? She's home and in bed. She was dead tired when I left at half-past nine. It just looked like her for a moment."

They were almost at Thirty-fourth Street. John leaned forward. "Stop here, driver." Late as it was there were bright lights and plenty of people. John got out. "Back in a minute," he said to Gabrielle. "I want to get cigarettes."

The driver remarked conversationally that it was a cold night and that it looked like it was going to be a bad winter and Gabrielle said yes, it did, didn't it, and put her head back and closed her eyes. She was almost asleep when John got in and they drove on. He had had to walk almost a block. "Now," he said, "what happened tonight? Why did you go down to that Jordon's?" She told him about the telephone call, and he swore softly under his breath. "Gabrielle." His voice was grim. He turned to her, put a gloved fist on her knee, tapped her knee lightly. "You were decoyed over there to that Jordon's for a purpose. I don't know what the purpose was—but I'm sure of one thing. If you're right, if Mark's death was murder, you're fooling around with dynamite."

"Not very volatile stuff," she said dryly. "I haven't had much of a reaction so far."

"No?" John's brows went up. "What about that fellow who followed you down to Jordon's and didn't go in?"

"Maybe he didn't join me because he saw you—and anyhow it was the first hint of any information about the round man. How could I *not* go?"

John didn't answer. The cab was pulling to a stop. He paid the driver, wouldn't let her get out until he had looked up and down the street, then he hurried her across the pavement and up the steps. Inside, at the foot of the stairs, Gabrielle said, "It's late, John. You only got back to New York this morning and you must be pretty tired. Tomorrow will be—"

He put a hand on her elbow. "I'm going up with

you." The alert and wary air still clung to him. He not only went up with Gabrielle, he switched on all the lights in the apartment and looked into every room, made her look. He said, "Is there any sign of anything having been disturbed, any sign of anyone having been here since you left?"

Gabrielle said no. Bedroom, kitchen, bath, living-room, and tiny maid's room and bath were just as they had been when she went out. But John's insistence, his precautions, had begun to infect her. She said tartly, "Do stop it, John, you're frightening me."

"Good," he told her trenchantly. "That's what I want to do. Now sit down. I want to know everything that happened on the day Mark died—again."

Gabrielle settled herself in a corner of the couch and tucked her feet under her. She talked, slowly and evenly. It took a long while to satisfy John. He made her go over not only the facts but into every random impression she had had. When Mark said, looking after the round man in the lobby of the Devon that day, "So that was it"—what she had thought.

Gabrielle listened to the clock tick, looked at the long-legged shadow of the stand lamp, at smoke from John's cigarette. Well, what had she thought? She said, "It seemed to me as if he had connected something up, had solved, bitterly and disagreeably, some sort of puzzle."

"Just by looking at the round man?"

"As far as I could tell."

"Was there anyone with the round man in the lobby, before he left?"

"When I caught sight of him he was alone."

The waiting car and the woman in it, then. Gabrielle shook her head. The woman was nothing but a face without features beyond the round man. The car—she fumbled with scattered patches of memory, caught at something, lost it as she had in Tyrell's study, found it again. The sea, the road along the sea up in Greenfield, a car in which old Mr. Bradley was being taken for an airing by his housekeeper-chauffeur—the car in front of the Devon had been the same make and model as the Bradley chariot. She said, "The car the round man got into was an old Packard cabriolet with a gray body and black fenders and black wheels."

"Ah!" John took a fresh cigarette from the glass box beside the green chair, lit it. "You don't know what year?" Gabrielle didn't, except that it must be in the late twenties. More questions, about Alice and Tyrell and Joanna Middleton and Claire and the Bonds and, surprisingly, about Brenda Holmes and Blake Evans; how they had taken Mark's death, whether they had agreed with her in the beginning that Mark's death was murder.

"All right," he admitted, with a grin at her expression, "maybe I. *am* shooting all around the bull's-eye. But I've got to get the picture. Don't forget I wasn't in New York."

Gabrielle could only say that all Mark's friends had been profoundly shocked, that Tyrell and Alice had been wonderful. They had had an open mind at first. She didn't know whether Brenda Holmes had been at the funeral or not, there had been a lot of people. Joanna Middleton had been there, shrouded in crepe, and Blake Evans had been there because of Mark's niece, Claire Middleton. He had been a help with Claire, who got hysterical—she had adored Mark.

It was the second time John had brought up Blake's name. She said, frowning, "What makes you ask about Blake Evans? He and Mark scarcely knew each other. Their only link was young Claire, and I don't believe Claire and Blake were even engaged then, at least not formally."

John Muir shrugged. "I have a notion that if Mark was killed, it was by someone he knew. His gun, for instance—he kept it in the drawer of that long table near the window, a matter of common knowledge to his friends and only his friends. Your round man would scarcely have known about it. And then his sending that housekeeper of his, Mrs. Pendleton, out. Maybe he didn't want her to see the person who was coming there."

Death by invitation—Gabrielle shivered. "You mean Mark sent for someone?"

"Could be."

It went on for a long while. John was insatiable, would have kept it up all night if there had been anything more to get. But she had emptied herself of every scrap of knowledge, was drained, grayly exhausted, when he finally got up to go.

He still wasn't through. He said, turning his hat in long brown fingers, "That woman in the cab down there on Sixth Avenue at Twenty-seventh Street that you thought was Alice—was the resemblance close?"

Gabrielle said impatiently, "It wasn't Alice. I know that now. It just looked like her for a second, in the dim light."

"Yes. Now about the telephone call that took you to that Jordon's. You're sure your caller mentioned the round man?"

Was John questioning her veracity? Gabrielle said flatly, "I don't know who else. The man who called me asked if I wanted information about the man who went to see Mark at lunch on June twenty-fifth."

"Well then"—John nodded as though a doubt had been dispelled—"I guess that's that, and I've got everything straight. . . . Mind?" He bent, scooped a handful of cigarettes from the glass box beside the green chair, thrust them into his pocket. "I'm going now. Lock up after me."

"You do believe I'm right, John, that Mark was murdered—no matter what the police say?"

His glance was withdrawn. She could tell nothing from his expression. He said slowly, "I think the whole thing will bear re-examination. That round man of yours will have to be found. He may be guilty, he may be innocent. We won't know until we get hold of him. I'll tell you what I'm going to do. The firm has a man we use for confidential work, fellow named Pete Basil. I'm going to put the whole thing up to Pete. When he's had a shot at it, we'll know more."

John did believe her—a weight fell from Gabrielle's shoulders. She straightened then, went with him to the door. He told her to lock it behind him. "And 'don't go down to the end of town without consulting me'—don't go answering any more telephone calls, Gabrielle."

He was close to her in the warmth and stillness, was looking down at her intently. There was an odd little pause.

John moved. He said abruptly, "You're tired, Gabrielle. I shouldn't have stayed so long. Go to bed and try and get a good sleep. As soon as anything develops I'll let you know. Good night." He opened the door, closed it behind him.

Gabrielle locked it, listened to his footsteps retreat down the stairs, and went back to the living-room. She looked at the chair in which John had sat, at the arms on which his hands had lain. Bending, she picked up the lid of the glass box, started to put the lid on, and held it still, staring down into the box's emptiness. John had stopped the cab near Thirty-fourth Street to go and get cigarettes, yet he had none when he came in. Without volition she recalled the random movements of his hands over his pockets, his overcoat pockets and his suit pockets, before he sat down in the green chair. No, he had no cigarettes, he had smoked hers. Then—what had he left the cab near Thirty-fourth Street to do?

Chapter Six: NEW FEARS

GABRIELLE DREAMED OF BALLOONS THAT NIGHT, great fat balloons with bloated heads and rudimentary feet dancing over marshland, that alternately turned into Tyrell and Blake Evans and Joanna and Tony Van Ness. The balloon that was Tony had a bottle and glass in its little hands and kept stamping something that had been Susan down into wet slime. . . . It was horrible. She awoke with a headache. No Freud need apply—the source of the dream was obvious, John Muir and his questions the night before.

An aspirin, a shower, a tall glass of orange juice, and three cups of coffee put her on her feet, made her feel immensely better. She no longer had to bear the weight she had been carrying alone. John Muir was going to help. She had convinced him that Mark's death was murder and once John put his hand to a thing he would carry it through to the end. That was one of the qualities that had made him a success in the business he had inherited from an uncle while he was fighting in Italy. He not only had judgment and strength and decision, he had a lucky touch. The suit against his firm that would have been crippling had been settled in his favor, and troubles at the South American end had ironed themselves out. He would probably be a very rich man before he was through.

It might take time but the round man would be found. The pin prick of doubt about the cigarettes John hadn't bought on Thirty-fourth Street vanished with the light. When he got to the store it might have been closed, or he might have left the cigarettes in the cab.

Gabrielle began the day by getting rid of tasks that

had accumulated during long weeks of inaction. There were letters to answer, friends to be contacted, business to be attended to—and she had lost a porcelain filling. She made an appointment with her dentist for two-thirty that afternoon and was dressed and ready to go when the phone rang.

It was Alice. Alice began to talk in her electric way about her party. It was a flop. There were too many people. Tyrell didn't care for that sort of thing. "I don't know why I bother. . . . Did you happen to notice Joanna Middleton, Gabrielle? She doesn't seem to love you dearly, does she? Do you suppose it's Mark's money? And by the way, what are you doing about that, darling? Tyrell and Phil Bond both say you'll have to exert yourself, that the estate has to be settled. Phil declares you're an eel, he can't get you to make an appointment. I don't know what Joanna has to kick about really—she gets fifty thousand and she has plenty of her own. But she's acquisitive, a magpie—always was. Perhaps it's on account of Claire. I suppose Claire and Blake Evans will be married soon. He's awfully good-looking. You really ought to warn that young man not to rave about you so. He did, at dinner. Maybe that got mother-dear's back up."

Alice wanted Gabrielle to go with her to the Larks' for cocktails. "I couldn't get out of it and I don't see how I'm to stand them without support. Tyrell promised faithfully, but he's deep in jugs and jars and retorts. Such smells in that laboratory of his, frightful. I might as well be married to the information booth in Grand Central for all the good I get out of him. And Joe Blanford's in Florida and Arthur broke his leg skiing in Quebec."

Gabrielle explained that she couldn't go to the Larks', she was in for a solid hour's session with her dentist. "I've been putting it off for ages. . . . Did people stay on last night, Alice? Did you get to bed late?"

There was the slightest of pauses. Then Alice said, "Not very. You looked wonderful. You do feel better, don't you?" Gabrielle said she did, and hung up.

The hot-water faucet in the bathroom was dripping. She went in to turn it off. If Alice had been downtown the night before she would have said so. Anyhow the woman huddled in the corner of the cab wasn't Alice. Alice didn't huddle.

Gabrielle was much more than an hour at her dentist's. When she arrived home a small man in a brownish-gray topcoat and a brownish-gray hat was waiting outside her door. He removed his hat. Neat hair that was neither gray or brown made him look like a mouse, gentle and sad. "My name is Todhunter," he said in a soft, whispering voice, adding, "from the Homicide Squad." He showed her his credentials. "I'd like to have a few words with you, Miss."

Gabrielle stared her surprise. Todhunter said humbly, "It's just for the record—to get things finished up, like."

For the record—a record of suicide. In the living-room Gabrielle waved him coldly to a chair. "Sit down —did you say detective?" She compromised on: "Mr. Todhunter."

Todhunter sat. He murmured on about the record and about his chief, Inspector McKee of the Homicide Squad. The Inspector was in the West. He had known Mr. Middleton for a long while.

Gabrielle had never heard of Inspector McKee. She answered the little detective's routine questions, said, as she had said a thousand times before, shadows around her again, that she had heard no one in Mark's apartment, but that she had heard the hinge of the front door creak as someone went out.

"Thank you, Miss. Now, while you were there that

afternoon, you didn't hear Mr. Middleton use the telephone, did you?"

Gabrielle said, "But I didn't know Mr. Middleton was there. I was in an upstairs room with the door closed. Oh—" She stared at Todhunter. "I did hear the phone downstairs. I picked up the instrument in my room and someone was dialing, so I hung up. I thought it was Mark's housekeeper, Mrs. Pendleton, but—Mrs. Pendleton was out then. It must have been Mark." Eagerness invaded her.

It died at Todhunter's prim nod. "That's what we thought." She gave him an emphatic no when he asked whether she had touched anything in the room after she had discovered Mark on the floor.

"I see. Now, since Mr. Middleton died, Miss—has anything occurred?"

Gabrielle hesitated. But she had nothing to conceal. She told him about the telephone call last night when she got home from the Amorys', and going to Jordon's, and her disappointment when her caller didn't turn up. "It was a wild-goose chase." She didn't mention John Muir.

At the end of five minutes the little detective rose. He didn't immediately go. He said, "Well, I guess that's about all, Miss. No. One more thing," and sprang it on her in his deceptively mild voice. "Who is Mr. John Muir, could you tell me? Was he a friend of Mr. Middleton's? We talked to most of Mr. Middleton's friends at the time, but I can't recall—was Mr. Muir in New York when Mr. Middleton died?"

Gabrielle sat very still. No one must know of John's flying visit to her on that distant, dreadful day. No one did know, she was sure of it, and she could answer truthfully. "Mr. Muir wasn't in New York at the time, he went to São Paulo in the early spring, only got back yesterday morning. . . . Just a minute, please."

She had been aware all along of a bubbling sound somewhere. It was coming from the bathroom. She crossed the hall, opened the bathroom door, and stared incredulously. The hot-water tap was on full. Water ran chucklingly, swirling and eddying in a pool in the basin, filling the air with clouds of steam. Gabrielle gazed at the tap blankly. She had turned the water off before she went out, she was positive of it. Besides, it was only dripping then, and now it was on full. Had someone been in the apartment while she was at the dentist's? Susan might have come into town, or Tony—Susan had a key. But would either of them have left the water on? Scarcely.

Was she mistaken? Had she meant to give the faucet a twist and forgotten? It seemed to her that she could feel the faucet's cool smoothness in her palm and against her fingers when she had turned it tight before going out, unless—coldness struck at her—the feeling existed only in her imagination. Yesterday she had imagined that someone was trying to kill her.

She roused herself, shut the water off decisively, and went back into the hall, to find the little detective looking at her interestedly. "Anything wrong, Miss?" he asked, and continued to gaze at her. Conscious of the whiteness of her face, Gabrielle said with unnecessary violence, "Nothing whatever, except that I left the water turned on."

Todhunter said, "Oh? Well, thank you, Miss," and picked up his hat. He had intended to query her about the affair on the subway platform yesterday afternoon, but she seemed upset, and the Inspector had said not to alarm her. If she thought anything of it herself, had any suspicions, she would have mentioned the incident. There were other ways. He took his departure.

Outside the closed and locked door, Todhunter heard the slam of the bolt going home and rubbed his chin

thoughtfully. In her account of where she had been last
night Miss Conant hadn't mentioned meeting up with
Mr. John Muir, whose name and address he had ob-
tained by following Muir home. What bothered him
still more was the tailspin she had gone into because
water was running in the bathroom. Was she—he fingered
a loose button on his coat meditatively—quite all there?
The little detective's doubt of Gabrielle's mental sta-
bility would have been enormously increased if he had
seen her twenty-four hours later.

On the following morning she got a surprise phone
call. Brenda Holmes rang her at a little after eleven and
asked her to a cocktail party. She was having some people that afternoon, and would Gabrielle come?

Gabrielle's brows rose. Word that she was out of seclu-
sion had evidently been passed around, but while she
and Brenda had been meeting at the houses of mutual
friends for a long while they had never been intimate.
Why this sudden attention? Go and see. Perhaps John
would be there and might have news, although it was
unlikely so soon.

Gabrielle thanked Brenda and accepted, and got into
a soft gray wool dress that made her skin very white
and her eyes a misty sea color. By that time she had
pushed the incident of the running water to the back of
her mind. She had more important things to think
about. It was half-past five when she arrived at her
destination and gentle dusk was falling over the square.
Trees made twisted charcoal-black patterns and birds
flew in the pearly shadows underneath. It was the love-
liest hour of the day, when darkness drew in and thousands of lamps were lighted against it and nighttime
existences were taken up.

Brenda welcomed her pleasantly to the small pretty
apartment on Washington Square West where she lived
with an elderly invalid cousin.

"Nice of you to come, Gabrielle. You're looking *so* much better. I said so to John the other night."

Proprietorship? *Don't be a cat,* Gabrielle told herself. "Thanks, Brenda. I feel much better." They chatted for a minute. Didn't Gabrielle loathe the new hats? Did she find winter dried her skin—nothing deeper than half an inch. Brenda led the way to the diminutive living-room. "You know everyone, I think."

Gabrielle did. Philip and Julie Bond were there, and the Ryecrofts and Simeon Clark and the Gasconys. "When," Phil Bond demanded, bringing Gabrielle a Martini, "am I going to be able to talk business with you?"

That was another of the tasks she would have to take up. "Soon, Phil," she promised. Big, ruddy, jovial, Phil Bond wasn't a miracle of tact. He said to Bob Ryecroft with whom Gabrielle was standing, "Gather ye round, boys, this young woman's going to be a catch."

Mark's dead, he's gone, forgotten, Gabrielle reflected bitterly, and watched Brenda moving about the room. What was behind those blue eyes, that golden look? Shrewdness, calculation, the intelligence to conceal intelligence?—or simply a moderate portion of brains that taught Brenda how to use her beauty to the most advantageous end, i.e., a wealthy marriage? Well, what was the matter with that? Why did you expect so much of beauty like Brenda's? And yet, in a way, it was fair enough. If the box was enchanting you expected the contents to be equally so, holding the mind and spirit as the outside held the eye. To be presented with mediocrity or worse was fraud.

Claire Middleton and Blake Evans came in then, diverting her thoughts. What little Gabrielle had seen of Mark's young niece, she liked. Claire was a tall shy girl with a long narrow face, a delicate skin and soft brown eyes, gentle and sweet. Blake at once crossed the room to Gabrielle. "Hello! I didn't expect to see you here." She said, "Hello, yourself," and they fell into gossip about Greenfield, and people they both knew. In the middle of it Gabrielle glanced up and got the impact of two brown daggers flashing at her from across the room.

She was blankly amazed. She and Blake Evans had gone to school together and she liked him and he liked her, and that was all there was to it. Was Claire Middleton jealous, or did the child dislike her for some other reason?

Gabrielle cut her conversation with Blake short and left a few minutes later. She got home at half-past six. When she opened the door with her key there were people in the living-room—a man and a woman—she could hear their voices. It must be Susan and Tony, she thought, and crossed the foyer to the living-room, to pause sharply in the doorway, again with that cold feeling of shock. There were no lights on and the living-room in twilit darkness was empty. There was no one in it. She switched on the lamps dazedly. The voices she had heard were coming out of the radio.

Gabrielle's glance touched it, moved away, returned to the cabinet. Her breathing was flat, shallow. What was happening to her? She hadn't had the radio on since yesterday morning. No one had apparently entered the apartment while she was at Brenda's, the door was locked. And yet the radio, silent when she went out, was on full blast. Gabrielle went to it. She snapped it off. Stillness rolled against her eardrums. There were voices buried in it. *Did you turn it on unconsciously—neglect to turn it off? Didn't you? Did you? Are you beginning to forget things?*

She went to the kitchen door. Like the front door, it was securely locked. The groceries she had ordered were in a box outside. She went back to the living-room, picked up the phone, and called Susan in Greenfield. That was it, of course. Susan had been there—or Tony. But when she got her cousin, Susan said no, neither of them had come into town that day, and asked why. Gabrielle said someone had been there while she was out, but it didn't matter, talked for a few minutes without knowing exactly what she said, and rang off. She went down to the basement and sought out the superintendent, busy coaling the hot-water fire. He shook his head at her question. He had admitted no one to her apartment that afternoon.

Gabrielle went slowly upstairs. The hot water on when she had thought she had turned it off, the radio playing when she hadn't touched it—well, she hadn't turned the hot water off, and she had turned the radio on and, face it, had—forgotten. That night she had to take two of the sleeping-pills Dr. Cutter had given her before sleep finally came.

She woke in midmorning to the shrilling of the telephone. It was John Muir. John was brisk, businesslike. He had nothing to report except that Pete Basil, his investigator, was on the job and that he'd let her know as soon as there was any news. Then Phil Bond called. Phil wanted to see her, something had come up. "How about this afternoon? I'll be in your neighborhood anyhow."

Gabrielle said listlessly, "Late this afternoon, half-past four. Not any earlier. I have to go up to McGrath's to get some stuff I left there."

McGrath's was the advertising firm for which she had worked until a week before the wedding that had never taken place. Gabrielle made tea instead of coffee, rinsed the cup, put it on the drainboard and dressed. Blank spots, memory lapses: "Everything went gray . . . I didn't know the gun was loaded"—they put people in asylums for that. *Oh, stop it,* she told herself wearily, *everybody forgets sometimes.*

There were two locks on the front door, the lower lock belonging there, and a special lock she had had put on when she first took the apartment and which she seldom used. She was the only one who had a key for the special lock. When she went out that afternoon she bolted the back door and double-locked the front door.

To empty out her desk and say good-by to Miss Hallstein and Jim Gregg and Barney, the art director, took longer than she had expected, and Phil Bond was on the sidewalk in front of the house when she got out of her cab. Tyrell was with him. Tyrell looked tired. He and Phil Bond had been inspecting one of Alice's apartments. She had a good deal of real estate.

They went upstairs. Gabrielle switched on the lights in the living-room and the two men took off their coats. "You've been working too hard," Gabrielle said accusingly to Tyrell and he admitted it. "Some day I'm going to take a long vacation and do nothing but sit in the sun." Phil Bond was his usual cheerful self. He was armed with a briefcase. He began to talk about a block of Industrial Products, Inc. of Mark's that had to be given immediate attention. "They ought to be disposed of at once, Gabrielle. They're at their peak now—hold them another couple of months and you may take a big loss."

She smiled at his earnestness. "Let me get my breath, Phil. What will you have? A drink? Coffee?"

Both men said coffee. Gabrielle threw her own coat down on top of theirs, pulled off her hat. "I won't be a moment." She started for the kitchen—and saw it. The cup out of which she had had her tea at noon that day, and which she had washed and put on the drainboard in the kitchen to dry, was upside-down over the upright of the stand lamp in the corner.

At her abrupt halt, Phil Bond and Tyrell stopped talking. She faced them slowly. They stared at her in alarmed amazement. Gabrielle felt herself swaying. Tyrell jumped up and came to her and lowered her into a chair near the window. "Just take it easy, Gabrielle . . . just take it easy." Phil Bond was bringing her whisky in a water glass. She drank it, shuddered, and fought her way back to sanity, or as near to it as she could get.

"It's that cup," she said, waving at the little china dome crookedly upside-down on top of the lamp and trying to keep her voice level. "Before I went out I washed it and put it away in the kitchen. Or I was sure I did. There were other things." She was shaking again. "Someone *must* have been in here. And yet you both saw me unlock the door, and I have the only key." Her voice rose. "But I did put the cup on the drainboard in the kitchen. I did put it there. I *know* I did."

Tyrell went to examine the doors. The bolt on the back door was in place, the lock on the front door didn't appear to have been tampered with. The two men looked at each other. Phil Bond said heavily, "Gabrielle, you've been doing too much. You're tired, overwrought. You ought to get away and have a good rest." Tyrell said worriedly, "Two keys come with a lock. Lose the other one? Well then, someone could have found it and come in here."

Why should anyone enter her apartment illegally to put a teacup upside-down on the stem of a lamp? Gabrielle could see the question in both men. Tyrell was examining the view from a window. Phil Bond took papers from his briefcase for her to sign, explaining whys and wherefores that sounded distantly in her ears. She did as she was told, stupidly, numbly. Tyrell had removed the cup, but the image of it was stamped on the retina of her eyes. Not to be sure of what you were doing, had done, not to *know*—the running water on Monday, the radio on Tuesday, the misplaced cup on Wednesday . . .

Phil Bond and Tyrell left, night came and went, and it was morning. Thursday and Friday passed without incident, and Saturday. Then, on Sunday, the full horror cascaded down over her in strangling folds from which there was no escape.

Chapter Seven: THE WHITE PILLS

SUSAN CALLED GABRIELLE early on Saturday morning. She was openly concerned. Evidently she had· heard something from the Bonds, or from Tyrell and Alice. Susan said, "You've got to come up to Greenfield. I won't take no. You haven't been here since"—she hesitated, and plunged—"since Mark died. You know deep down you hate the city—and there's nothing to keep you there. Now listen, you take the three-thirty from Grand Central and I'll meet you at the station."

It was almost, Gabrielle thought, listening apathetically, as though they had changed places. It was Susan who was decisive and clear and knew her own mind, she who doubted and questioned and in the end did nothing. A recognized phobia, wasn't it?

Gabrielle agreed without argument to what her cousin proposed. The thought of getting out of the apartment, knowing that she wasn't going to have to sleep there alone another night—waking to who knew what?—brought a faint release of pressure. She packed hastily, taking only essentials, among them her sleeping-pills. There weren't many left. She would have to get Dr. Cutter to give her another prescription. The nights were the worst.

She had planned to walk to the station but rain was

coming down drearily and there was a cold wind from the east. The usual cab was in front of the florist's shop on the corner. The usual man wasn't at the wheel. She got into the cab, said, "Grand Central, please," and asked about the other man. She knew him well, knew his politics and that he liked the Giants and hated the Yankees and what he was going to do when his horse paid off. The new driver said without turning, "Joe? He's sick. I'm playing that corner for a while," in a surly voice. He was a disagreeable brute with a bullet head, a long thick nose, and a large brown mole on his forehead under the peak of his cap.

The three-thirty left on time. It was purple dark when Gabrielle reached Greenfield. Susan was there waiting at the station in the familiar beaten-up sedan, green beret sideways on crisp copper curls, and just for a moment as she climbed in, the world Gabrielle had once lived in came back, a world in which she had known her way about, who she was, where she was, what she did, intended to do.

She kissed Susan and said she was fine and asked about the children and about Tony. You always did ask in that fashion about Tony, as though he were something on the fire that might boil over with disastrous results. Were things going well? Susan said they were. Arrived at the sprawling house in the fields beyond the town's rim, Gabrielle kissed little Joan and young Anthony, patted the dog, and admired some new furniture, with the proper responses. "Susan, the room's lovely. Isn't that bookcase an innovation, and those two chairs—and haven't you done something with the curtains?"

Susan said absently that Tony had picked up a lot of stuff at auction, scrutinized Gabrielle in the fuller light, and frowned. "Are you all right, Gabrielle? You've lost weight and your eyes are enormous. I think you ought to go back to that Dr. Cutter for a checkup—I really do."

Gabrielle laughed and said she hated doctors and that she was perfectly all right. The effort to be all right carried her through the evening without mishap. Susan apologized for not serving cocktails on account of Tony, but when Tony came in he brought a cargo of bottles with him. The liquor helped.

Tyrell and Alice had a house on the shore a few miles away. Gabrielle didn't want to see anyone, but at ten-thirty, when Susan went to her bedroom, a big, rambling, pleasant, shabby room in the west ell, she said they were coming over for breakfast in the morning.

Sunday-morning breakfasts were an institution in Greenfield. People dropped in at other people's houses in droves. It didn't really matter. Susan switched on another lamp, turned down the bed, and Gabrielle roused herself. "There's something I've been wanting to say to you, Sue. Mark's estate will be settled soon and there'll be a lot of money, so—you don't need to worry any more."

Susan began to cry. Gabrielle was distressed; it wasn't in character. For all her lightness, there was a stoical quality to Susan. "You're so damn *good*, Gabrielle," she said, through tears, "so—so *swell*." She wiped her eyes, smiled. "That's enough of that, but—thanks. Tony's got plenty to do at the moment—but if we get into the doldrums again I'll let you know." After five difficult years, in spite of what he had done to her she still loved her charming, unscrupulous, irresponsible husband.

"Now go to bed and get a good sleep, Gabrielle," she said at the door, added, "Brenda Holmes and John Muir are at the Amorys', they'll probably be over—and I want you to look nice."

John Muir in Greenfield. She hadn't heard from him since Wednesday, perhaps he would have news.

Gabrielle undressed quickly, switched off the lamps, got into bed, tried to sleep and couldn't. Her mind was too alive, awake. Hadn't she, contemplating her own burden, forgotten the main issue? Perhaps John Muir's Pete Basil had picked up the round man's trail. . . .

Almost two hours later, Gabrielle got up and did what she hadn't intended to do, took her sedative. She would look like a scarecrow tomorrow if she didn't get some rest. Brenda Holmes always looked marvelous. Her beauty didn't depend on light and shade, the emotion of the moment. She had the changeless perfection of a marble or a bronze. Yes, it was a wonder that she hadn't married. She would make a perfect wife for a man of wealth and position.

There were only six pills in the little box. Gabrielle swallowed two, smoked a cigarette at the window. The frosty November night was very still. There were no sounds as there were in the spring and summer, and then there was a sound. It was low, distant—and hurting. Susan was crying again. What *was* the matter with Sue? Gabrielle climbed into her bed worried and uneasy until the sedative took hold, then drifted off.

Thunder woke her. The thunder was Tony Van Ness rapping resoundingly on her bedroom door. "Hi, Gabrielle. Up, up, the British. It's half-past eleven and Susan's shouting for you."

A clutter of voices drifted through the open window; someone laughed. Gabrielle got out of bed. She was stupid with sleep and her eyelids had weights on them. A shower would help but there was no time for one. It was the maid's day off and Susan would have her hands full. John would be there, perhaps already was, and Brenda Holmes. . . . Why couldn't you always sleep, she thought, getting into dark-blue slacks and a yellow pullover. When you were asleep nothing mattered.

There were no hurts, no problems. Twice she got her lipstick on crooked before she was ready. The sun was shining. It came in and lay down in bars on the wide old floor boards. Soon there would be snow. She felt oddly peaceful, indifferent. Sleep was still in her freeingly. It would have been good to sleep the day out.

The big old-fashioned dining-room was down the hall and around the corner to the right. Voices and laughter again. Gabrielle went through the dining-room door. They were all there, in the living-room beyond, Alice and Tyrell and Brenda and John and the Hardens. Tony was fixing drinks for some of the men. Susan, smart and pretty in green wool, was at the buffet laden with covered dishes, manipulating her coffee urn. There was no trace of the tears of the night before. She looked up with relief as Gabrielle came in.

"Thank heavens! I hated to wake you but I'm all thumbs this morning. Sleep well? Good. Make the tea, will you, darling? Everything else is ready." She called to her guests. "Breakfast—come eat it."

Gabrielle turned her back on the advancing throng and began to busy herself with the tea things. Cups were ready on the Georgian silver tray that had been her uncle's, the silver kett'e was hissing over its flame next to the big Derbyshire teapot and the canister and spoon. People called greetings to her and Gabrielle answered over her shoulder, her hands busy, listening for John Muir's voice, waiting for him to come up to her.

"How are you, Gabrielle, dear? It's ages since you've been here." That was Celia Harden. Gabrielle said she was fine, asked how Celia was, poured water in a long stream, put the lid on the pot, and swung round. John was looking at her from across the room. He threw up a hand in salute, tall and straight in breeches and boots and an old tweed jacket.

Gabrielle smiled at him. Brenda Holmes was also in

riding-clothes, propped on the arms of a chair, biting into a small crisp sausage on a toothpick. She had no hat on. Her fair hair shone like satin above silvery whipcord and her eyes were dazzlingly blue. "Can I have a cup of tea, Gabrielle?" she begged. "I'm simply dying of thirst." Alice and Celia Harden wanted tea too. Most of the men were drinking coffee. Gabrielle lifted the big teapot and poured, handing out the three cups. The sugar and cream and lemon were on the buffet.

Chit chat, banter, sunlight on warm paneling, the children running around outside, Tony, geniality at large, a glass at his lips . . . Suddenly someone, Alice, gave a little scream. The scream was followed by laughter. Brenda said in an amused tone, gazing down into her cup, "Me, too. Is this something new? Or what?" All three women looked at Gabrielle. She felt heavy, helpless, didn't know what they were talking about, what was going on. The others had stopped talking. Everyone was staring. Alice explained.

"Look what Gabrielle's done to us. Hot water. She forgot to put in the tea."

Gabrielle took an unsteady step. *No,* her mind shrieked. And *Yes,* another part of it said, *yes. This time you're caught. You meant to put in the tea, thought you put it in—and you didn't.* Barriers hemming in sanity loosened. She was foundering in fog, with chains dragging her down. Her elbow struck something a sharp blow. It was the Derbyshire teapot. She staggered drunkenly among the fragments, would have fallen except that John Muir caught her.

"Get some more cushions."

"Her head ought to be down."

"What do you suppose made her—?"

"She hasn't been well, never really recovered from—"

"Where's that liquor?"

Gabrielle was on the divan in front of the living-room fire. She hadn't lost consciousness, had kept her eyes closed as a protection, burningly aware of the scrutiny directed at her, the wonder, the guesses, the alarm. She opened her eyes. Susan was kneeling beside the sofa, chafing her hands. The others stood around in a semi-circle.

Gabrielle sat up a little. The tip of her nose itched and her lips were dry. She had to make some kind of explanation—and there was one of sorts. "I'm all right . . . what I need is coffee. It was those pills."

"Pills!" Susan exclaimed, and Alice demanded, "What pills?"

"The sleeping-pills Dr. Cutter gave me."

She told them, sipping a cup of hot black coffee Tony rushed to her, about having taken two of the pills the night before and how drugged she felt when Tony called her at eleven-thirty. "I couldn't seem to wake up." If only it was the pills, she thought, if only it was nothing more than a drug.

Understanding, relief; they accepted the pills. "That's exactly what happened to me once." "Me, too. I took the stuff after I had pneumonia and I want to tell you . . ." Sedatives I have known was a popular subject.

Breakfast was resumed. Alice thought Gabrielle should have something to eat and Tyrell, looking worried under his cockatoo brush of flaxen hair, brought her toast and bacon, and Tony, lean and dark and Machiavellian, brought her more coffee. They all seemed to be wearing masks. Inner fear was a hard tight core behind Gabrielle's surface recovery. She bemoaned the teapot. Susan said, "It was yours, darling; anyhow, perhaps it can be patched up."

Could her mind be patched up, Gabrielle asked herself grayly, or was the disease incurable? Not to know what you were doing, always to be afraid of what you might do next. . . . People drifted about, groups mingled, broke up, re-formed; John Muir didn't approach Gabrielle directly, but twice, across the width of the room, he sent her a message with his eyes. She couldn't interpret it. The Deans came, and Ellen Tribeau and Oscar Force, and then Joanna Middleton and Claire and Blake Evans. They were week-ending with the Amorys—so like Alice, she could never get enough guests.

The same old group, tied together by long association. Gabrielle had a sudden longing to be free of it. Neither Joanna nor Claire came near the couch on which she was propped up. But Blake Evans did, and she wished he wouldn't. Manlike, he was oblivious of under- or overtones.

"What's the matter, Gabrielle? You look all in—don't bother answering if you don't feel like it. When I'm sick I want to be left alone."

Blake was nice. He was quiet and perceptive and able to interpret your mood. He had an almost feminine gentleness. It was that rather than his looks that made him popular not only with men but with women. Susan had been crazy about him when she was seventeen. Too bad Susan hadn't married him instead of Tony. . . . She said, "I'm fine now, Blake. I just got dizzy, that's all. Go and get something to eat."

Her curtness puzzled him. He gave her a quick glance and sauntered off to join Claire Middleton.

Gabrielle was beginning to feel stronger physically, more wide-awake. Perhaps it was the sleeping-pills that had made her forget the tea, perhaps there was nothing wrong with her. Ten minutes later she was plunged back into the depths. Her mind played another trick on her.

She had gone to one of the long windows at the front of the room, was gazing out at the wintry landscape, when she went rigid. The two children and the Airedale romping with a ball, cars, sun shining on the coats of the horses John and Brenda had ridden over on, a couple of chauffeurs chatting and smoking, three women with canes walking past on the road; a face came into view around the clump of cedars near the gate, was abruptly withdrawn. But not before Gabrielle thought: *It's my cab man—the man who drove me to Grand Central yesterday afternoon.*

It wasn't her cab man. She went outside, walked quickly across dry grass. There was no one behind the cedars, no stranger in sight. Standing there under the leafless trees Gabrielle shivered uncontrollably. She was overwhelmed. Now she was beginning to *see* things. . . . She returned slowly to the house.

Suddenly she couldn't bear to face people. Inside the hall she went left and down the passage to her own room in the ell. The hall was dark. Opening her bedroom door she stood still, the knob in her hand. What was that sound? Had the other door, the door leading to the roofed-in terrace on the north, just closed? Had someone just gone out—or were her senses fooling her again? She advanced into the room and studied the door leading to the veranda. The bolt was pushed back, was free of its socket. It had been in place last night—hadn't it? She swung sharply. A breeze was blowing her hair. The window to the right of the dressing-table was open. Beyond it a thick planting of overgrown pines that extended almost to the road obscured the light. Susan continually talked of having them thinned but Tony said they acted as a windbreak.

Gabrielle went to the window and thrust her head out. Thirty feet from her, back turned, a man was making his way through the pines toward the front of the house. He was moving fast and surreptitiously, as though he didn't want to be seen. The man was John

Muir. Gabrielle retreated into the room—and saw it.
The box that held her pills had been moved. It was on
the wrong side of the lamp on the table beside the bed.
She moved across the rug, took the cover off. There
had been four pills left in the box. There were no pills
now. The box was empty.

The full implication of that emptiness was like a
flash of blinding light. The pills—the pills weren't what
they were supposed to be. She wasn't mad. There was
nothing the matter with her mind. Her forgetfulness
with the tea wasn't psychological. It had a purely physical base. She had been drugged, deliberately, as witness
the removal of the remaining four pills once she had
called them to public attention. Relief as tangible as
a flood of cleansing water washed through her healingly.

It ebbed, was succeeded by a wave of pain. Someone
had removed the pills in order that they shouldn't be
found, perhaps analyzed. And less than half a minute
earlier John Muir had walked away from this isolated
wing, fast and secretively.

Chapter Eight: MISSING FORTUNE

KATY DID, KATY DIDN'T—John did, John didn't . . .
Gabrielle finally managed to have a word alone with
John Muir in the hall before he and Brenda rode off.

"John, someone took my sleeping-pills, the four that
were left in the box, from my bedroom a little while
ago. I looked out—and saw you walking away."

John didn't say anything for a moment. Then he
nodded. The nod was somber. Oddly enough, and it was
frightening, he used the same words Mark had used in
the lobby of the Devon on the day he died. "So that
was it," John said softly. "I thought it might be—" He
stared at the newel post, at Gabrielle's face, narrowed
eyes smolderingly bright, drew a long breath.

"Yes, I was there. I was over on the north side of the pines when I heard someone leaving your room by the veranda door. I didn't think it was you. I tried to see who it was, and didn't succeed. Gabrielle—" He was harsh suddenly. "Don't take any more pills. If you can't sleep, stay awake. There's something pretty nasty going on—far more than we two know about." Then his tone changed. It became light, bantering. "You're a fraud. Now how about you and I and Alice and Tyrell getting together for dinner and the theater one night soon? I'll give you a ring."

They were standing near the front door. Claire Middleton and Brenda were coming down the stairs. John left Gabrielle.

The question mark remained in her mind. What was John doing away from the others at the northern end of the house? It wasn't that she disbelieved him exactly, it, was that she thought he wasn't telling her all the truth. He wasn't trying to shield her. She knew him too well for that. He faced up to facts, however disagreeable they might be, expected other people to do so. Then why was he being evasive? Because he was. Let it go, she decided wearily, he would probably tell her when there was time.

One thing was certain. What John had said about more going on than they knew about was true. Someone in the house, or with access to it, had removed the four remaining pills from her bedroom. Remaining? Hadn't other pills been substituted for her own and then taken away? Because, back again on safe ground, with her feet firm beneath her, Gabrielle knew that the other manifestations of mental instability had been superinduced, the running water in the bathroom of her apartment, the teacup upside-down on top of the lamp, the radio in her living-room turned on. Someone had managed, with pass keys or skeleton keys or whatever had been used, to get into her apartment at will. There was no other conclusion possible. Why? To undermine her faith in herself, make her shaky, indecisive, useless, to discredit her with her friends, with Tyrell and Phil Bond, and again that morning over the tea—all this in order to stop her talk of the round man and break her conviction that Mark had been murdered.

The surly taxi driver who she thought had followed her up here and who had slipped away when she went outside, might be a confederate of the round man's, he might have been the one who made the appointment with her at Jordon's and didn't keep it. Tell John about him as soon as she got back. She had to be in Phil Bond's office on Tuesday afternoon, Phil was getting things into shape, wanted her to sign some papers.

It was on Monday morning that she found out about Tony Van Ness.

Susan had said they were doing all right and certainly the evidence of it was there, in the new furniture and draperies, the furnace properly fixed, any number of odds and ends. Tony had told her at Alice's party that he had delivered the cover to Drake's, which accounted for it; he got good prices.

Tony hadn't delivered the cover. On Monday morning Susan was doing her marketing in the village and Tony wasn't around when the phone rang. It was the art editor of Drake's calling. He demanded Tony. She said Tony wasn't there and the irate voice, addressing her as Mrs. Van Ness, wanted to know where the devil the May cover was? Gabrielle corrected the editor and hung up.

So that was the explanation of Susan's tears last night —Tony hadn't done the cover. He was gambling again, and Susan knew it, and didn't want her to know. Poor Susan, with her almost passionate desire for order, normality, engrossed in her children, her home, her garden, her friends.

Gabrielle had only turned away from the phone when it rang again. It was New York calling. This time the call was for her. A voice she didn't know, a man's deep resonant voice, said, "Miss Conant?" and when Gabrielle said yes: "This is Inspector McKee of the Homicide Squad, Miss Conant. Something of importance in regard to the late Mark Middleton has come up. We'd like to talk to you as soon as possible."

Gabrielle caught the two o'clock train.

"Try this, Miss Conant. It's not very comfortable, I'm afraid."

The Inspector waved at a chair facing his desk near the single window in the long narrow room on the third floor of the Twenty-seventh Precinct.

Gabrielle sat down. McKee was a very tall man, with a thin clever face, a strong mouth, deep-set brown eyes, and a courteous manner.

Studying Gabrielle, the Scotsman was faintly surprised. She was younger than he had anticipated, not, somehow, the sort of girl he would have expected Mark Middleton to have chosen for a wife. Middleton was pretty much of an extrovert, and his tastes were simpler, more obvious. This young woman was a delicate piece of mechanism, highly civilized and very sensitively adjusted. Gray-green eyes at a slight tilt under long brows, dark hair, a white skin, high cheekbones, a fine jaw line; she wasn't conventionally beautiful. Her charm was too subtle for that, took time to register.

McKee was favorably impressed. It was beginning to look as though the girl had been right all along. The discovery Middleton's lawyer, Bond, had dug up pointed that way, unless there was some adequate explanation. He told the girl about it, baldly.

Gabrielle listened with amazement. A little more than eight weeks before he died, Mark had converted eighty thousand dollars' worth of blue chip securities into cash. The eighty thousand in cash had disappeared. If Mark had disposed of it himself there was no record of such disposal, at least none had yet been found.

"What can you tell me about this, Miss Conant?" the Inspector asked.

Gabrielle shook her head. She could tell him nothing.

"Mr. Middleton didn't speak to you about any such transaction?"

"No." She didn't add that Mark wouldn't have unless it concerned her. He didn't believe in bothering women with business.

"You have no inkling, no idea—?"

A very terrible idea had darted through Gabrielle's mind. Tony Van Ness—Tony, who had been pressed for money and who had miraculously found it some-where. . . .

"I have no idea whatever." She couldn't control the whiteness of her face, the too steady cadence of her voice.

McKee noted these items and went on talking, giving her dates. It had taken Mark several days to realize on his securities. He had asked his brokers for cash, had carried the cash away with him from their offices on the morning of the twenty-fifth of June.

"June the twenty-fifth." Gabrielle sat forward, her eyes brilliant. It was coming at last. "The round man!" she exclaimed. "It was on that day, the twenty-fifth, that the round man arrived at Mark's apartment during lunch. He had a briefcase with him. Mark could have given him the money—and then, to keep from having to account for it, or pay it back, he killed Mark."

McKee moved a pencil on his desk. Gabrielle Conant had been rather badly frightened. Her recovery was quick. She was offering them a stranger, a man whose existence as an important factor had never been substantiated. Clearly a re-evaluation of the whole case was called for. He had been out of the city when Mark Middleton died, had been away for a good part of the autumn. No use interrogating the girl in detail until he knew a good deal more.

Gabrielle leaned toward him eagerly. "This does prove, doesn't it, Inspector, that Mark's death was murder—and not suicide?"

McKee said, "We'll have to see. It's not possible at this stage to say anything definite. Certainly the disappearance of eighty thousand dollars of Mr. Middleton's money in cash calls for further inquiry. Well, thank you for coming, Miss Conant. We'll keep you informed." He rose.

When the girl was gone the Scotsman pressed a button, had File No. 136-704 brought, and sent for Todhunter.

Gabrielle went home a prey to violently conflicting emotions. The Inspector had admitted that the disappearance of the eighty thousand dollars in cash changed the picture, that Mark's death might have been murder and not suicide. But suppose Tony—Susan's husband, the father of Susan's children—was mixed up in it somewhere? She told herself that there was no evidence, nothing to connect the modest sum spent on the house in Greenfield with Mark's missing eighty thousand, that Tony might have won money at cards, or on a horse.

She was only just in when Alice called her, full of this new development. She said, "Almost a third of what Mark had, Gabrielle—Phil Bond and Tyrell are stunned. I hope they find it, for your sake, darling. Did Mark ever say anything—I mean he told us he was going to give you a nice wedding present and he might have—"

Gabrielle said she knew nothing about the money. Later Susan called from Greenfield to find out what the Inspector had had to say. She was shocked when she heard the news, but not at all apprehensive—and she would have been terror-stricken if Tony had had anything to do with it.

Before she went to bed Gabrielle put the chain on the front door and a chair under the knob of the kitchen door. Get new locks tomorrow, she decided firmly. At half-past eleven on the following morning she was preparing to go around to the hardware store when a lawyer from the District Attorney's office rang her bell. Assistant District Attorney Simpson introduced himself pleasantly. He was a brisk fellow in his thirties with a sharp nose and glasses. Gabrielle thought he had come to talk to her about the money. He hadn't. District Attorney Dwyer had received an anonymous letter accusing her of having killed Mark.

For a moment Gabrielle was too astounded to speak. Then she got breath, and her voice back. The anonymous accusation was too absurd for anger. She smiled at Mr. Simpson, said gently, "I killed Mark—why, Mr. Simpson? We were engaged, were about to be married. What was my motive supposed to be?" Watching Assistant District Attorney Simpson she decided she didn't like him much.

He was apologetic, and evasive. "We don't pay too much attention to letters like this, you know, but we've got to look into them, Miss Conant, so if you wouldn't mind putting me straight about a few things . . .? That's fine." Mr. Simpson stared at the toes of his polished black oxfords and then directly into her face. "Another man has been mentioned. Who was the man who visited you here in your apartment on the afternoon of the day Mr. Middleton died?"

Gabrielle sat motionless. Was Mr. Simpson guessing

or had the anonymous writer mentioned a visitor? Probably. But the writer didn't know her visitor was John Muir, or he would have been mentioned by name. What was this? An attempt to smear her? Admit nothing. She covered her pause with: "Sorry—I was trying to think back. To the best of my recollection no one came to see me that afternoon."

Mr. Simpson didn't insist. He was almost elaborately civil. She must understand that their office had to check on all sorts of screwball letters, complaints. Gabrielle said she quite understood, and they parted with mutual civilities. She thought of calling John Muir but decided against the phone; five minutes later she was on her way to his office.

The surly cab man with the big nose and the mole on his forehead wasn't in front of the florist's on the corner. To make assurance doubly sure that she wasn't being followed, she took the subway. John was in and saw her at once. He sent his secretary out of the room, said, "Gabrielle!" in a pleased tone, put her into a chair, and gave her a cigarette. "Is it this money of Mark's that—?"

"No." She poured it all out at once, the anonymous letter to the District Attorney, the accusation of a covert connection with another man, what she had told the Assistant District Attorney who had come to see her. "I said there was no one with me on the afternoon of the day Mark died."

"Hmmm—an anonymous letter." John drew concentric circles frowningly on a pad in front of him, thought it over. "You did the right thing, Gabrielle. At this stage—"

His phone rang. He lifted the instrument impatiently, said, "Yes, oh—all right. I'll be there in a minute," and hung up. "Some men I've got to see." He gestured toward a conference room opening out of his office.

"Look, Gabrielle, what are you doing later on today?"

"Nothing much." Gabrielle said she had to see Phil Bond at four but that she wouldn't be too long. "There are a lot of things I want to talk to you about."

"And I want to talk to you," John said. "Suppose I come along to your apartment between five and six and we'll go somewhere for dinner. Right?"

"Right." Gabrielle fastened her furs and picked up her gloves with a feeling of release. It was good not to be always alone. John took her to the elevator. Three glossy, plump, well-fed men were waiting in the conference room; he waved to them as he went past. At the elevator he said cheerfully, "See you at around five-thirty," and for no particularly good reason, Gabrielle went out into the cold November afternoon with a lightened heart.

She had a sandwich and tea in Schrafft's and walked to Phil Bond's office. Phil was ready for her. They talked of the missing eighty thousand before getting down to work. Phil Bond was very troubled and upset about it. "I suppose we should have unearthed it long ago," he said slowly, "but we were sure the stuff, the securities Mark sold, were in one or the other of his safe-deposit boxes. It wasn't until we opened the third one yesterday morning that we got on the trail." He reached for a file of papers.

Gabrielle left his office at ten minutes after five, her bright mood persisting. She drew the keen air into her lungs with a feeling of pleasure. Her senses were waking from sleep, from the atrophy of Mark's death. It was the hour of magic in New York, twilight, with the first star twinkling high overhead and the tall towers arrowing up into the fading sky, dark against the lambent west, and hung with millions of square yellow spangles. Busses and private cars and taxis filled the streets, neon lights flashed and the crowds were a flowing sea.

It was dark when she got home. The darkness prevented her from immediately seeing the traces of recent excitement when she got out of the cab in front of her door. But once inside the house she smelled the smoke. She sniffed, startled. There had been a fire somewhere close by.

The fire had been in her apartment. The door was wide open. The first person she saw was a big fireman in a rubber coat making his exit. He brushed past her indifferently. Gabrielle ran toward the living-room, came to an abrupt stop on the threshold.

The room was a complete wreck, the disorder indescribable. The rugs had been rolled up and the furniture moved aside. The bookcase spilling books was lying face down on the wet floor. The curtains on the middle window were gone. The frame and the wall beside it were black and blistered, and the air was filled with a sharp odor of charred wood and chemicals.

There were half a dozen men in the room. One of the men—Gabrielle's eyes widened—was the Assistant District Attorney she had seen earlier in the day.

Simpson looked up and saw her. He said in a peculiar tone, "Here's Miss Conant now," and a short thickset man with hair as yellow as butter and a bright blue stare, swiveled sharply. It was District Attorney Dwyer himself. In one hand the District Attorney was holding the smashed base of her blue pottery lamp, in the other what looked like some crumpled dollar bills.

They weren't dollar bills. They were thousand-dollar bills. The District Attorney spoke in a voice as hard as his eyes, and Gabrielle put her shoulders gently against the door jamb. What he said was, "We found these bills tucked up into the base of this lamp, Miss Conant. What did you do with the rest of it?"

"The rest of what?" Gabrielle's voice was just above a whisper.

"The rest of Mark Middleton's missing eighty thousand dollars."

Chapter Nine: A PUSHING HAND

"I KNOW NOTHING ABOUT THE MONEY. I never even heard of the eighty thousand dollars until yesterday. I didn't hide three thousand-dollar bills in the base of the lamp. I never saw a thousand-dollar bill in my life until just now. . . ."

For more than an hour Gabrielle repeated that steadily. Nothing she said had the slightest effect on the District Attorney. They struck sparks from the beginning. Dwyer had an eye for a pretty woman. Gabrielle's slim distinction didn't appeal to him. The poise of her dark head, her very quietness, a quietness he couldn't break, merely deepened his conviction of her guilt. Even before McKee said so, he realized he hadn't enough evidence for an arrest, which was why he worked over her so hard in an effort to drag more out of her by main force.

"You took that eighty thousand of Mark Middleton's. We have the numbers of the bills. A fire started here in your apartment while you were out. Three of the missing bills were found in the hollow base of that lamp over there. You hid those three bills in that lamp. Only that they were found by accident— What did you do with the rest of the money?"

"I never had it, don't know anything about it."

"Give it to some man, the man who was with you here on the day Mark Middleton was shot? Who is he?"

"There was no man here."

Assistant District Attorney Simpson came in. He handed Dwyer a slip of paper.

Dwyer was pleased. He beamed. "Memorandum from

your bank, Miss Conant. So you never gave money to anyone?"

"No."

"Then what did you do with seven thousand dollars of your own you drew out of the bank last May, May the eleventh, in hundred-dollar bills?"

He almost had her then. Not quite. She grew paper-white but got hold of herself. To Dwyer it was the old story: an infatuated woman and an illicit lover with a taste for honey . . .

"Who's the other man?"

"There is no other man."

·"Then what did you do with the seven thousand?"

"That's my affair."

The effort to break her didn't succeed. Dwyer refused to listen to what she said, made mincemeat of her assertions, danced around on the fragments.

"Someone has been in and out of your apartment secretly, someone who planted the money? Convenient, Miss Conant, very convenient. A visitor who passed through locks and bolts at will—after the event. Did you tell anyone about this mysterious visitor? Oh, you didn't have time. Well, well. But you have time now. You'll have to do better than that, Miss Conant."

He was fighting a losing battle and knew it. McKee arrived. He listened for a few minutes and then talked to Dwyer in another room. Dwyer said, "She's guilty, Inspector, guilty as hell." He made his case trenchantly.

Gabrielle Conant was engaged to Mark Middleton. They were going to be married. She was carrying on with another man—"We know that from the letter we got—and then there's the seven thousand of her own she disposed of last May. Middleton found out about the other man, confronted her with him—and she shot him."

"Why?"

"Because she was in love with this other guy and wanted to hold him, because she's a poor girl and Middleton was a rich man, because the marriage was off, because he was going to change his will. He called his lawyer, Bond, on the afternoon of the day he died, couldn't get Bond. Perhaps Middleton knew she took the money, perhaps she grabbed it after he was dead."

"Ah, the eighty thousand." McKee gazed pensively at an etching above Gabrielle's dressing-table. Dwyer glared at him suspiciously.

"Well, what about it?"

"My dear fellow, that's the point. What was Mark Middleton doing with eighty thousand in cash?"

That stopped Dwyer, but only for a moment. "How do I know? There are any number of explanations. Maybe the girl asked him for it, told him some tale. Maybe he was engaged in some transaction that called for cash on the barrelhead."

"Mark Middleton was not a criminal."

"What's that got to do with the price of potatoes? Lots of deals calling for cash are perfectly legitimate, on the up and up, simply have to be kept under cover."

"Yes, of course. But why, if Gabrielle Conant killed Middleton and his death was pronounced suicide, did she keep on insisting to anyone who would listen that he was murdered?"

"Ha!" Dwyer was triumphant. "Because she's smart. Because she knew she might come under suspicion when the loss of the eighty thousand turned up. That anonymous letter—someone knew something phony was going on. She was afraid of just such a development and decided to beat her antagonist to the draw. . . . If she didn't shoot Middleton, who did?"

"You're convinced now that his death was murder?"

"Well, with these bills found in this girl's apartment—"

"Exactly. The money, the cash—is the crux. Until we find out why Mark Middleton wanted cash for his securities, why he sold them to obtain the cash, we won't get to first base. Did you know," McKee asked, "that someone tried to kill Gabrielle Conant by pushing her under a subway train early last week?"

He described the incident Todhunter had witnessed. Dwyer was contemptuous. "Todhunter *thought* she was pushed. He was a good distance away and that was just his idea. Nothing to substantiate it. Absolutely nothing."

McKee didn't insist. "Perhaps not. What happened here? How did the bills happen to be found?"

"There was a short circuit on an extension cord in the living-room. A fire started. One of the tenants on the floor below called the fire department. The lamp in there had overturned, wind blew it over, the window was up. The base of the lamp is hollow, and there's an opening in the bottom. The bills were in it. One of the precinct men first on the scene recognized the numbers on the bills. I understand the numbers were sent out yesterday afternoon. As soon as I got the flash I came straight up here. Then the girl walked in."

McKee said slowly, "If someone did try to—eliminate Gabrielle Conant, then the bills were planted and the fire started, deliberately, in order that exactly what happened should happen."

"*If!*" Dwyer breathed fire and brimstone. But he knew when he was licked. His conviction of Gabrielle's guilt remained unaltered; from McKee's attitude, objections, he realized that there wasn't enough to make a case, yet.

"But mark my word," he said heavily at the end of five minutes of arguing, "you leave that girl running around loose and you'll have another homicide on your hands."

"That," McKee said softly, "is what I'm afraid of."

Presently the choleric District Attorney stamped away with his entourage and the Scotsman talked to Gabrielle alone. But the harm had already been done. Dwyer's hammer blows had had their effect. They had lost her confidence. McKee did what he could. "You think, Miss Conant, that someone has been coming in and out of this apartment, that . . ." It was useless. She was a small iceberg, unapproachable.

"I really don't know what I think at the moment, Inspector—except that I would like to get this mess in here cleaned up. . . . Unless I'm going to be taken to jail," she added politely.

Give her time, McKee decided. There were other things he had to do before the scent cooled. He took his departure.

Back at the office he sent men out to check thoroughly on Gabrielle's apartment, the exits and entrances, the neighbors and what they might have seen, and on who had called the fire department. Then he tackled another facet.

Whoever was out to get Gabrielle Conant knew her habits, where she was going, how long she'd be out of the apartment; had to, to get into it, plant the bills and set the fire. Then there was the telephone call taking her on that abortive trip down to Jordon's where she was supposed to receive information about the round man. The call had come after her return from a party at the Amorys'. In the light of what has since occurred, the visit to Jordon's was assuming a new and darker value. The pattern was old, and familiar. Gabrielle wouldn't have met the unknown Mr. X. she was supposed to meet. Instead she would have met an acquaintance, a friend. Surprise, surprise. "What are *you* doing here, Gabrielle? Did you get a telephone call, too?" After that a sortie out into the street. An excited

"Come on—your round man. He just made off in a car. We'll follow him. I've got a car here." In the car into which Gabrielle Conant would have unsuspectingly stepped she would have been slugged into oblivion without knowing what hit her, an oblivion from which there would probably have been no awakening. Something had interfered with the plan, perhaps the presence, unseen by the girl, of a third person on the scene.

McKee's gaze moved to the calendar on his desk, stood still on the date November the twelfth. It was on the twelfth of November that death had threatened Gabrielle Conant twice, first on the subway platform, and again on a dark street on the West Side at close to midnight. November the twelfth. It was on the morning of November the twelfth that John Muir, a friend of Gabrielle Conant's, *and* of Mark Middleton's, had come back to New York from South America. There had been no attempt on the girl between Middleton's death and John Muir's return. None whatever. McKee leaned forward, put his finger on his buzzer and kept it there.

Alone in her apartment after the Inspector had gone, Gabrielle set about the task of putting the wrecked living-room straight. This attack was the worst. She felt soiled, unclean, after the tussle with the District Attorney. Bad luck that he had found out about the seven thousand dollars of her own she had given Tony Van Ness six months ago. If she hadn't given it to Tony, he would have gone to jail. It was a miserable, sordid business. He had raised a check, clumsily, in an attempt to cover his losses. The forgery had been discovered. Only Gabrielle's intercession and her seven thousand had let him escape with a whole skin. To tell the truth about it would be to crush Susan.

Gabrielle had cleared away the worst of the disorder

when John Muir arrived. He stood still in the living-room doorway and looked around. "Good God! What—?"

Gabrielle told him. She had never seen him so angry. His anger was almost frightening. "Someone is going to pay for this, plenty. Oh, yes. Framing you! A short circuit—what's easier to arrange than a short circuit? Bait the trap and then spring it." He walked the floor like a tiger hungry for food. He questioned her exhaustively, grew livid and very quiet at the revelation of the water running in the bathroom, the radio turned on, the teacup upside-down last week.

It was a comfort to have him there. His glance was gentle when it touched her, his concern was warming. Gabrielle said she had seen no one loitering around the building and nothing suspicious, except the strange cab man who she thought had followed her to Greenfield. She wiped smudges from her hands with a crumpled handkerchief. "I'm inclined to think now he was a detective, John. The police have a lot of information about my movements, seem to know where I've been, and what I've been doing."

He was bleakly furious. "And the pills were removed from under their noses up there in your room at Susan's. The police! Damn the police."

They discussed the anonymous letter to the District Attorney and who could have sent it. John said, "It is whoever's at the bottom of this whole business."

"Yes." Gabrielle hesitated, but he'd better know. "The District Attorney asked me again about the man mentioned in the letter as having been here on the afternoon of the day Mark died."

"And you said—?" John looked at her over the flame of his lighter.

Gabrielle shrugged. "I repeated what I told his bright young assistant, Simpson, this morning. I said there was no one here."

John thought that over frowningly. "I don't see what my visit could have to do with Mark's murder."

Gabrielle didn't either, except . . . "It's just that they think I was in love with another man, and that Mark found out."

John wheeled on her.

"Were you? Are you?"

The demand was abrupt. Gabrielle was already bruised and sore. His roughness startled her, and his lack of faith was a shock. Once, in another life, she had loved him. That was over and done with, but there had never been anyone else. If John chose to believe there was, and he seemed very ready to, let him.

He crossed the floor, towered over her. His hands were on her shoulders. They had been there before on one occasion, but not like this.

"*Please.*" She tried to twist away from him.

His grip tightened. "Answer me, Gabrielle."

"Of course there was no other man." To say it was a humiliation. She thought, *I'll never forgive him for this.*

"Then why did the *police* think there was another man? They don't dream these things up."

She wrenched out from under his grasp. "It wasn't the police, it was the District Attorney." Her words were icicles.

"Same thing."

If she told him about Tony Van Ness and the seven thousand he would go to Dwyer and Susan would find out about the forged check. Pictures of Susan, doing her housework, the tip of a pink tongue between her parted lips, going to the Yale prom with Blake Evans in a white tulle dress . . . No, she couldn't do it.

"The District Attorney decided there was another man because of that anonymous letter. Someone must have come here that day while you were here. The bell was out of order. Whoever rang and didn't get any answer heard us talking in here—heard a man's voice."

She was exhausted, drained, and deeply angry at his insistence, didn't know whether he believed her or not, scarcely cared.

"Could be." He nodded thoughtfully. "It must have been someone you knew, who came with a gift, or to talk about the wedding."

Someone she knew. She had been fighting that for days. "Yes. I suppose so. . . . I'm tired, John."

"What . . .? Oh, no wonder." He roused himself from inner brooding, left in a few minutes after vainly trying to get her to go to a hotel to sleep. "You're not safe here, with these locks." She said, "I'll bolt the kitchen door and put the chain on the front door."

He wanted to hear the chain going on. She went with him into the foyer. At the door he stood still and looked down at her. Gabrielle looked up at him. Her heart began to race, and there was a hollow under her midriff. His face, his eyes and mouth, were different. The hardness was gone out of him, the detachment, aloofness. Gabrielle's anger died. They were close, there was no separation between them. This was the John Muir she had once known, had once loved. Had loved?

He took her hands. "Gabrielle . . ." His voice was gentle.

The ice began to fall away from Gabrielle's heart, the tensions that had built up since Mark's death to release their hold. She kept on looking at him, and waiting.

There wasn't any more.

John dropped her hands and turned. He opened the door and went out. The door closed. From the other side of it he said, "Put the chain on," and when she did: "Good night, Gabrielle."

"Good night, John."

Gabrielle remained where she was in the little hall,

listening to his footsteps recede down the stairs. John loved her, and she loved him. She had seen it in his eyes, in the way he looked at her. He didn't need to put it into words, nor did she. The time for that hadn't yet come. When all this was over, when the round man had been found and the truth about Mark's death revealed, then . . . She went to bed and slept profoundly, woke rested and with a sense of well-being that even an avalanche of telephone calls couldn't disturb.

The news of the finding of the three thousand-dollar bills in her apartment was out. As one of the executors, Phil Bond had it first. Phil was portentous, grave, thought she ought to have someone to look after her interests. Tyrell called, and Alice, and later Susan called from Greenfield and after that, surprisingly, Blake Evans. They were all outraged, took her innocence for granted without question. Blake Evans agreed with Phil Bond. He said awkwardly, "I was with Claire last night when the District Attorney came to talk to Joanna. I'd—if I were you I'd get a lawyer to see I wasn't pushed around, Gabrielle. That Dwyer's a damn fool."

Joanna Middleton, who disliked her; was it Joanna who had been outside her door on that August afternoon, Joanna who had sent the anonymous letter to the District Attorney?

Gabrielle thanked Blake, refused to go to Alice's to stay, wouldn't let Susan come down to New York. Then the superintendent of Mark's apartment called. The lease of the apartment had been terminated by mutual agreement between the executors and the landlord. Mr. Middleton's effects **were to** go into storage the following day. What did Miss Conant want done with the things that belonged to her, the pictures and books and ornaments in the upstairs room?

Gabrielle didn't want anything done with them. She couldn't leave them there. Ticket them and have them brought back to her own place and pack them away out of sight; she went to the apartment on Central Park West that afternoon. To walk into the building was difficult. Upstairs in the softly lighted corridor it was still more difficult to unlock the front door with the key Mark had given her. She opened the door. The hinge creaked when she closed it behind her, recreating the smell of cordite, the echo of a shot, Mark lying on the study floor with blood welling.

Grayness filtering through the living-room windows, darkness was beginning to come down outside, silence, dead air, a faint film of dust on everything. Mark's housekeeper, Mrs. Pendleton, had long since gotten another job and only the executors had come here since Mark had been lifted to the stretcher and carried away. Gabrielle swallowed in a stiff throat, turned her back on the study, started for the stairs, and stood still. The door of the closet under the stairs was wide open.

She walked over to it. Clothes of Mark's, three or four coats, were lying in a heap on the floor as though they had been hastily flung down. The pockets of a chesterfield were inside out. Gabrielle was standing there, her back to the foyer, staring down at the inside-out pockets when it happened. A hand between her shoulder blades thrust her sharply forward and she went to her knees in blackness on top of the piled coats. Behind her the closet door slammed and a key turned, locking her in.

Chapter Ten: SHADOWS OF DOUBT

POUND. Call out. Rest a minute, and think. What good did thinking do, or pounding, either? Someone in the apartment when she got there and who didn't want to be seen or identified, had locked her in the closet. Whoever it was was far away by now. The prospect of immediate release was dim. No one knew where she was. The moving men would arrive tomorrow morning. But until then—

The blackness was the worst. It made her dizzy. There was no limit to it. The door fitted tightly into the frame. If only there was one thin line of light. How much air was there in the cubicle? She had always hated confining spaces. Claustrophobic terror got its claws into her. Without her intending it her fists were battering again on the panels, fiercely, insistently.

So suddenly that she almost fell forward on her face, the key turned and the door was jerked wide. Light. Escape. Gabrielle opened her mouth, drew a gulp of air into her lungs, and stared whitely at Tyrell Amory, knob in hand, staring whitely at her.

"Gabrielle!—Good Lord!"

Gabrielle told him about it, in a chair in the living-room, with all the lights on.

Tyrell was stunned. "Thank God I came when I did. I almost didn't come." He wiped his forehead with his handkerchief. "I heard the pounding when I opened the front door, but not when I was outside. Who was it, Gabrielle?"

"I don't know."

"You didn't hear anyone—see anything?"

"No." There was a smudge of dust on Tyrell's right cuff. There was dust all over the apartment. If Tyrell had come straight from the front door to the closet, how had dust gotten on his cuff? Oh, silly. He could have gotten it anywhere. She was losing her sense of values. Tyrell was her friend, he had been a friend of Mark's, he was a man of probity, a scientist with an established position, happily married and with everything in the world he wanted, his laboratory, and Alice. To imagine him in connection with chicanery and deceit and subter-fuge and lies and—she was mad.

Return to the problem. Who had been searching the

apartment, and why? For it had been searched, pretty thoroughly; she and Tyrell went over it together. Mark's bedroom had been ransacked. Drawers had been pulled out, pushed in crookedly. Books and periodicals were in scattered heaps and the closet and the clothes in it were in wild disorder.

"But why?" Gabrielle said helplessly. "There couldn't be anything undiscovered here—anything important. The police practically took this place to pieces after Mark died, and since then Phil Bond has been through Mark's records, papers." Tyrell agreed. He had come to get some books he had lent Mark, first editions, and they discussed the search while he helped her ticket her own things in the room upstairs, without getting anywhere. But Tyrell wasn't being frank with her. He was concealing something. Gabrielle taxed him with it. "Tyrell, what is it? What are you thinking—and not saying?"

He stared at her, reddening, turned away. Hands in his pockets, jaw set, gazing at nothing, he said explosively, "Damn it all, Gabrielle—I still don't think Mark's death was murder."

Gabrielle was astonished. "No? Then what about those three thousand-dollar bills that were found in the base of my lamp?"

He gave his cockatoo flaxen crest a shake, as though he were trying to get rid of a hornet. "I know. They were put there, but—" He hesitated and went on doggedly: "Did it ever occur to you that—there might have been another woman?"

Gabrielle's eyes widened. Her astonishment grew. "You mean Mark—that he was mixed up with some woman and gave her eighty thousand dollars? And that, to remove suspicion from herself and throw it on me, those bills were planted in my living-room?"

For a man schooled to clear thought and exactness Tyrell was being peculiarly muddle-headed.

"I don't know. . . . Maybe I'm wrong, maybe you're right, but I still—"

"You still think Mark killed himself?"

Tyrell was wretched but firm.

"I—yes."

According to Alice, once he got hold of an idea he was immovably obstinate. Gabrielle said coldly, "Well, it's a free country and you're entitled to your own opinion."

He was honestly disturbed, loathed hurting her. "I hate to be like this, but . . ."

Gabrielle stopped listening. They were standing near the open door. The whine of the front door drifted up. Someone had just come in. She went to the rail of the gallery, looked down. It was Joanna Middleton.

A figure in black caracul that managed to have about it something of majesty, and mourning, Joanna moved diagonally across the floor to a heavy pseudomedieval table-desk at the far end of the living-room. Back turned, she started to pull out the drawer. Gabrielle said, "Hello," and at the sound of her voice Joanna gave the drawer a quick shove with her hip, put down her gloves and purse as though that was what she had gone to the table to do, and turned.

She looked up. Her pale face was blank. Had there been fear in it, and a flicker of hatred? She said, "Oh—Gabrielle. I understand that the apartment's been rented. I came to get a gold toilet set I left here. I hope you don't mind my removing my own property?" Her tone was falsely civil, almost arch. There was venom under it.

Gabrielle said curtly, "Don't be silly." Was Joanna trying to be deliberately insulting? There was more to it than that. The gold toilet set was in the spare bedroom that Joanna Middleton used to occupy occasionally when she stayed in town overnight while Mark was alive. It wasn't in the table drawer.

Downstairs, when Joanna had gone, Gabrielle looked in the drawer. The little key was in the keyhole but the drawer wasn't locked. The riding-crop Mark had valued was there, and silver trophies and his war medals, not things Joanna could reasonably have wanted, without asking for them, anyhow. "Here, let me," Tyrell said. He lifted the heavy drawer out. There was nothing in the aperture behind it.

"You think Joanna was looking for something, Gabrielle?"

"That was the impression I had."

When they left the apartment a few minutes later Tyrell asked Gabrielle to go home with him. "Alice has been moping a bit lately, she'll be glad to see you. I think all this, coming up again, has gotten on her nerves. I wish I could take her away, but I'm in the middle of an important experiment."

Gabrielle wanted to call John, tell him about the closet and about Joanna; she could do it just as well at the Amorys' as anywhere else.

Alice didn't seem particularly glad to see her, not at first, anyhow. When Tyrell unlocked the door of the sumptuous apartment in the East Sixties Alice was in the foyer. Warmth, light, a stretch of violet broadloom. She was at the telephone, had evidently just come in herself, had on her mink coat and mink tricorne. As they came in she turned her head and Gabrielle had a fleeting impression that she was displeased. She said into the mouthpiece, "Well—thanks very much," dropped the instrument into its cradle, and stood up.

"Gabrielle, this is nice! . . . I thought you were going to Mark's place, Tyrell?"

"Did. We just came from there." Tyrell kissed her. She moved away from him, impatiently pulling off her hat and running thin jeweled fingers through her dark hair. "Come on into my room, Gabrielle. I just got in myself. Bridge—I'm broke and broken-hearted—I lost a fortune. . . . That dreadful Betty Lawrence, her face—two currants in a stale bun. Mix a drink, will you, Tyrell? I need support."

Tyrell was right, Gabrielle thought, listening to her restless flow of chatter. Alice had a drawn expression and there were now lines in her small vivid face. Gabrielle left her in her beautifully appointed bedroom, changing into a hostess gown. Tyrell was in the serving-pantry. There was a phone in his study; call John there. She went through the living-room, across the corridor, opened the study door—and saw him.

John was on the sofa at the far side of the big dim room. Firelight danced over the walls, the books and pictures, over John's head and shoulders above the back of the sofa. He wasn't facing the door, and he wasn't alone. There was someone on the couch with him. Before Gabrielle could speak or move, white hands reached up and cupped his face and a voice said chidingly, "Stop looking at me like that and stop asking questions. Kiss me, darling, I'm blue today."

The woman with John was Brenda Holmes. Neither of them had seen her. Gabrielle stepped soundlessly back into the corridor and pulled the door closed with the most minute care.

She was saying good-by to Alice and Tyrell in the living-room when John and Brenda sauntered in. They had arrived separately half an hour earlier and the maid had admitted them. There was no sign whatever of the intimacy of the little interlude Gabrielle had witnessed in the study. Friends dropping in on friends; they were all friends together. Before Tyrell could tell them about what had happened in Mark's apartment, Gabrielle made her escape.

It was dark out, and the air was icy. It was going to

snow. A few random flakes drifted lazily. Down on the street, Gabrielle started south on foot. Her wild, violent anger was anger at herself. Since John Muir's return over a week ago the personal equation between them had been in abeyance. Last night she had concluded that it was she who had kept it that way, because Mark's death had numbed her. She had even been able to smile at her own flash of jealousy at John's casual interest in Brenda Holmes. She had fooled herself to the top of her bent. John Muir didn't love her and his interest in Brenda wasn't casual. Brenda was the woman he loved.

Walk fast, let the wind blow, be cold, shiver and shake, and face facts. . . . Turning the last corner fast, Gabrielle collided with someone in front of the drugstore. "Upps . . . Hurt, Miss Conant? I came over on the chance that you'd be in, had about given you up. I was just going."

Gabrielle pulled herself together, straightened her hat, smiling mechanically. It was Inspector McKee.

There was nothing unusual in the Inspector's manner, his voice or bearing, and yet she was warned in advance, so that when he told her, upstairs in her living-room, what he had come to say, she received the burning thrust of it without the flicker of an eyelash. The police had built up a man with whom she was infatuated, to whom she had given money, for whom she would lie and cheat and steal and kill.

It wasn't true. She had lied about John Muir's flying visit to her on the afternoon of the day Mark died because she thought it had nothing to do with Mark's death, couldn't possibly have anything to do with it. She was wrong. John's plane was supposed to have left LaGuardia at five-thirty that day. It didn't leave at five-thirty. It had been delayed by weather. John wasn't flying south when Mark was killed, he was in New York City.

Chapter Eleven: THE SEARCH

IF YOU COULD ONLY KEEP YOUR MIND FROM TALKING, from
being a separate entity, small and clear and reminding
and deadly. John had said on that distant afternoon,
"Don't marry Mark. I'm warning you. . . ." She had
refused to take advantage of the warning, and John
Muir had walked out without another word. Less than
four hours later Mark was dead.

Subconsciously, without ever bringing it out into the
open, Gabrielle had assumed that at least one of the
reasons why John Muir had come thousands of miles
to stop her marriage to Mark was because he loved her
and didn't want her to take the irrevocable step that
would permanently separate them. But John Muir
didn't love her. He was in love with Brenda Holmes.

The Inspector was watching her. She forced herself
to outward stillness, listened without visible evidence
of shock to his documentation. McKee said that everyone
on Mark's horizon, everyone even distantly connected
with Mark, was being scrutinized. John had been a close
friend of Mark's. A check with the South American
offices of John's firm, and Pan-American Airways, had
put John in New York on August the twentieth, from
ten in the morning until 9:42 that night.

"You didn't happen to see Mr. Muir that day, Miss
Conant?"

Careful, she warned herself. She was already committed. And she could honestly say, she thought with a
sardonic flash, that she hadn't "happened" to see John—
he had deliberately sought her out. In any case she
must stick to her story.

"No, Inspector—but I'm afraid I don't understand."
She moved to the coffee table, picked up a cigarette, lit
it. "Granting that Mr. Muir was in New York on busi-

ness that day and that the departure of his plane was
delayed, why is it important? Mark had hundreds of
other friends besides Mr. Muir, a great many of them
right here in town."

The Inspector nodded pleasantly. "True. But it does
seem rather odd that Mr. Muir didn't mention to anyone later on that he was up here on the day his best
friend died. Moreover, his visit doesn't appear to have
had anything to do with business. He didn't turn up at
his office at all. . . . No matter. We'll talk to him, of
course. What I really came for is this. I want you, if
you will, to go back carefully over the weeks preceding
Mr. Middleton's death, with particular attention to the
day on which he died."

Gabrielle did.

It was that recital, long-drawn-out and interrupted
with probing questions, that gave Gabrielle a directional
hint to the one safe path out of the black morass into
which she was slowly sinking. It was the only possible
thing she could think of to do—and she had to do something. She was under suspicion by the police. In spite
of the Inspector's affability, John Muir was under suspicion.

After McKee left she walked the floor endlessly. To
call John and warn him that the police knew he was
in New York when Mark was killed would imply doubt
—and she had no doubt. He might be in love with
Brenda Holmes, and their ways in the future, her own
and his, might lie far apart. That was beside the point.
John had had nothing to do with Mark's death, she
knew that with certainty.

What then? The path the Inspector had indicated
began to open up a little more clearly. The round man
—and the truth; before she slept that night Gabrielle
made up her mind to try and find the round man herself.

Her resolution still held on the following morning.

From the first she was under no illusion as to the difficulty of what she proposed to do. Trained people were trying to do the same thing, John's investigator now, and formerly the police. But no one believed in the round man as she did, or had actually seen him in the flesh. Gabrielle set about her improbable task with businesslike precision. She had two leads, the man himself, and the car in which he had driven away from the Devon.

The car was the one point on which she had been less than frank with the Inspector. "The car the round man got into? I don't know what sort of car it was. . . ." All right—the round man, and the car. But the car might have been driven into New York from any place in the United States, and the round man had vanished into thin air. More than once hopelessness invaded her. She pushed it resolutely aside. Go back to the place where she had seen both the round man and the car. Start from there.

Before she left the house that day Susan called. She wanted to come down to New York. Gabrielle put her off firmly. "I'm perfectly all right, and I'm up to my ears in a rush free-lance job for McGrath's." That settled that. She told Alice the same thing unsolicited. It would explain why she wouldn't be available.

At eleven o'clock on Thursday she entered the Devon bar, almost empty at that hour so that she had no trouble getting a seat at one of the little tables that commanded a view of the main lobby and also of the Avenue outside, through a wide plate-glass window. She drank ginger ale until she was nauseated, ate a luncheon she didn't want, bore the inquiring glances that gradually began to be directed at her until she could bear them no longer. Then she transferred herself to an armchair in the lobby itself. At three o'clock she left the hotel and walked the surrounding streets until it was almost dark. A return to the Devon bar;

perhaps the round man might come in for a cocktail. Vain hope. At eight that night she went home exhausted.

On Friday she widened her circle, using the Devon as a central point, radiating from it and returning. Washington Place, Waverly, the park itself, north, east, south, and west, neighboring streets. Again and again the futility of the search she had undertaken pressed in on her; New York had almost eight million people in it, how was she going to find one man among them? It had millions of cars rolling through its thousands of miles of streets. How was she going to find one car? She refused to give up. And then, without warning, she struck gold.

She was walking up Fifth Avenue at around four-thirty on her way back to her apartment, when near the corner of Twenty-first Street the car she was beginning to think she had dreamed up, black body, gray top, old-fashioned but smart lines, appeared before her startled eyes, outstanding in the procession of sleek new models and trucks and busses in which it was embedded.

Gabrielle stood still with a gasp. She was headed north. The Packard cabriolet was going south. She reversed herself and started to run, but the light was green and the flow of traffic continued without interruption. Before she had taken more than three steps the Packard cabriolet was out of sight.

Her disappointment was bitter but at the same time her spirits soared. The Packard in which the round man had driven away on the day of Mark's death, she was convinced it was the same car, was not only in New York, it was going in the direction of the Devon. That made twice. Why not a third time? She retraced her steps to the Devon's canopy. The Packard was nowhere in sight. After that she toured the Village without success until sheer fatigue sent her home. But tomorrow was another day.

Gabrielle went to a movie that night in order to keep out of reach of possible droppers-in, and of telephone calls. Early the next morning she started out again with renewed vigor, vigor that waned gradually as the long November day darkened and drew down. More ginger ale at the Devon, more patrolling of the streets as far south as Bleecker, as far north as Fourteenth, as far east as Broadway. There was no sign anywhere of the Packard cabriolet.

Late in the afternoon she was on University Place between Tenth and Ninth, her eyes ceaselessly roving the traffic and the pavements, for there was always the possibility that just as she had caught sight of the car so she would catch sight of the round man, when she saw Alice Amory.

Alice was on the southwest corner of Ninth Street talking to a short dumpy woman with a bundle in her arms. Wondering vaguely what Alice was doing so far downtown, Gabrielle quickened her pace. She was tired and discouraged and had a sudden longing to return to her own world, if only for a little while. And she was anxious for news of John Muir and what the police were doing, if anything. Alice had parted from the woman and was walking west fast. She was almost at Fifth Avenue when Gabrielle caught up with her.

"Alice," she called, and Alice stopped and turned sharply around. "Gabrielle! . . . What are you doing in this part of the world?"

"Out for a walk," Gabrielle said. "I've been chasing you for a block and a half. I saw you talking to that woman on the corner of Ninth when I was on the block above."

Alice pulled folds of mink more tightly around her. It might have been the low light or perhaps the cold, but her face looked suddenly pinched, almost old. And then Gabrielle did get a shock, for Alice said, too quickly and too brightly, "Woman? What woman? You must have been seeing things, darling. . . . Oh, you mean the woman who asked me the way to the subway? I've just come from Wanamaker's. They sent Tyrell the wrong shirts. . . . How about a cocktail at the Fifth Avenue?"

Gabrielle said she'd love one. Seated at a table in the Amen Corner, she listened to Alice's light voice, watched the restless movements of her jeweled hands—and again, as it had with Tyrell in Mark's apartment last Wednesday afternoon, a gauze curtain descended, making Alice strange, different, a travesty of her normal, secure, established self. Why had she tried to deny the stout woman with the bundle she was talking to on the corner of Ninth Street, and then thought better of it? What was making her so nervous, keyed up?

She spoke of Gabrielle's adventure at Mark's place. "Frightful for you, darling—perfectly frightful . . ." Of the police: "They're being utterly ridiculous. Imagine questioning John Muir, of all people—not your horrid District Attorney but that tall Inspector, the one who looks like Lincoln, only with milk and vitamins and nice ties. Just because John missed his plane the day Mark died. I suppose he dashed up on that business, the suit against the firm. No, that was settled, wasn't it? It might have been Brenda Holmes. . . ."

The way Alice spoke Brenda's name, lingered over it, not caressingly, focused Gabrielle's attention. They were supposed to be friends. Alice's intonation was anything but friendly. "You know," she said suddenly, "I thought, I hoped, when John first came home, that you, that he—oh, damn, Gabrielle, John Muir seems to be head over heels about Brenda now, but it won't last. Dear Brenda cares only for Brenda—and nothing whatever for God. John will find that out, just as Mark did."

"Mark?" Gabrielle's brows drew together. She was sharply surprised.

Alice said, "Oh, yes, didn't you know? Mark had money, and our Brenda's been trying to marry money for years. . . . He was interested for a while and then"— she shrugged—"it petered out." She looked at her watch, and moaned. "I've got to fly. The Larks are coming to dinner. Of all the deadly bores—maybe I'll poison them." She signaled the waiter.

They parted on the pavement in front of the hotel. Alice was taking a cab and wanted to give Gabrielle a lift but Gabrielle said she was going to walk. Moving up the Avenue in the wintry dusk and watching the traffic, she thought of what Alice had told her about Mark and Brenda. Why should she be surprised? Brenda was a beautiful woman. . . . Perhaps it was because Mark had never mentioned her name, had seemed, when they met at the Amorys' or the Bonds', to be indifferent to her.

Dusk was thickening. The wind was cold. It blew gustily down the Avenue. Gabrielle was tired. She changed her mind and decided to take a bus home. One came along as she reached Tenth Street. The only other passenger who got on was a man muffled up in a heavy ulster, with his hat down over his eyes. He remained near the doors at the front. Gabrielle edged toward the rear, got a single seat near the doors at the middle, and settled back. She didn't stay that way long. The ride was the shortest she had ever had.

Two blocks to the north a southbound passenger car cut sharply across in front of the bus and swung into Twelfth Street. Gabrielle stared after it idly—and woke up. It was the Packard cabriolet, and there was a woman at the wheel. By the time she got to her feet the bus was already at Thirteenth Street. The next stop was Four-teenth. A jam of people waiting to get on, she was out of the bus the moment it stopped and eeling her way nimbly through the crowd.

Not so the man muffled up in the ulster who also got
out at Fourteenth, after a delaying harangue from an
immense woman with three chins. The man looked
around, up and down and in and out, for his quarry—
in vain. He sought a telephone and called the Homicide
Squad and said dolefully into the receiver, "Chandler
here. I lost the Conant girl," and gave his location.

Chapter Twelve: SECOND CORPSE

MEANWHILE Gabrielle had reached Twelfth Street out
of breath but with a high heart. In all probability the
woman driving the Packard was the woman who had
driven the round man away from the Devon on the day
Mark died. The car had turned east into Twelfth Street.
Go over it from end to end.

The Packard wasn't between Fifth and University, it
wasn't between University and Broadway. To the south
the spires of Grace Church thrusting up into the darkening sky; nothing in the short block there. Fourth Avenue
then, a river of traffic, beyond Fourth, office buildings
and a Delehanty's and St. Ann's church, then Third
Avenue with an el train pounding overhead. Still nothing. It was almost completely dark by that time. Gabrielle kept on walking east. Run-down houses and small
shops, overflowing garbage cans, litter in the gutters,
children playing in the streets, narrower pavements,
women in shawls in basement stores with queer smells
drifting through the doors; east of Second Avenue the
neighborhood began to improve. Rows of tenements
had been replaced with modern housing. Cars of every
other make in the world lined the curbs—but no ancient
Packard. And then, when she had almost given up hope,
she saw it. Long and lean and rakish, the Packard cabriolet was drawn up in front of an apartment building
midway between First Avenue and Avenue A.

Gabrielle approached it cautiously. The car was empty and the lights had been turned off. The apartment house in front of which it stood was a great ugly modern building that housed hundreds of tenants. The Packard had reached its destination not less than a good twenty minutes earlier. How was she to find, to isolate, the woman who had driven it here?

Her luck was in. She was standing there, whipped by a wind off the river and racking her brains, when a woman, approaching from the opposite direction, paused beside the Packard and unlocked the door. Reaching in, the woman took a package from the front seat, re-locked the door, and walked briskly across the pavement and into the apartment house.

Gabreille started in after her. What she had to do was to find out in which apartment the woman lived and what her name was. But when she entered the long white-tiled antiseptic lobby it was empty. Gabrielle paused and listened. Heels were clicking up the stairs to the left at the back. She sprinted for the staircase, and unexpectedly came up against a great fat man with a wrench who appeared out of an embrasure. The man was evidently the superintendent.

Gabrielle slowed, smiled pleasantly, and tried to control her breathing. She said, "I know I'm foolish, because I saw your no-vacancy sign outside, but I was wondering whether—this time of year with so many people going south—you have any sublets?"

The superintendent nodded ponderously. "As a matter of fact, Miss, we have. There's Mrs. Smith on the eighth, she's moving into the country, bought a house . . ."

The heel taps had stopped, not very high overhead. Would Mrs. Smith have walked to the eighth floor? There was a self-service elevator off on the right and it was not out of order.

"And let's see," the superintendent went on, "there's Miss Nelson on the second floor. She was speaking to me just today. She'd like to get out of New York for a couple of months—don't know as I blame her."

Gabrielle agreed enthusiastically. "I don't either.". Miss Nelson had a four-room apartment on the second floor. The superintendent didn't know what rent she was asking, said, "She just come in, now. Why don't you go up and talk to her?"

There was nothing Gabrielle craved more than to see and talk to Miss Nelson. Her heart pounding, she mounted the stairs and rang the bell of 2B. The woman who had been at the wheel of the Packard cabriolet opened the door. Miss Nelson was tall and thin, in her thirties, with strawlike, elaborately waved blond hair and glasses. Her rouge didn't match her lips and her purple wool dress was the wrong color for her skin, but she wasn't bad looking. She looked at Gabrielle and said, "Yes?" stiffly.

Gabrielle said, smiling, "The superintendent sent me," and Miss Nelson opened the door wider. "Oh, the superintendent. Come in."

Inside the little hall Gabrielle explained that she was looking madly for an apartment. "Well, I do want to sublet," Miss Nelson admitted, "but I'm not so sure just when. Now that you're here, though, you might as well look around."

Looking around didn't take long. The apartment consisted of a bedroom and bath to the left, a kitchen straight ahead, with a view of a wilderness of backyard fences beyond a fire escape, and the living-room with a dinette attached to it, on the right.

The moment Gabrielle entered the living-room she found what she had been seeking for so long. He was there, the man who had lived so intensely in her mind, the man in whom at times she had almost begun to disbelieve under the pressure of universal skepticism. He wasn't there in the flesh. He gazed at her unblinkingly out of an elaborate frame on top of a radio cabinet between the windows.

Hold it, Gabrielle warned herself. *Don't let this woman* see.

Apparently Miss Nelson did see something. Her prominent blue eyes behind glasses studied Gabrielle intently. There was wariness in them. "I'm not sure about subletting. . . . If I did, I'd have to have references. When would you want the apartment?"

Gabrielle kept her gaze carefully away from the beacon on top of the radio cabinet, tried frantically to put all thought of the round man from her mind—there was such a thing as thought transference. She knew what she was going to do, but that was for later.

"As soon as I could get it," she said brightly. "But if I even knew I was going to have a place, I'd be happy. Do you know what it is to live in a hotel room? Or don't you?"

Miss Nelson thawed, ever so slightly. "Sure I know—it's tough."

She worked for a living, Gabrielle decided, and had just come in. There were no cigarette stubs in the ash trays, no litter, and a scrap of paper cuff was attached to one of her sleeves. Apparently she lived alone. Gabrielle pretended to look around judiciously. "My brother and I do want some place where we can cook our own meals. . . . One bedroom—does that davenport open out?"

The davenport did. She chatted for another minute or two with Miss Nelson, burning with excitement held firmly in check. Was the round man a relative of this woman's, a boy friend? No matter, his photograph was there. At last she could prove that he actually existed. Any last lingering doubt John Muir might have of his existence would be finally removed when he saw the photograph—if only she could get him here. She turned to Miss Nelson. "I hate to bother you like this, but I'll be frank. My brother's a—bit of a fuss-budget—you know what men are." That won a faint smile and she went on: "The rent won't bother me if I can only keep him happy. Would it be possible for me to get my brother and bring him here to see the apartment tonight? If he likes it, I'm sure we can agree about the price, then, when you get ready—well, I'd know I had some place to come to."

Miss Nelson had to go out in a few minutes and again later on, but she was interested. "I guess it'd be all right. Could you make it about seven-thirty?"

Gabrielle looked at her wrist watch. It was twenty after five. Get hold of John right away, he might have other plans for the evening, but to come here with her wouldn't take long. "That would do nicely, Miss Nelson."

Five minutes later she was in a phone booth in a drugstore in the next block. About to drop a coin into the slot, Gabrielle hesitated. Why call John Muir? Why not Tyrell, or Phil Bond, or better still, Inspector McKee? No, she thought, her gaze cold on brightly colored jars of bath powder beyond the glass door, Phil Bond and Tyrell had been kind and patiently indulgent, but they had never really believed in the round man. John Muir had, up to a point. As for the Inspector—she shrugged slim shoulders—she hadn't been fortunate in her encounters with the police. She inserted the coin, listened to its tinkle, and pressed the receiver firmly to her ear.

John Muir wasn't at his office. She got him at home. "John," she said quickly, "I found the round man."

"*What?*"

"Yes." Gabrielle was triumphant. "At least—not the round man himself but—"

John guessed. "The woman who drove off with him from the Devon?"

"In person—a Miss Nelson. You and I are going to see Miss Nelson in a little while."

John sounded almost incoherent with worry. Indistinguishable mutterings . . . "What have you been up to, Gabrielle?"

She didn't want to say too much over the phone. "Never mind. I'll explain when I see you." She told him where to meet her, and when—553A East Twelfth Street at seven twenty-five. "Can you make it?"

John said of course, repeated the address and the time. "Where are you now?" She said, "I'm in a drugstore on First Avenue," and waited for him to ask her to have cocktails with him or an early dinner, to pass the time. He didn't. She said quickly into the mouthpiece, "See you, then," and rang off and left the drugstore, angry, and enraged at her anger. She hadn't asked John Muir to dine with her, hadn't intimated that she was at a loose end. Why should he be expected to drop everything at a moment's notice, and rush over here now, when she had specifically asked him to meet her at seven twenty-five? He had his own affairs to attend to, his own commitments.

She thought again of what Alice Amory had told her, and of John Muir's conversation with her on the day he had come up to New York. She had no doubt that Mark had loved her, but it might have been in much the same way she loved him, tenderly and protectively. John Muir could have known that Mark's interest in Brenda Holmes wasn't dead, that could have been why he warned her. If so, how bitterly ironical it was that she should have fancied herself torn between two men in a dream world of her own, while all the time the real three emotionally involved were Mark and John Muir and Brenda Holmes.

Water under the bridge, over the dam—Gabrielle went
into a beanery down the block, ordered a roast-beef
sandwich she couldn't eat, drank coffee, and fastened
her thoughts firmly on the round man. Miss Nelson was
the lead to him, the only lead. She had unearthed Miss
Nelson. Her job was done, once John saw Miss Nelson,
saw the picture of the round man; he could carry the
ball from then on in.

An odor of frying meat, shouted orders; the dingy
little restaurant was beginning to fill up. She couldn't
stay in the place. There was still an hour and a half to
be disposed of. It was too cold to walk the streets; besides, she had had enough of walking, had been doing
little else for three days. A movie sign down the block
caught her eye. She entered the theater at ten minutes
past six, left it at twenty past seven and arrived in front
of the apartment on Twelfth Street with a minute to
spare.

It had grown colder and there was a low mist. Passers-
by huddled in coats, a trickle of traffic, windows pouring
light faintly out into the street; the wind from the river
blew patches of fog about and the cries of the boats were
louder. John Muir was late. It was seven-thirty and then
it was seven thirty-five. Gabrielle was angry again. She
was tired and on edge and her feet, her whole body,
ached. Moreover, Miss Nelson had said she was going
out. If she left now there would be no way of getting
into her apartment. Go in, she decided, talk to the
woman, give her some excuse and try to detain her.

At twenty minutes of eight Gabrielle turned on her
heel, entered the lobby, and mounted the stairs. She
rang Miss Nelson's bell. There was no answer. Gabrielle
frowned. The woman might be in the bathroom taking
a shower. . . . She looked exasperatedly at the closed
door. The door wasn't closed, not quite, it had simply
swung to, the latch wasn't caught. She gave it a push,

stepped into the narrow inner hall.

"Miss Nelson." Silence. Curious . . . The living-room door was closed. Suppose John was in there with Miss Nelson, hadn't waited downstairs. Her patience tore. Aware that she was doing an unwise thing, she walked to the living-room door, opened it. Lamplight, stillness. no voices; the room was empty.

Gabrielle's glance went to the radio cabinet between the windows. The top of it was bare. There was nothing on it. The photograph of the round man was gone.

Gabrielle stood staring at the slab of polished wood. So she hadn't been as clever as she had thought she had been. She hadn't deceived Miss Nelson for a moment; it was Miss Nelson who had taken her over the jumps. The woman had suspected her from the minute she entered the apartment. When John Muir came he wasn't going to find anything. Once more, at the zenith hour, the round man had eluded her. Miss Nelson was gone, and the photograph with her—but gone where? Women didn't walk out of their apartments at night leaving their front doors open. And yet Miss Nelson wasn't here. . . . Make sure . . .

Gabrielle turned. A dinette opening out of the living-room, and then the kitchen; she didn't get any farther than the rim, the very edge of the dinette. The plaster arch separating it from the living-room was hard between her shoulder blades. It was solid, something to lean against.

Two settles and a table in between, a sugar bowl, a salt and a pepper shaker on a paper doily on the table, that was all. But underneath the table, on the floor, and quite close to her, so close that she could have reached out and touched it with the toe of her sandal, a saw-dust figure was sprawled, a great jointless rag doll.

Overhead light poured down on twisted limbs, on the greenish white face, the big nose in profile against the

beige rug. The beige was stained with purple wetness.
The twisted limbs would never move again. The eyes
staring at a credenza against the far wall would never
flicker. The mole on the balding forehead, the bullet
head; the man lying at her feet was the cab man who
had driven her to Grand Central last week, and who had
then appeared and disappeared beyond the cedars on
Susan's lawn in Greenfield.

The room was swinging to and fro. She was going to
faint. . . . She mustn't faint. She was alone in the apartment with a dead man. A faint sound jerked her head
up. She tore her gaze from the floor. She wasn't alone
in the apartment with the dead man. There was someone
else there. The door from the kitchen was being pushed
open slowly, inch by careful inch.

Chapter Thirteen: THE BLOOD-STAINED ENVELOPE

GABRIELLE KEPT HER EYES ON THE OPENING DOOR. Run,
her mind shrieked at her, scream—get help. She couldn't
stir. Whoever had killed the man on the floor, so
twisted, so horribly still, was there, was coming in, coming toward her. A hand, an arm, a face . . .

Gabrielle sagged and began to slump.

The room was gone altogether now. There was nothing but greasy billowing smoke with the dead man hidden in it, and above waves of grayness the man who had
stepped into the dinette.

"John." Her cry was the merest thread. She stumbled
forward, fell.

John Muir was across to her, was lifting her to her
feet. They were out of the dinette and in the living-
room, standing in the middle of it. John was holding
her elbows, supporting her. His face was carved brown
stone, the bones of it, under a taut skin, sharply ac-
cented in a bleak pattern of light and shade. His eyes

were darkly bright. There was an air of poised wariness about him. He was speaking. His voice was quiet.

"Gabrielle—what happened?"

She tried to draw back. "I didn't kill him."

"Don't be foolish." John gave her a shake. "Get hold of yourself, Gabrielle. You shouldn't have come up. I meant to stop you." He held her off, looked down. "Damn . . . I was afraid of that."

The front of Gabrielle's polo coat was stained with brown redness that was the dead man's blood. Folds of it had trailed in the pool under his head when she fell to the floor. The stains stood out hideously on the soft pile of the cloth. Her stomach took an ascending lurch. She controlled sickness with an effort.

"Wait here." John left the room. She heard him rummaging in a closet. Hangers clashed. He came back with a coat. It was the brown coat with the hood Miss Nelson had worn earlier that evening. It had a plaid lining.

"Here," John held it for her. "Put this on. You can't go through the streets like that." The coat was too large and too long. Over her own it felt bulky, uncomfortable. It hid the spots.

"Did you touch anything?" he asked. Gabrielle said no, extended her gloved hands.

John's hands were also gloved. "All right, come on."

Gabrielle didn't move. How dreadful the little apartment was, how forlorn and boxlike and drab. The small attempts at decoration, the few possessions, the painstaking cleanliness, smashed and despoiled by the great ugly stain of murder. Shadow banked the walls. Light was only there when you looked at it directly. The whole place had an uneasy, impermanent air, seemed to wait for noisy discovery, for sirens shrilling urgently in the night, for brass-buttoned official voices and the tramp of implacable footsteps.

She said, "But John, we can't . . . What are we going to do—about him?" and glanced toward the dinette. Her stomach surged again, and she looked away.

"We'll take care of him later." John was impatient.

Gabrielle said, "I didn't kill him, John. You didn't kill him." There was no question in her voice but she wanted to hear him say it. He didn't say it. He said carefully, restraining himself, "That's fine. That's splendid, dear. All you have to do is to say so to the police. They'll believe you, of course. They're such trusting fellows. You've already been accused of murder by a loving correspondent. Bills of Mark's were planted on you. The District Attorney thinks you killed Mark. Gabrielle, use your wits—what do you suppose will happen if you're found in this place?"

"Where's Miss Nelson? Where did she go?"

"I haven't the slightest idea."

"Then—who let you in?"

"Nobody. I walked in. The door wasn't locked. He"— John motioned with his head—"was there, just as he is now. No one else."

"Who is he?"

John shrugged. "All I know is that he was the man who followed you down to that Jordon's the night you were decoyed there. Come on, Gabrielle. You had nothing to do with his death. But if you're found here—"

John was right. And yet . . . The decision was taken out of their hands.

The doorbell rang.

The peal was loud, insistent, a blow with a fist. The walls moved in on Gabrielle. The grayness thickened. The door was unlocked. It was the only door. There was no other way out of the apartment. They were pinned there, bottled up. This was the end. There was no escape for either of them.

The doorbell rang again.

The call went into the precinct at seven fifty-three.
The prowl car was there as quick as a wink, the first
contingent of the law. The call was made by a Mr. E. T.
Brown, who lived opposite Miss Nelson and who had
heard the screams issuing from her apartment. The
screaming was done by Mrs. Mabel Tash who was calling on Miss Nelson by prearrangement. Mrs. Tash and
Miss Nelson, who were friends, were to have gone to a
movie together. Finding the door unlocked and getting
no answer to her ring, Mrs. Tash had walked in, and
almost into the dead man. Except for the corpse the
apartment was untenanted. Miss Nelson was not at
home.

The prowl car was followed by precinct detectives, by
men from Headquarters. An Assistant Medical Examiner arrived, a man from the District Attorney's office,
and a detective from Homicide.

The dead man's pockets had been rifled. They were
empty except for a handkerchief, a crushed cigar, some
change, and a watch. The watch had stopped at seven-
fourteen. The dead man's skull had been smashed in
with a heavy metal vase. The metal vase was Miss Nelson's, she had won it at bingo. Miss Nelson had not yet
put in an appearance. Her car, a Packard '28, was in
the garage two blocks away. She had garaged it herself
at around six forty-five, after which she had returned
to her apartment, letting herself in with her key, according to her next-door neighbor Mrs. Elmo, at a few
minutes of seven. No one had seen her leave.

The terrain looked over; Miss Nelson's departure had
been hasty. An ordinarily neat bedroom was in disorder.
Clothing had been snatched from closet and bureau
drawers, at least two dresses, a robe and slippers, other
articles.

"Florence didn't kill that man. Florence wouldn't kill
anyone!" Mrs. Tash sobbed.

"Sure, she didn't," Mrs. Tash was told soothingly. "We just want to talk to her, that's all. What kind of a coat would she have been wearing, what kind of a hat?"

At a few minutes before nine the alarm went out from the small gold room at the top of the long gray building on Centre Street to all prowl cars and all personnel within the city limits to pick up and detain a woman aged thirty-two or -three, five feet eight inches in height, with blue eyes, fair hair, and glasses, wearing a brown coat with a brown hood and possibly carrying a brown leather suitcase.

The detectives went on talking to Mrs. Tash and the tenants and building the picture. Florence Nelson had lived in the Sycamore for a little over a year. She was employed as a stenographer by the firm of Enderby and Horsch, lithographers, in Queens, where Mrs. Tash also worked.

Miss Nelson was quiet and steady, didn't drink or run around. Boy friends? Mrs. Tash couldn't say, except that there was someone named Bert; his picture was on the radio. Bert's picture wasn't on the radio. Miss Nelson had apparently taken it with her when she left.

An examination of a desk in the living-room revealed that Miss Nelson paid her bills promptly, that she had a sister Ethel in Montana and two thousand, three hundred and twenty-seven dollars and twenty-three cents in the savings bank.

The savings bank book was gravy. Miss Nelson might want it. There were other things she might want more. Wait and see.

The police asked about visitors to and from the apartment between Miss Nelson's return at around seven and Mrs. Tash's arrival at 7:45. A Mr. Sturgeon (5A) had passed the man who was now dead, in the lobby at perhaps 7:10 or thereabouts. For the rest, Miss Nelson, they said, had thought of taking a good long vacation and subletting her apartment.

"Florida," Mrs. Tash said.

The airports and railroad terminal and bus lines were covered. The tenants were dispersed, the dead man was carried away in a basket, Steinmetz, the Homicide detective, went back to the office, and two precinct men settled down in the apartment to wait. Nothing more happened there that night. Miss Nelson did not return.

Gabrielle was a block and a half away when she first heard the siren. It was á dreadful sound. She sat back hard against the cushions of the long green convertible and tried to iron out the hollow between her shoulder blades. The hollow was fear, an atavistic fear of the unseen, of a hand clapped on her arm from behind, a harsh voice calling on her suddenly to stop. She was still breathless from the journey through the window of Miss Nelson's kitchen and down the fire stairs in darkness with a woman's screams banging against her ears. She and John had made their way across the hard cement of a back yard into a vacant lot strewn with debris that led to Thirteenth Street, and along Thirteenth to First Avenue where John's Cadillac was parked.

Refuge had never been so sweet. She wore Miss Nelson's coat. Her own, stained with the dead man's blood, was in the back. John was going to have it cleaned at some cleaners a long way off, said it would be safer. It was good to be in motion, to be putting distance between themselves and the horrible apartment and the sprawled sawdust man lying on the floor of the dinette in a pool of blood.

John drove west steadily while they talked. When he entered through the unlocked door, the man in Miss Nelson's apartment was only just dead—he didn't go into details and Gabrielle didn't ask for them. Standing looking down at the dead man he had felt a breeze on the back of his neck. The kitchen window was wide open. He went to it, looking down. A shadow on shadows in the yard below, darting, disappearing; he had given chase futilely, which was how he knew about the fire stairs, to return and find her.

He was angry at himself for having let that happen. "I didn't want you to go upstairs, Gabrielle. I was a fool, thought I had more time."

Sleet tapped at the canvas above their heads and the black winter wind blew. The night was bitter. The streets were almost empty. Gabrielle discussed the dead man, who he was, why he had been killed, whether Miss Nelson had killed him.

John answered in monosyllables. He was abstracted, engrossed in his own thoughts. He pulled to a stop near a drugstore, sat for a moment gazing absent-mindedly in front of him, then shifted into gear and drove on. "It's no use," he said with a shrug. "I was going to phone around, but it wouldn't get us anyplace. If someone we know was mixed up in that business back there, there's been plenty of time for whoever it was to get clear."

Gabrielle sat up sharply. "But, John, surely it was Miss Nelson who—"

He wouldn't accept it. "There's no such word as sure in any of this. What do we know? Precisely nothing. We're about where we were when we started. If we could only establish one clean line." He struck the wheel lightly with his hand.

The drugstore and a telephone; Gabrielle had a sudden intuitive flash. "That was what you did that first night, the night you came home, the night that you followed me over to Jordon's. After we left, when we were on the way uptown, you didn't get out of the cab to buy cigarettes. You telephoned to—to see where everybody was?"

John nodded, taking the big car carefully over ice between holes.

"Whom did you call?"

"Everyone at Tyrell and Alice's who knew Mark even distantly. It seemed like a good idea at the time. It didn't pan out. No one answered except Julie Bond." He corroborated her earlier guess. "Someone was listening outside the door of Tyrell's study the other night, while you were telling me about Mark. If you remember, you had just recalled that there was a woman in the car with the round man."

"Did you—have you any idea *who* was listening in on us?" Gabrielle asked. John said no. Did he hesitate before he said it? Gabrielle thought of Tony Van Ness and of how Tony had tried to stop her on the way into the study—Tony who had come into possession of unexplained money—and eighty thousand dollars of Mark's was missing.

John slid deftly between two trucks, accelerated. "There's more than one person mixed up in this, Gabrielle. There's the round man and Miss Nelson and that fellow back there—and God knows who else. If we could only establish a single positive." He struck the wheel again, this time sharply, with an edged palm. "Well, perhaps we can."

"How?" Gabrielle said tiredly.

"Take a look at this." He shoved an envelope at her. The envelope was empty. It had gone through the mail, the stamp was canceled. It was addressed to Mr. E. P. Glass, Room 416, Jenkins Building, East Twenty-second Street. There was a list in pencil written on the back of it: blades, soap, bread, rye. The dead man's name was presumably Glass.

John said, "Someone emptied that fellow's pockets. I think that's what whoever killed him had just finished doing when I walked in. There's a bloodstain near the stamp."

Gabrielle looked at the envelope with revulsion. "Where did you find it?"

"Under the stove. I imagine it dropped there when the murderer went through the window in a hurry."

"What are you going to do, John?" But she knew before he spoke.

He said calmly, "I'm going to have a look at that office, now, before the police get there. Maybe I can pick up some information in the building, from the janitor, superintendent, elevator boys—if someone's there. If not, I can get in touch with some of the other tenants when I know who they are—the names will be on the doors. Unless you'd rather I took you home first."

"Of course not."

But Gabrielle didn't like it. She very much didn't like it five minutes later, after John's tall thrusting figure had disappeared and she was alone in the convertible parked down the block and across the street from the Jenkins Building.

Wind shook the canvas impotently. It broke without effect on the stone flanks of the city, lost itself moaningly in the black throats of the avenues. An occasional pedestrian huddled under an umbrella, trucks shouldering past at intervals; it was just after eight o'clock and at that hour the business section was dark and empty.

To wait, she thought drearily, above hands clasped in her lap, to sit and do nothing, a prey to a million fears. It was the second time that night she had waited. Suppose something happened. Suppose the police came or, worse still, suppose they were already waiting in Glass's office, and John had walked straight into a trap.

It was too much to have to take. She couldn't stand it. At the end of another five minutes Gabrielle got out and slammed the car door behind her. Icy rain was coming down hard. It spat at her cheeks coldly. Miss Nelson's coat was heavy, hampering. It had the virtues of its faults, it was an excellent disguise. She pulled the hood more closely around her head.

Reconnaissance. The Jenkins Building was old and soot-stained and dilapidated. Three lighted windows on the second floor, they were a dentist's windows; two on the sixth. There was nothing but blackness in between. Display fronts on either side of the entrance, a scissors house, a corsetiere—beyond the glass of the doors the hall was empty. Gabrielle went in.

Overhead light, pallid and cheerless, fell on dingy tiling, on two elevators to the left, stairs beyond them. She started for the elevators, didn't put her finger on the bell. Both cars were in the basement, the indicators stood at B. Take the stairs. There was no danger of missing John. The old-fashioned elevator shaft was an iron grille affair you could see into.

The building had a curious hollow stillness to it in which a cough would have sounded like a shout. She found herself walking on tiptoe up the stairs. Out in the country you expected isolation. Here where people dove to and fro like bees, where voices called and typewriters clacked and telephones rang and people saluted each other in passing, the cessation of all human activity was strange, unnatural. It was like stepping aboard a floating ship ablaze with lights and with colors flying and finding it empty and unmanned.

Hurry drove her, and the whip of fear. Second floor, third floor, fourth floor—she was breathless when she stepped out into a long corridor parallel with the elevators. Other corridors branched off right and left. She looked at numbers. The one she wanted was to the left

and some distance away. She went around a corner into
a tomblike tunnel walled with tiles and broken only
by dark ground-glass doors with names on them—*Jones
P. Jones, attorney; Friedburg Fabrics; James Murray,
Cutlery; Bletman Brothers, Inc.* Her heels clicked on
the marble floor. *Reesman, Ribbons—410—*the door she
wanted according to the envelope John had shown her,
was three farther along. There was no sound anyplace,
no one in sight. Where was John? He had certainly entered the building. She had seen him with her own eyes.
Perhaps he was in the basement talking to the superintendent. The emptiness of the silent spaces mocked her,
the stillness pressed grindingly on her taut nerves. She
was an intruder in a dead world—a sleeping world that
might suddenly rouse.

Her steps slowed. A light flickered behind the ground
glass of 416. She looked at the door. Was John there?
Had he managed, somehow, to get in? Perhaps it wasn't
John. The hesitant light beyond the ground glass went
out. Gabrielle reached the door, paused in front of it.
The legend on it read *Acme,* and in smaller letters, *E. P.
Glass.*

There was certainly someone in E. P. Glass's office. A
voice spoke. It was a strange voice, and yet there was
something familiar about it. The voice was saying,
"Yes, Mrs. Harper . . . Oh? . . . Well, thanks very
much." The telephone dropped into its cradle with a
click.

Dragging footsteps, hesitating and slow, approached
the door from inside. Gabrielle went on staring at the
ground glass. She had recognized the voice. The door
swung inward and she threw a balled fist hard against
her lips to keep the cry from coming out.

It was John. He stood tall and curiously wavering in
the shadow of the doorway. He was hurt, injured. There
was a cut on his temple. A trickle of drying blood ran

down his cheek. There was dust on his coat and his tie was pulled drunkenly sideways. He looked at her with angry despair and then resignation, as though giving in to the uncontrollability of women, accepting it.

Gabrielle said shakily, "John . . ." and stopped. John was staring past her fixedly, his head on one side. She listened then and heard it, the distant whine of the elevator, the clang of an opening gate. People, men, were advancing on the spot on which they stood.

Chapter Fourteen: AFTERMATH OF TWO MURDERS

ON THE FOLLOWING MORNING, in his office, McKee absorbed the death of an unidentified man in an apartment on East Twelfth Street with a second cup of coffee and the day sheet and talked to Steinmetz, the detective who had handled it. Steinmetz said, "Looks like Miss Nelson." McKee said, "Yes . . . I wonder why she left her door unlocked behind her when she took off."

Miss Nelson hadn't left by the front door. With the fuller light certain discoveries had been made. The fleeing woman had gone down the fire stairs on which the kitchen window opened. A thread from her brown coat had caught on a rough place on the window sill and there were several more threads on the iron railing that led to a cement court at the back of the house, from which she could have reached Thirteenth Street, via an empty lot, without being observed.

The dead man was still without an earthly habitation and a name. His pockets had been emptied and there were no papers on him. "Fingerprints, Steinmetz?"

"Not in our files, Inspector. We sent his prints to Washington and Albany."

The unlocked front door bothered the Scotsman. Under ordinary circumstances a woman fleeing an apartment with a dead man in it, a man she had killed, would

certainly have locked her door behind her to stave off
discovery, particularly as she expected a friend to drop
in. He tapped a pencil thoughtfully on the desk in front
of him.

"Well, keep after it," he said, "and let me know."
Steinmetz went and McKee turned to other things, and
presently reached the report on Gabrielle Conant.

Chandler, the detective who had been covering her,
had lost her at Fourteenth Street and Fifth Avenue at
around five o'clock the evening before. McKee pressed
his buzzer for Chandler, and they went over the report
together. The Scotsman recognized Alice Amory from
the description: "Smallish, dark, money, in mink."
Chandler said, "Miss Conant ran into this dame late
yesterday afternoon on Ninth Street and they went into
the Fifth Avenue together for a drink. When they left,
the dame in mink waited for a cab and Miss Conant
started to walk up the avenue." He told McKee what
had happened. "She got off the bus at Fourteenth Street
so fast you couldn't see her for dust. I tried to—"

McKee nodded. Interesting to know why Gabrielle
Conant had shaken off her tail, whether it was deliber-
ate. "Pick her up later, Chandler?"

"Not until around ten o'clock, Inspector. She turned
up at her apartment then in a Cadillac convertible belonging to a John Muir. Big, good-looking fellow. But
Miss Conant had been home between the time I lost her
and then, she had different clothes on."

Alone in the long narrow inner room the Scotsman
looked at the slip of paper on the desk in front of him
and then at assorted roofs, drab and dwindled under the
heavy November sky. The slip of paper was a canceled
check of Mark Middleton's made out to a famous Fifth
Avenue jeweler for the sum of four thousand, two hundred and thirty-five dollars and seventy cents. On the
morning of the day he died Middleton had bought a

string of pearls from the jeweler, giving the check in payment and taking the necklace away with him. Like his eighty thousand dollars in cash, the pearls had also vanished. They were not among his effects.

Over the phone Middleton's lawyer, Philip Bond, had been acrimonious. "Everything seemed to be in order, Inspector, and there was a lot to do. There was no reason why we should go into what Mark did with his money while he was alive. He probably bought the pearls for Gabrielle Conant. They were going to be married in a couple of days."

About to reach for the phone and call the girl, McKee sat back. Gabrielle's peregrinations through the Village with the Devon as a focal point, continued through three days during which she had divorced herself from her friends and normal occupations, had already engaged his uneasy attention. Mark Middleton had lunched with her at the Devon on the day he died and according to her story it was in the Devon that Mark had stared after the round man in a rage. Was it possible that she was taking a hand, trying to find the round man herself? He frowned blackly, got up with a violent movement, got into his coat, and descended to the street.

Gabrielle Conant showed surprise in which there was no pleasure when she opened her door and found McKee standing on the mat. There had been no diminution of her rancor. It was still in full bloom.

"Oh! Good morning, Inspector."

There was an interrogative note in her voice. She was definitely not hospitable, blocked the door, gave way with reluctance. In the attractive living-room, with fresh paint over the ravages of fire and new curtains at the windows, she sat on the edge of a chair in a yellow housecoat that made her skin very white, her hair very dark, added to the shadows under her tilted eyes. She looked as though she had been dissipating the night before, and yet she had been home by ten o'clock.

McKee showed her the canceled check and explained. "Miss Conant, on the day Mark Middleton died, he bought a string of pearls."

Relief was her first reaction, then agreement. "Yes— of course. I forgot them." She told him about Mark's having shown the pearls to her in the Devon, said, "The catch was defective. Mark was going to have it fixed. Did he take the pearls back to the jeweler's after I left him that afternoon, Inspector? Are they at the jeweler's now?"

McKee shook his head. The filling up of Mark Middleton's afternoon on the day he died was a major project. So far, backtrack as they would, they had dredged up very little—but there were certain things Mark Middleton definitely hadn't done. Returning the pearls was one of them. He said, "The necklace would appear to have been in Mr. Middleton's possession when he died, Miss Conant."

"The round man!" Gabrielle exclaimed.

McKee looked at her.

"You've been searching for him yourself, haven't you?"

Gabrielle returned his look steadily. She didn't deny it, she didn't say yes. John had warned her to avoid committing herself, to say as little as possible until they found out how the land lay. There was nothing to do now, not after last night, but to follow his instructions.

McKee warned her with gravity and with a disturbing conviction that his warning would have no effect. But it had to be done, anyhow. He said that her accentuation of the round man, the way she had dwelt on him to everyone who would listen, had already endangered her life. "A better way of finding out the truth and resolving the case, Miss Conant, would be to tell the truth yourself—all the truth."

She flashed, "I don't know what you mean." She was very much on her guard.

McKee was mild. "Well, now, Miss Conant, there was that incident at Mark Middleton's Central Park West apartment the other day, when you went there to ticket your things."

More relief.

"Oh, that," she said. "I was frightened at the time, but there has been so much . . ." She gave him the details, described Tyrell Amory arriving and letting her out, Joanna Middleton's entrance, and what Joanna had done.

McKee said musingly, "You think Mrs. Middleton was looking for something in the desk in the living-room and didn't want you to know it?"

"That was the impression I got, Inspector."

The evidences of a search of Mark Middleton's effects, which McKee had discovered for himself and which had sent him to Tyrell Amory for information, was important. The key piece, the foundation stone on which Mark Middleton's murder had been built, was still hidden from them. That it had something to do with the missing eighty thousand dollars, the most important development in the case to date, was a fair assumption. Perhaps there was a physical clue of some sort, something in writing, and the killer was looking for it. He had an advantage. They were forced to work blind.

He studied Gabrielle thoughtfully. What was worrying her? What was making her hold herself so tightly inside the yellow gown? "Miss Conant, yesterday afternoon at around five o'clock you got off a bus hurriedly at Fourteenth Street and Fifth Avenue. Why?"

This is it, Gabrielle thought. Don't rush, take it easy. John had coached her well after their escape the night before. All she had to do was to stick to the story they had arranged, producing bits of it as the need arose.

She smiled an enamel smile. "I forgot a pair of gloves I'd bought, Inspector. I met Mrs. Amory and we had a drink at the Fifth Avenue. After I left Alice Amory and got on the bus I missed them. I got out and turned back. Then I remembered that I didn't have the gloves when I went into the hotel, so"—she shrugged—"I gave it up."

Chandler's report hadn't mentioned any purchases, any package. The girl appeared to have done nothing but perambulate the streets, except for an occasional stop at the Devon or a neighboring bar—and yet she showed no sign of being an alcoholic. He said dryly, "I see."

Gabrielle sat silent, waiting. To lie hurt her pride; it was a confession of guilt where no guilt existed. And yet what else was there to do? She and John had been in Miss Nelson's apartment within minutes of Glass's death, they had been hot on the trail of the murderer in Glass's office later on. It was the murderer lying in wait beyond the door, who, when John incautiously opened it, had knocked John down and escaped. But neither of them had seen him, had the slightest idea of his identity, who he was, what he looked like—so it wasn't as though they were concealing anything of value to the police. They themselves had escaped, in turn. No one knew they had been there, but she was afraid of the tall man sitting quiet and relaxed in his chair. Did the Inspector believe in her lost gloves? And how did he know she had gotten off the bus at Fourteenth Street? Alice—could Alice have seen her from her taxi? But Alice wouldn't have gone to the police. Or would she? Alice had changed in the last few months. Her careless volatility had taken on a feverish cast and there was an edge to her ordinarily sweet temper. A woman could have killed Mark, a woman could have struck John and

knocked him momentarily senseless in Glass's office the
night before, if she had used a weapon instead of her
fist—and John didn't know what had hit him. Alice was
small, but she was strong and wiry.

Gabrielle stopped thinking, tried to make her mind
a blank. She had an almost superstitious fear of the Inspector, of his penetration, insight.

She was wrong, she did him too much honor. All
McKee knew with certainty was that Gabrielle was at
high tension and in a state of nerves and that she wasn't
going to give. Force, with such a girl, would get him
nowhere. The harder he pressed, the more adamant she
would become. And there was a peculiar quality of de-
fenselessness about her brow, the troubled glance of her
eyes, that aroused his unwilling sympathy.

He was on his feet when the phone rang. Gabrielle
went to it quickly, yellow skirts swirling. Odd that he
hadn't thought her beautiful at first, he reflected, watching her.

The call was for him. He took it, listened, and hung
up. He turned. He hadn't taken off his coat. He put
down his hat and said quietly, "Better get your things
on, Miss Conant. I've just had a report from my office.
I want you to come with me."

Chapter Fifteen: EX-WEDDING GIFT

SLEET TAPPED AT THE WINDOWS of the Middleton suite
in the Waldorf. Joanna Middleton was playing solitaire
in the sitting-room when they went in. She obviously
didn't expect them. Her careless "Come" had been directed at a maid, a bus boy. She didn't leap to her feet,
didn't tip over the table in front of her on which the
cards were laid out, at their entrance. She gave the effect
of doing so with the rigid posture of her full-bodied
figure in arrested motion, the prominent stare of her

china-blue eyes.

There was fear in her, a quick leap of it, instantly suppressed; the fear was followed by recovery, and calculation. She inclined her head stiffly at McKee's "Good morning, Mrs. Middleton." No form of greeting was exchanged between her and Gabrielle. When their eyes met, Joanna's slid away, as though they had touched something obscene.

Why does she hate me so, Gabrielle thought, marveling, and knew the answer. It was, Claire. Joanna Middleton hated her because Mark had been going to make her his wife. Alice Amory had said so more than once. "When he got over Brenda in his middle thirties Joanna thought she was safe, that Mark would never marry. You were a blow, darling. Claire would have got everything from a bachelor uncle if you hadn't happened along." Nevertheless, what Joanna had done was . . . Gabrielle was still dazed by what the Inspector had told her coming up in the cab.

He didn't waste any time. "Mrs. Middleton, I believe you hired a private detective named Edward Glass to keep Miss Conant under surveillance?"

Joanna stacked the cards neatly, put them into their container. "Yes, Inspector, that's correct."

No compunction, no embarrassment; her expression didn't change. She might have been talking about a dog license, an order to a florist.

The Inspector was equally detached. "Would you mind telling me your whereabouts last night between six-thirty and nine o'clock, Mrs. Middleton?"

Joanna drew herself up a little, recognized that she was dealing with the vagaries of a policeman, and indulged him, frigidly. "I was here in the hotel."

"You didn't leave it at all during that time?"

"I believe I did go out for a brief walk and a breath of air before dinner." Her tone sarcastically begged him to forgive her for having done so. "We dined at nine, my daughter and myself and Mr. Evans, my daughter's fiancé."

"Then your daughter can corroborate your whereabouts?"

"Pretty well, I should say. I'll go and get her."

"Don't bother, Mrs. Middleton. I'll talk to her myself later. A few more questions." McKee managed, unobtrusively, to get between Joanna and the door to the adjoining bedroom. "Why were you having Miss Conant watched?"

Joanna said coolly and without a trace of emotion, "Because I finally decided that Gabrielle Conant might very possibly have shot Mark. I was at her apartment on the afternoon of the day he died. I rang the bell but there was no answer."

Gabrielle said, "The bell was out of order; you must have known it was, or you would have heard it ring."

Joanna ignored her interruption blandly. "There was a man with Miss Conant. They were talking confidentially together, as lovers talk. I had always suspected her motives in marrying my brother-in-law. Mark was thirteen years older than she was, and he was a sick man. In spite of his illness she kept hurrying the marriage on, wouldn't hear of its being postponed. I decided to try and find out why. I understand that she has since denied that she was shut up in her apartment with a man that day. The very fact that she did deny it—" Joanna shrugged.

The chips were down. Gabrielle pleated the suède cuff of her gauntlet. The police knew John Muir had been in New York on the day Mark died. She could speak out. She said, smiling faintly, "I denied it because it was my own business and had nothing to do with Mark's death. Yes, John Muir came to see me that afternoon."

Joanna looked at her for the first time. It was a long look. Her lips were compressed. She removed her glance, focused her cold blue stare on a hand lying on her knee. "Poor Mark," she said softly, "and poor Brenda Holmes."

The amount of insinuation she managed to get into the words was amazing. McKee was watching both women closely. Blood rushed up under Gabrielle Conant's skin, ebbed, leaving her very white, very still. The reason why he had brought Gabrielle with him was to clear the decks, get the real relationships of these people out in the open. Joanna Middleton hated the girl who had been going to marry her brother-in-law, would go to any lengths to injure her—and two attempts had already been made on Gabrielle Conant's life.

"Mrs. Middleton, Mr. Glass was killed last night."

A frown, an intake of breath. "Killed! You mean—?"

"Murder," McKee said smoothly.

It was Joanna's turn to change color. She moved sharply in her chair, faced him directly, used anger as a shield. "So that's why you asked me where I was last night between six and nine o'clock. Have you asked Miss Conant?"

"As far as motive goes, Mrs. Middleton, Miss Conant is not involved."

Gabrielle stared at him, startled. She was filled with gratitude, and remorse. She could have told the Inspector the truth, after all. . . . No. She came back to reality. She couldn't, on account of John.

Joanna would have none of it. She was cold, scornful. "Who had a better motive? Mr. Glass was watching her, found out things about her. He found out more than she bargained for, so she took steps—"

The Inspector shook his head. "I'm afraid not, Mrs. Middleton. I'm afraid your inquiry agent was—ah—unfaithful to his trust. Glass was watching Miss Conant carefully for you until last Tuesday afternoon, it's true —but after that he transferred his attention to someone else."

"Tuesday? I'm afraid I don't—"

"Last Tuesday was the day of the fire in Miss Conant's apartment. Glass didn't follow Miss Conant when she left home that day. A man answering his description was seen leaving the house in which she has an apartment a minute or two before the alarm was turned in. I think Glass went there that afternoon to examine Miss Conant's belongings, letters, papers, and so on—and that while he was there someone else arrived."

"Someone else? I—"

"Yes," McKee said, his voice cold. "Someone else— someone who planted three one-thousand-dollar bills of Mr. Middleton's missing eighty thousand, and set the fire that brought about their discovery. This visitor wasn't seen, evidently left hastily by the rear tradesmen's entrance. Glass then made his own exit through the front door—with valuable knowledge in his possession, knowledge that he hoped could be made to pay off. In some fashion or other, how we don't know, he tried to collect payment in the apartment belonging to a Miss Nelson on East Twelfth Street last night—tried and failed. Instead, he was killed."

Weight rolled away from Gabrielle, and at the same time her compunction deepened. The Inspector didn't believe her guilty.

He was speaking again. He didn't speak to her or to Joanna. He had turned, was facing the flat ivory door in the opposite wall. The door was slightly open, so slightly that you wouldn't notice unless you looked closely.

McKee said in an easy voice, "Come in, Miss Middleton."

Joanna was suddenly on her feet. The Inspector fore-
stalled her. The door didn't move of itself. He reached
it, sent it wide with a swinging, purposeful motion. Five
feet inside the bedroom Claire Middleton stood with a
balled fist pressed to her mouth. Above it, her eyes
were blazing brown disks with something disordered,
sightless, in them.

"Claire!" Joanna's voice was sharp, commanding.

It roused Claire. She had something of her mother's
power of dissimulation, control. Her hand fell to her
side, her eyes veiled themselves, and a small grimace
intended for a smile quirked her lips briefly.

"Yes, Mother?" She looked at McKee, at Gabrielle,
politely, a poised and restrained young woman with excellent manners about to enter the sitting-room and
surprised at the presence of strangers. "I heard voices,"
she murmured, "didn't know—"

She advanced into the room, crossed it, propped herself gracefully against a broad window sill, tall and slight
in green wool, and continued to look gentle and inquiring. But Gabrielle had a sudden new view of her. Claire
was shy, yes, but you could attribute too much to her
shyness. There was force behind it—rather a terrific
force.

Joanna took over, the calm secure matron with an
established background and an orderly way of life
that nothing must be allowed to disturb. "The Inspector's come about that man Glass. Mr. Glass is dead.
The Inspector wants to ask some questions about where
we were last night at between six and nine o'clock."
A smile held amused communion with Claire. "I told
him—"

"Better let your daughter tell it, Mrs. Middleton, then
we'll have everything straight." McKee joined them in a
display of disinterested courtesy.

Claire traced arabesques on a green-wool-covered knee,

her hair falling forward around her face, partially
concealing it. "Last night between six and eight, Mother? What time did we get home from shopping? About
five? Yes—and then we had tea and then I went out
for a walk. I watched the skaters at Radio City. I . . ."
She filled an hour and a half with chapter and verse,
brought herself back to the hotel at around seven-
thirty or so and went down to dinner with her mother
and Blake Evans at nine o'clock. "Does that answer?
Will it do, Inspector?" She was anxious to please, do
the right thing, lifted her eyes with a candid look, flut-
tered her lashes.

"Very nicely, Miss Middleton, thank you." McKee
put the notebook in which he had scribbled back in a
pocket, reflecting that Joanna Middleton might have
remained here in the hotel and that Claire Middleton
might have been walking around the city. There was no
proof either for or against. Check it, or try to, with the
hotel staff.

Mother and daughter quite evidently felt alike about
Gabrielle Conant. Their treatment of her was a study
in insult, very well done. She might have been a shadow,
imponderable, not there. The mother's dislike was the
stronger, the girl's more burningly violent. The fact
that Gabrielle Conant was to have married Mark Middleton, and Mark's money, scarcely accounted for it.
There must be something else. There was.

According to Joanna, neither she nor her daughter
had ever heard of Miss Nelson. Joanna was saying so
when there was a tap on the door and Blake Evans, the
man Claire was engaged to, walked in. He had a paper
under his arm. It was a tabloid. McKee had already
seen it. The missing-woman angle in Glass's death had
been heavily played up. It was a tasty piece.

Evans halted just over the threshold, narrowly straight
and easy and debonair. He was blond, in his late twen-

ties, and rather remarkably, and pleasantly, good-looking. He was jarred by the Inspector's presence and surprised at Gabrielle's being there. He betrayed very little; his manners were excellent. He greeted the three women, nodded civilly at McKee.

It was Claire Middleton who gave the show away. A stiffening, a heightened color, a close and instant watchfulness of Evans and Gabrielle Conant; her eyes went from one to the other probingly, assayingly. She was very much in love with Evans, and she was jealous.

There was no doubt in the Scotsman's mind that Glass had been eliminated because he knew who the person was who had planted the three thousand-dollar bills in Gabrielle's apartment. The purpose of that planting was to convict Gabrielle of Mark Middleton's murder. If proved guilty she would have forfeited her inheritance. Middleton would have been considered to have died intestate and his money would have gone to his next of kin, i.e., young Claire. And Evans was going to marry Claire.

Joanna Middleton was explaining McKee's presence. "Mr. Glass, that private detective I hired, was killed last night, Blake."

"I know," Evans said. "I saw it in the paper. That's why I came." At the mention of Glass, he looked unhappy, and glanced quickly at Gabrielle, who continued to lean lightly against a chair, her face, her whole manner, polite, indifferent, and unyielding. She smiled at Evans, said in a clear expressionless voice, "Don't worry, Blake. There was nothing you could do."

Evans flushed. He put the paper down carefully, thrust his hands into his pockets, looking like a troubled small boy. He was caught between two fires, his allegiance to the Middletons and his friendship for Gabrielle Conant, who went on: "If Joanna chose to have me watched because she thought I killed Mark, *you* couldn't help it. For your information, I didn't."

Evans said firmly, "Of course you didn't." He glanced imploringly at Joanna, who refused to meet his eyes, crossed the room, and propped himself on the window sill beside Claire. She drew away from him mutinously, a sulky child staring at the floor.

"While we're on the subject of Glass, Mr. Evans," McKee said mildly, "would you mind telling me where you were last night between six and nine o'clock?"

The question disconcerted Evans. He half rose, sank back. Looking at McKee without friendliness, he said evenly, "I was at my office writing copy for a double-page spread in the *Leader* until almost nine, when I came here and had dinner with Mrs. Middleton and Claire."

Once again Claire Middleton was revealing. As Evans spoke, the hands clasped in her lap tightened sharply and she turned a shoulder to him. Absorbing her gesture, her averted face, her whiteness, her downcast eyes, McKee made a guess at a venture.

"I think not, Mr. Evans. You told Miss Middleton you would be at your office, working late, and she either went there or phoned, and found you weren't where you said you'd be."

It was an arrow into the heart of the target. Claire gave a little gasp. Her mouth opened, and stayed open. Blood swept darkly under Blake Evans's fair skin. His blue eyes went hard. He was furiously angry. He held his anger in check, ignored the girl beside him, and addressed the Scotsman coolly, with an affectation of amused good humor.

"I'll tell you, Inspector—I don't think it's any of your damn business where I was or what I was doing—but I was willing to answer and did. You can take it or leave it. I've said all I intend to say on the subject." He turned to Claire and his voice softened. "If you phoned and couldn't get me, Claire, if you came to the office and couldn't find me, I was probably over in statistics getting some figures, or in the art department checking on a copy block."

He did it very well; he was lying in his teeth, McKee was sure of it. Gabrielle, too, was convinced that he was lying. She was dismayed. She had known Blake for a long time and liked him. She appreciated his predicament as far as she was concerned; Claire's jealousy put chains around him. She bore him no ill-will for concealing his knowledge that Joanna was having her watched—he had tried to warn her obliquely, had told her she ought to have a lawyer to look out for her interests. But why in the name of Heaven wouldn't he say where he really was last night? Unless he was with another woman—that was always possible with Blake.

"Then you'll stand on your statement, Mr. Evans?" McKee asked, and when Evans said, "I will," the Scotsman threw his bombshell.

He did it quietly. He closed the red-leather notebook with precision, slid it into his pocket, and turned to Claire. "That box you threw aside as you left your bedroom and came in here a few minutes ago—will you get it, Miss Middleton, or shall I?"

Pure panic. Claire sprang to her feet with a thrusting, defenseless movement. She was shaking. Her lips parted. No words came out.

It was Joanna who spoke. She looked tired, sighed, said composedly, "Sit down, Claire, dear," and to McKee, "A foolish error, Inspector, a mistake. Nothing more. Mark had promised her, you see—and it was close to her birthday and quite naturally she thought— Just a minute." Joanna was proceeding toward the bedroom as she talked. She went in, came out again, handed a slim green-leather case to McKee. He sprang the lid on a string of pearls glowing softly on their satin bed.

Gabrielle looked hard at the pearls. The lost found; as far as she could tell they were the pearls Mark had shown her in the Devon on the day he died, that he had bought for a wedding present.

McKee examined the necklace carefully. It corresponded with the jeweler's description—and Gabrielle's initials, or the initials that would have been hers, *GM*, were on the lid. "Yours, Miss Conant," he said, and extended the box.

Gabrielle made no motion.

"Take them." Joanna's voice was a rasp. "Now that we know they're yours, *we* don't want them."

Gabrielle took the box without a word, dropped it into her bag. McKee turned to Claire. "Where and when did the pearls come into your possession, Miss Middleton?"

Claire was a lifeless mannequin, holding confusion and humiliation and, yes, disappointment, tightly in check.

She said tonelessly, "They were in the drawer of Mark's desk in his apartment. I found them when I went there to get some things for Mother last week."

McKee shook his head. "I'm afraid not, Miss Middleton. I was talking to Mr. Bond this morning. Not only the desk but the entire apartment was gone over immediately after Mr. Middleton's death and the pearls were not there. The last time they were seen they were in your uncle's possession—which was on the afternoon of the day he died."

Chapter Sixteen: THE LONG FINGER OF SUSPICION

GABRIELLE RATIOCINATED STUPIDLY. The pearls in Mark's possession when he died . . . They were gone afterward . . . Claire had them. . . . Was it Claire who had fled from the apartment, running through the door, the hinge of which had creaked, after the shot that killed Mark was fired?

If she was guilty she didn't look it. She looked young and innocent and proud and stricken; she stuck to her story with passion. She said the pearls were in the drawer. "The desk drawer where Uncle Mark kept things he valued. I went to it. I wanted his crop with the silver mounting, I didn't think anyone would care. He taught me to ride. . . . I saw the box. Mother had told me that Mark had bought the pearls. It was near my birthday. He always said he'd give me a string. The initials on the box were mine."

Joanna had risen. She looked old and sick. She said with perfect composure, "Don't worry, dearest, it was a mistake. Inspector McKee, my daughter came back here with the pearls last Wednesday afternoon. She was perfectly frank, didn't try to conceal them. I told her that she was mistaken, that they weren't for her, that the initials were GM, not CM." She appealed to him with a gesture, suddenly throwing herself on his mercy.

The Scotsman gazed from mother to daughter thoughtfully. It was on Wednesday afternoon that Gabrielle Conant had been thrust into the foyer closet in Mark Middleton's apartment. Was Claire the thrustee? He asked her, and got an icy "No. No, I didn't. There was no one there when I went in, no one!"

He returned his attention to Joanna, "And you yourself, Mrs. Middleton? You took the pearls back to the apartment, I presume, meaning to return them to the desk, and the presence of Miss Conant and Mr. Amory stopped you." Joanna nodded grayly. Evans had an arm around Claire. Her face was against his shoulder and he was smoothing her hair. Her shaking had stopped. She was listening.

"And then, Mrs. Middleton?"

Joanna sat down tiredly. "I brought them back here

with me. The more I thought of it the more I began to think that perhaps I *was* mistaken, that the initials might be CM, not GM—that Mark had bought the pearls for Claire, after all. I met him at the jeweler's that morning, we always go there, and I was taking my watch to be repaired, and he showed me the pearls on the way out. He didn't say they were for—Miss Conant. He just said, 'Pretty, aren't they?' and put them in his pocket. And then, there was something else." She smoothed a sleeve. "Mark was very generous, very. It occurred to me that his wedding gift to Miss Conant would have been more—more magnificent. The pearls are good, as they go, but the string is rather small."

Joanna Middleton had said all she intended to say. McKee thanked her pleasantly. *Always leave them smiling when you say good-by.* He was not ill-satisfied. Neither Joanna nor Claire—nor Blake Evans—had an alibi for the time of Mark Middleton's death. All three had both motive and opportunity. In addition, Glass's murder had provoked a direct lie from Blake Evans as to his whereabouts the evening before. Wherever Evans had been, he wasn't in his office working late. And then there were the pearls—very much the pearls.

His good-morning was general. Joanna responded with a stiff nod. Over Claire's bent head Evans sent a long glance to Gabrielle. The glance said: *She's only a child —and Joanna can't help herself. Don't be too hard on them.*

The Inspector was holding the door. Gabrielle went through it with a sense of escape. Claire's jealous dislike, Joanna's hatred; her malevolence, had been queerly shocking. You didn't expect people to hate you like that when you had done nothing to deserve it. Traversing the lobby downstairs McKee spoke of the pearls. He said that either Claire's story was true or it wasn't. Granting that it was true, it was presumably the murderer who had returned the pearls to Mark's apartment after his death had been pronounced murder instead of suicide. Gabrielle asked why. "Because," McKee said, "when the case was reopened they would have been too hot to handle."

He wanted to know about keys. Gabrielle said there were four. Philip Bond had two, one of which he had loaned to Tyrell. Joanna had one and she had one.

McKee did a little mental arithmetic, not aloud. It was beginning to narrow down. A certain number of people, and only a certain number, could have had access to Middleton's desk. Just as only a certain number of people could have lured Gabrielle to the Jordon's, entered her rooms at will, planted the bills, and set the fire. Outside, sleet was still coming down. The day was dark, forbidding. He put Gabrielle into a cab, went back to the office, and found an interesting report waiting for him on the missing Miss Nelson.

The report had come deviously, via a janitor, the local precinct, and Headquarters. Glass's office had been broken into the night before. At around 8:30 p.m. a man had called a dentist who occupied space two floors above in the same building to report that a burglary was in progress in Room 416. The dentist, a friend, and the night watchman had promptly investigated. They had found Glass's door unlocked and his office in wild disorder. The desk had been ransacked, the drawers of a filing-cabinet in which he kept records of his cases were pulled out, and papers littered the floor. The thief was gone, but hearing a noise in a transverse corridor that sounded suspicious, the three men gave chase. They hadn't caught up with their quarry. They *had* caught a glimpse of a flying woman at the foot of a staircase, a woman in a brown coat with a hood over her head who answered Miss Nelson's general description.

McKee used the telephone half a dozen times and sat

back, frowning. On the face of it, it was simple enough. Miss Nelson had killed Glass, taken his keys, and gone to his office to collect material incriminating her. But, the Scotsman thought, if he was right, if Glass had been wiped out because he was putting the finger on the man or woman who had planted the bills on Gabrielle Conant—Miss Nelson couldn't have done that. She was at work at the time, he had checked with her employers. Moreover, the "Bert" of the photograph that had vanished with her, was not in New York, according to Miss Nelson's friend Mabel Tash. Mabel Tash was very positive. "Bert went away somewhere. Florence was planning to join him, she missed him a lot." When had Bert gone away? He had gone away in August.

It was in August that Mark Middleton had been killed. And the Bert who had gone away had "kind of a round face—plump—with glasses."

Gabrielle Conant's round man? It could be. The Scotsman brought the front legs of the chair in which he had been teetering to the floor, pressed his buzzer, and went to work.

Gabrielle, meanwhile, was being steadily maneuvered into the last position in the world McKee wished her to occupy. When she got home she found her cousin Susan and Susan's husband, Tony Van Ness, waiting for her. They had come into town to go to a cocktail party and exhibition at the Solcoldt gallery. Susan looked well, but there was a suggestion of tightness, strain, under her lively chatter. Tony again? Gabrielle wondered. His imperturbable and rakish front was much as usual. It would be; it always was, up to the moment he was confronted with his sins, when he became a small boy pushed into a corner, alternately indignant and contrite.

They both professed anxiety about her, asked whether there had been any new developments, and were horrified when they heard of the death the night before of the private detective Joanna Middleton had hired to watch her. "A private detective watching you!" Susan exclaimed. "That dreadful woman! How could she, how dared she!" Tony applied a more forceful epithet to Joanna.

Not even to Susan could Gabrielle tell the whole story. She kept her own counsel as she had all along. Tony pressed for details. Where had Glass been bumped off? Why? Who was Miss Nelson? Alice and Tyrell arrived in the middle of it. It was Tyrell's day off and they had come to take Gabrielle to lunch at a new place Alice had discovered. They too were outraged. More cries, exclamations, questions—Gabrielle's discomfort grew. To remain silent as to what had happened the night before with the police was one thing, to do so with her cousin, her friends, was another. The time element saved her from getting in too deep. The contingency for which John had prepared abruptly arose.

There was a clamorous ring at the front door and the District Attorney entered the apartment accompanied by three other men. The men remained in the hall. Dwyer brushed unceremoniously past Tyrell, who had admitted him, and walked into the living-room. He ignored the others, stood still just over the threshold, and looked at Gabrielle, slender and relaxed in a chair near one of the windows. He said in a hard voice, without preface or apology, "Miss Conant, what do you know about an Edward P. Glass who was killed last night in the apartment of a Miss Nelson on East Twelfth Street?" and watched her closely.

She remained cool, unflurried. Her eyes steady on his, she said, "I know nothing you don't know—simply that Mr. Glass was a private detective employed by Mrs. Middleton to watch me, and that he was killed."

"That's all you know?" Dwyer smiled unpleasantly.

"Come, Miss Conant, this isn't going to do you any good." He dropped wheedling, became harsh. "Who is Miss Nelson—and where is she now?"

Gabrielle bore the onslaught unflinchingly. "To both questions—I haven't the slightest idea."

The blond stocky District Attorney looked as though his skin had grown too tight for him. He swelled visibly. Glancing over his shoulder, he gestured to someone in the hall, and a man walked through the doorway, an enormous man, clean and combed, in a badly fitting overcoat that was too small for him. It was the superintendent of Miss Nelson's apartment building. His name was Alden. Dwyer said to him, "Mr. Alden, I want you to look around this room for the young woman who paid Miss Nelson a visit at around five o'clock yesterday afternoon under the pretense of wanting to sublet her apartment. Do you see the young woman? Is she here?"

The superintendent nodded. He raised a hand like a small roast of pork and pointed at Gabrielle. "Yes, sir. That's her, sir—over there in the corner."

A truck went past in the street. A radiator hissed. The clock ticked. No one spoke. Alice and Tyrell, Susan and Tony, sat still, bewitched, under a spell. Dwyer took over. His truculence had subsided. He was as smooth as butter. He dismissed the superintendent with a wave, returned his regard to Gabrielle. "And now, Miss Conant, your whereabouts last night at between seven and—say, nine o'clock?"

Gabrielle let the pause lengthen. If only John Muir were there to support her. He had said he would come today as early as he could. Footsteps along the hall; John was there, just inside the door, tall and commanding and calm, his gaze lazy, interrogative. It wasn't John who answered the District Attorney, it was Brenda Holmes. Brenda had come in with John, stood beside him, as beautiful as a dream in a gray squirrel coat with a gray squirrel cap on her fair hair. Looking at Dwyer directly, she said in her soft full voice, "I heard your question just now. I can answer it. I can tell you where Miss Conant was last night between seven and nine. She and Mr. Muir were with me in my apartment on Washington Square West."

The tension in the room gave way crashingly. A long-drawn breath from Susan, a small clap of triumph from Alice, faces relaxed, postures were shifted. Tony Van Ness grunted scornfully at the District Attorney, Tyrell sat back and lit a cigarette.

"I don't believe it," Dwyer said in what was almost a shout. He was flabbergasted, outraged. He had come there prepared for the kill and his prey was being snatched from him. It was not to be borne. He had to bear it. Brenda's statement was explicit. Listening to her make it, Gabrielle relived those hours last night, hours of confusion and pain. After she and John had made their escape from Glass's office by a narrow margin, John had called Brenda and they had gone to her apartment, taking care not to be seen going in, a simple matter as the building was small and the elevator a self-service one.

The alibi John wanted from Brenda was not quite so simple. Between them they had managed it. Brenda had had cocktails with John in his apartment at around six o'clock. They had intended to dine together but Gabrielle's call had taken John away and Brenda had gone home, getting there at a little before seven. Her elderly cousin, Lucy Morrow, with whom she lived, was in bed with one of her headaches and Brenda had been in and out of the room doing various small things for her. The question was whether Lucy Morrow would know whether or not Brenda had friends with her in the living-room from seven o'clock on. After consideration Brenda thought the deception could be managed, with a little manipulation. The manipulating had been done.

The faith she had in John, the way, after a startled and concerned glance at his face, the cut on his temple, she had agreed to what he asked of her, without explanation, made Gabrielle ashamed. She wouldn't have been so complaisant with anyone. But Brenda was very much in love and she was one of those women made for love, content to surrender her will to the man's, to sink her identity in his, secure in the conviction that whatever he did was right.

Everything she was saying in answer to Dwyer's barrage was the truth, except the time element. They had arrived at her apartment at close to nine instead of at around seven. They had had sandwiches and coffee, they had looked in for a moment on Lucy Morrow before leaving and John had said to the old lady, "I hope we didn't disturb you when we trooped in here on Brenda's heels a couple of hours ago. We tried to be quiet."

At the end of it Dwyer demanded corroboration— and Brenda offered him her cousin, Miss Morrow, quietly, gold-brown brows delicate semicircles on her white forehead. The District Attorney would check, of course, but Gabrielle saw that he believed Brenda, however unwillingly. He retreated. He wasn't yet through with her; he hammered at her about her visit to Miss Nelson during the late afternoon. Here, however, Gabrielle was on firm ground. She told him the story as it had occurred up to the time when she had entered Miss Nelson's apartment, told him about seeing the round man's photograph.

"And after that, Miss Conant, what did you do?"

Gabrielle shrugged. "What could I do, then and there? I didn't want to frighten Miss Nelson, make her suspicious. She said she wasn't sure she wanted to sublet

but that if she did she would let me know. So I left.
When I got home Mr. Muir was waiting for me outside
my apartment with an invitation from Miss Holmes. . . ."
The rest of the evening was accounted for.

Dwyer was openly incredulous. "I'll change the shape
of my question. You searched for the car in which your
so-called round man left the Devon, for three days. You
found it, found the woman who drove it—and did nothing. What did you intend to do, Miss Conant?"

Gabrielle said crisply, "I intended to get advice from
my lawyer, Mr. Bond."

"You didn't mention your visit to Miss Nelson to the
Inspector when you were with him this morning?"

Gabrielle shrugged. "No, I didn't mention it. As far
as Mr. Glass's death was concerned I had no information
whatever. And to tell you the truth, Mr. Dwyer"—she
smiled at him amiably—"my encounters with you, with
the police, have not been pleasant enough to make me
attempt new ones."

Dwyer refused to let go. "Mr. Muir knew of your visit
to Miss Nelson?"

Gabrielle said mendaciously, "Yes, but I don't think
he took it too seriously."

John nodded. He said soberly, "I didn't last night,
but when I saw the paper today . . . That's why I came,
Gabrielle. I thought you really ought to go to Inspector
McKee."

Dwyer was furious, and baffled. He disliked Gabrielle
Conant intensely. He admired Brenda Holmes. If Miss
Holmes was telling the truth—talk to the cousin—then
Gabrielle Conant couldn't have killed Glass. And yet
he had an obscure feeling that he was being given the
runaround. The blasted girl's friends would do anything for her. . . . To be on the safe side, so they
couldn't spring anything later, he got statements from
them, all of them, as to where they were between seven

and nine o'clock the night before. Tyrell Amory had
been in his laboratory working, Mrs. Amory at home,
Susan Van Ness up in Greenfield, Tony Van Ness in a
series of bars in a neighboring Connecticut town.
Dwyer's retreat was orderly and threatening. He must
ask Miss Conant to remain available for further questioning, not to leave the city; he clapped his hat on his
head and strode out.

With the District Attorney's withdrawal, the atmosphere in the room changed. There was constraint in it,
and coolness, and the stir of unspoken questions, con-
jectures. Gabrielle saw that Susan, Tony, the Amorys,
could understand her reticence with the police; that she
should have kept the finding of Miss Nelson from them
was another kettle of fish. Alice put the combined feeling into words as soon as the front door closed behind
Dwyer and his men.

Alice said, playing with a charm bracelet on her thin
wrist, making the pendants jingle, "Gabrielle, pet—why
didn't you tell us you'd tracked down this woman?
Very clever and exciting of you—but why didn't you
want us to know?" Her tone was amused; her eyes were
bright, watchful.

Gabrielle said calmly, "Why should I have told you,
Alice? You didn't believe in the round man, any of
you—didn't believe he existed."

Tyrell turned from the window where he was standing looking out into the wet street. He thrust a hand
through his brush of fair hair and grinned wryly. "She's
right, Alice. . . . Gabrielle, what was this woman like?
What was your round man to her? Husband, relative,
friend?" Tony was interested too. Only Brenda Holmes,
lovely and erect on the sofa beside John, her shoulder
lightly touching his, seemed incurious. But was she?
Gabrielle wondered. Brenda must know by now that the
alibi John wanted from her covered the time Glass was

killed. What did that faintly smiling golden surface cover? How much did she suspect?

Gabrielle said she had no idea what the relationship between the round man and Miss Nelson was, simply that his photograph was there, on top of her radio, and John said lethargically, lighting a cigarette, "Why bother, now? When the police find her—and they will—we'll know."

Something in the word "know," in the way he pronounced it, sent a deep shiver through Gabrielle. To know, at last—to have deceiving veils stripped aside. To see—what?

Suddenly she wanted them all to go. They did go—but not before another visitor arrived, and she surprised a glance that made her heart turn over. It was Phil Bond who came, his well-fed, well-fleshed face harried. He had had the story of the pearls from Inspector McKee. Intercepting the glance not meant for her, Gabrielle knew that Claire Middleton's story was true, knew, devastatingly, who had placed the pearls in the desk in the living-room of Mark's apartment on Central Park West after his death had been pronounced murder.

Chapter Seventeen: THE THIRD MURDER

IT WAS TONY VAN NESS who had replaced the pearls. The glance Gabrielle had intercepted, a terrified, lightning glance, was from Susan to her husband. When John and Brenda and Phil Bond and the Amorys finally went, at the end of what seemed like an eternity—Gabrielle had asked Susan and Tony to stay—she walked slowly back to the living-room.

Susan abruptly stopped talking as she came in. Under coppery curls her face wore a closed look. Gabrielle's heart sank. She knew that expression of old. Like Tyrell Amory, Susan could be immovably obstinate—and she had much more strength than people gave her credit for. Propped on the arm of the couch, Tony was pouring himself a drink with elaborate care.

Without a word, Gabrielle took the slim green-leather case from her bag and stood turning it in her fingers. Then she said quietly, "Sue—tell me, please. I've got to know,"

Susan twisted in her chair with a movement of violence, and Gabrielle thought, *I don't know her any more. She's changed since her marriage,* and said again, "Sue—please!" Susan capitulated. She did it defiantly and with more than a touch of bitterness. "You've got the pearls back, Gabrielle, so what does it matter? Oh, Tony was wrong. I know it, he knows it himself, but he was thinking of me, and of the children."

Tony Van Ness had never appeared to better advantage than he did then. He threw aside evasion, interrupted Susan harshly. "I *wasn't* thinking of you, Susan, I was thinking of myself. From beginning to end the whole thing was my fault. There was no excuse for it. I danced the tune and refused to pay the piper. . . . The hell with that. Gabrielle's got to know."

He told her in bald phrases. On the day of Mark's death, knowing that she and Mark intended to lunch at the Devon, he had gone there. "To touch Mark," he said flatly, "to get a loan from him. Yes, I'm not going to deny it. I'd lost every cent of Borah's check and more." When he got to the Devon, Gabrielle had just driven off and Mark was standing under the canopy waiting for a cab. Mark had given Tony the pearls, asking him to take them to the jeweler's and have the clasp fixed. "I meant to do it," Tony said, and shrugged lean shoulders. "I didn't do it. I met Carlo Dwight and we had some drinks and then it was after six o'clock and the jeweler's was closed and it was too late. That night Mark died."

Tony swung on Gabrielle. "Don't tell me I'm a heel, and worse. I know it. It doesn't matter to you particularly, but it does to Susan." His handsome, haggard face was contorted, the lines in it deeply grooved. He went on talking.

The long and short of it was that Mark was dead and no one seemed to know about the pearls and Tony needed money—so he had pawned them. With the proceeds, twelve hundred, the curtains and the new furniture in the house in Greenfield had been bought and the mortgage interest and his life insurance paid. As soon as he got a decent check Tony had meant to get the pearls out of hock and give them back to Gabrielle. He had gotten them out of hock. Then Mark's death was pronounced murder, and he was afraid to give them back, afraid of getting mixed up with the police. When Gabrielle was up in Greenfield he had taken the key of Mark's apartment from her purse and on Sunday night, while she was still there, he had driven to New York and had put the string of pearls in the drawer of the desk in Mark's living-room.

Gabrielle was inexpressibly relieved. Tony hadn't killed Mark, he wasn't the one who had thrust her into the closet in the foyer of the apartment on Central Park West. It was all she cared about. Susan was crying quietly, huddled down in her chair. It was the pearls that had made her cry that night up in the house in Connecticut. She loved Tony, no matter what he did she would always love him. For the first time Gabrielle understood something of her feeling for him. His frankness was disarming. Whatever he was, he wasn't a hypocrite, knew the score.

Gabrielle went to Susan and comforted her, held out a hand to Tony. She said that no real harm had been done and that no one but themselves need ever know what had happened to the pearls.

After they had gone, Susan radiant with relief, re-vivified, Gabrielle sat down in the slipper chair beside the desk, opened the box, and looked at the pearls. They were Mark's gift but she would never wear them. There was too much tragedy connected with them and with the day on which they had been bought. Later on she would give them to Susan. She lifted the little string and let the smooth cool stones run through her fingers. The clasp would have to be fixed. She sprang the tiny diamond-studded catch absently—and sat sharply still. Staring down fixedly, she sprang the catch again and again—and let her hands fall to her lap as though the pearls had become too heavy to hold.

Tony hadn't taken the pearls to the jeweler's, the necklace had reposed in the pawnbroker's until it went back to Mark's apartment. The clasp was just as it had been that day in the Devon. And the clasp was perfect. There was nothing wrong with it. Why had Mark said there was? Why had he deceived her?

All that day, all the next, the enigma of Mark's statement about the pearls teased her without surcease. To make sure she checked with Tony, and went to the pawnbroker's. She called Joanna and got a frigid answer in the negative. The string of pearls had had no attention from a jeweler since Mark had given it to Tony in front of the Devon on the day he died. The more she dwelt on the subject, the more mysterious it became. Mark had bought the pearls for her as a wedding pres-ent, her initials were engraved on the box, and yet, in the Devon, he hadn't given them to her, he had kept them in his possession on a pretext; only that the box had dropped from his raincoat pocket outside the cloak-room, she wouldn't have seen them at all that day.

The whole thing was senseless, and Mark had been an eminently sane man. There had to be an explana-tion, if only she could find it. . . . There was no one to

whom she could go for assistance. To talk of the riddle
to Alice or Tyrell, to Phil Bond, or even to John, would
be a reflection on Mark, would cast a slur on his memory—and she couldn't bear that.

It was a miserable interval, worse almost than anything
she had been through. Inaction deepened her depression.
Her occupation was gone. All her thought, her endeavor
had been fastened fiercely on finding the round man,
and the thread to him had broken in her hands. Miss
Nelson had vanished as completely as though she had
dropped through a hole in the earth.

Gabrielle wasn't alone in her feeling about the missing woman. McKee was almost as exercised as she was.
Talking to Gabrielle over the phone, he neither re-
buked nor reproached her for failing to tell him about
her visit to Florence Nelson's apartment prior to Glass's
death; to do so would still further have alienated her—
and Dwyer, he reflected grimly, was in charge of the
alienating department, and doing very well at it. Gabrielle had nothing of importance to add to what they
knew of the missing woman. But there had been an advance in a different direction, a distinct advance. The
round man finally established himself in time and space.

Mark Middleton's eighty thousand in cash had been
in bills of large denomination. In addition to the three
planted in Gabrielle's apartment, four more had been
tracked down, or rather the numbers of them. In mid-
July, almost a month before Middleton's death, a man
answering Gabrielle's description of the round man had
changed four one-thousand-dollar bills for bills of smaller denomination at three separate Newark banks.

So the fellow existed; he wasn't a figment of the girl's
imagination. He began to take on shape, character.
There was no record of him in Mark Middleton's life,
he was neither servitor, employee, acquaintance, nor
friend. The only slot into which he fitted was that of

an emissary, a tool, a go-between, a messenger.

Very slowly the pattern of Middleton's death was etching itself with more clarity. It was inherent not only in the circumstances but in the character of Mark Middleton himself. Big, open, genial, direct, he was a man to whom right was right and wrong was wrong, with nothing in between. He had been a good friend and an implacable enemy, living by his heart rather than by his robust and unsubtle intellect. His generosity was immense. Impose on it once and you were finished.

That, obviously, was what had happened. Someone had borrowed or begged eighty thousand dollars in cash from Middleton. "I will carry the message. . . ." The round man had carried the cash, taking it away from Middleton's apartment in late June. Eight weeks later, in the Devon, Middleton had seen the round man again, and had gone into a tailspin. Why? Because, in the meantime (and it might have been then and there, in the lobby, or the bar, through association with someone or something else) the round man had revealed himself as not what he had seemed but, monstrously, what he was. Middleton had realized that he had been done, tricked, lied to. Going over Gabrielle Conant's testimony and the physical facts, McKee saw what must have happened almost as clearly as though he had been present.

Mark Middleton had gone back to his apartment and summoned the round man's principal. The accusation direct: "I know the truth. I am going to send for the police." In the act of calling McKee's private number, the receiver had been replaced and the shot that killed Middleton had been fired.

So far so good; it wasn't far enough, by a measured mile. The identity of the principal remained a complete blank. There were a few controlling factors. It had to be someone with a reasonable claim on Middleton's help, therefore someone close to him, a friend, or relative. And there was his call to Philip Bond that Bond's wife had taken. "I want to see Phil first thing in the morning." That, however, wasn't much help. Bond was Middleton's lawyer and Middleton might have needed his counsel in whatever steps he had intended to take. On the other hand, Middleton might, as Dwyer insisted, have been going to change his will. But Gabrielle Conant wasn't the only legatee. Joanna Middleton benefited to the tune of fifty thousand dollars.

Too many mights, buts, ifs. One thing was certain: the round man, Miss Nelson's "Bert," had been removed from his normal sphere, sent out of New York because he was a sure lead to the murderer. Once the round man was located and forced into the open, not only the killer but the reason for killing would stand revealed. Florence Nelson might or might not know where her Bert was; she certainly knew something about him. But Miss Nelson had vanished like a puff of mist. Find her.

Easy to say; difficult to do. They had a description of her and the clothes she had been wearing, true, but there was nothing distinctive about either the woman or her apparel—you could probably pass a baker's dozen of her on any busy midtown street. Nor was there anything in her past that was at all helpful. Detectives had gone out to her place of employment, had talked to her boss, her fellow-workers. Police in Montana had interviewed the sister there. The net result was a large zero. The woman appeared to be exactly what she seemed, a good stenographer in her middle thirties with a respectable background and a boy friend named Bert to sweeten and add romance to the monotony of existence and her advancing years. She might be anywhere in the country by this time.

She wasn't anywhere in the country. She was in New York. Two days after Glass's death, she was finally located. The call came in from the Hotel Rothingham at 9:21 a.m.

"That's all for now, as far as I'm concerned." In the bedroom on the third floor of the Rothingham, McKee stood erect and stepped back from the body extended on the carpet at his feet, halfway between bed and bureau. He spoke to an Assistant Medical Examiner, who promptly went to work. Miss Nelson had been dead quite a while. Rigor was already well developed. Standing looking down at her, the Scotsman's mouth was wry. A gun for Mark Middleton, a metal vase for Glass, a noose of some sort here—the killer had a taste for variety. Miss Nelson had been strangled.

The body had been discovered by a chambermaid entering the room with a pass key at nine o'clock. Miss Nelson was supposed to have checked out early that morning, had told the desk that she would be doing so and paid her bill the afternoon before.

She had checked out very thoroughly, in a direction she hadn't intended to take, McKee reflected moodily. It was one of the things he had been afraid of. Like Glass, Florence Nelson had brought about her own death by playing ball with the murderer. In her case, however, he was inclined to think it was unconscious, that she hadn't known the score, or even which team she was on.

There was something pathetic in the woman's natural innocuousness, she was not a forceful creature, never had been; anger tightened in him. Her procedure, the course she had followed, wasn't difficult to chart. She had checked into the Rothingham at around ten o'clock on the night Glass died. As a hiding hole it wasn't a bad choice. It was bold, out in the open, one of the huge West Side midtown hotels filled each day with thousands of transients constantly coming and going. In the search for her, all hotels had been checked as a matter of course, this one among them, but Miss Nelson had registered under a false name, her appearance was nondescript, and she wasn't wearing the clothes described by her friend, Mrs. Mabel Tash. Instead of the brown coat with the hood she had turned up at the hotel in a black coat with a fur collar and a black hat pulled well down over her head and concealing her hair. She had either disposed of the brown coat in transit, or it had been disposed of for her. Unless it was at the cleaners—check on that. The other articles of apparel she had taken with her in her hurried flight from her apartment were in her suitcase, open on the trunk rack. The suitcase told the tale. The garments in it were neatly folded, except for the top one, a brown wool dress, the skirt of which she had dragged with her to the floor when she fell.

She had evidently been packing when her lethal visitor arrived. A knock, a voice, an entrance; a moment's talk, perhaps; Miss Nelson had returned to her task. Then, while she was bending over the suitcase, a noose had been thrown around her neck from in back and the ends pulled tight until suffocation ensued.

The photograph of the round man, Bert, was not among her meager possessions, nor was there any clue to him or to his whereabouts in the contents of her purse, which included a ten-dollar bill, four singles, some change, and the usual feminine make-up paraphernalia. For the rest the hotel had very little information about her. The chambermaid was the only one who had seen her, and she had nothing of importance to contribute. As far as was known, Miss Nelson had remained in her room for the most part, and when the maid was doing it she had sat at the window with her

back turned, reading a magazine. No one had asked for
her at the desk, no one had seen a visitor arrive or de-
part. She had had several telephone calls, but they were
local calls and there was no record of them. The switch-
board operator didn't know whether the voice asking
for room 517 was a man's or a woman's.

As in Glass's case, it looked like one of those blatant
and uncomplicated murders that were so difficult to
resolve. It had most certainly stemmed from Mark
Middleton's. From the moment the investigation into
Middleton's death was reopened, Miss Nelson was
doomed, as a direct lead to Bert. Well, it was done now;
and they were further from finding the round man than
ever.

At the end of another half-hour McKee left the Rothingham and returned to his office to begin a check on
all concerned, or all who could have been concerned, in
Mark Middleton's death. He was not optimistic. They
were dealing with a nimble and adroit mentality. An
alibi has been arranged and will take place . . .

The check-up took time. The net result, when it
came, wasn't negative; it was positive. It knocked the
Scotsman back on his heels. If it had been possible to
doubt, he would have doubted then.

Dwyer had no doubt. He said exultingly, "Who was
right all along, eh? Who was right, Inspector? Well,
well, now we can really go to town."

Chapter Eighteen: PIECES OF A PUZZLE

"I COULDN'T TELL YOU, Gabrielle. I didn't dare tell you.
I was afraid of what you might do, that you might try
to find the woman yourself. You must see that."

John Muir stopped pacing the floor, paused in front
of the chair in which Gabrielle sat lifelessly, held upright only by her will. In a blank white face her eyes

were large and dark with terror, and remorse.

They were in the living-room of the apartment on Hammond Place left to John by his uncle, a heavy handsome room with thick maroon curtains at the tall windows and great pieces of furniture built apparently for mastodons. The heavily shaded lamps fought with encrouching shadow, and lost. It was almost seven o'clock. Gabrielle had read the account of Miss Nelson's death in the evening paper an hour before. The false name that Miss Nelson had registered under had hit her between the eyes. It was Mrs. Harper—and John Muir had been calling a Mrs. Harper over Glass's telephone when she reached the door of the private detective's office on the night Glass died.

John said urgently, "You do believe me, don't you, Gabrielle?" He was unhappy, distressed.

She responded with the slightest inclination of her head. Yes, she believed him. It was impossible not to. Her first fear had been allayed, but what did it matter? Their personal concerns seemed small, unimportant. Miss Nelson was dead—and it was her fault. It was as though, in her pursuit of the round man, she had unloosed a deadly plague that struck at the innocent instead of the guilty. Whatever he was, Glass hadn't killed Mark; neither had Miss Nelson.

As though he guessed what she was thinking, feeling, and wanted to divert her thoughts, John went on talking, calmly and evenly. He said that outside Glass's office the other night he had heard someone talking softly over the phone. The voice was low. He had heard the words "Mrs. Harper" and "Hotel Ellmore," and that was all. "Whoever was in the office must have turned then and seen my shadow on the ground glass. I didn't know who Mrs. Harper was from Adam, but I thought I might get something revealing out of her. After I was socked, as soon as I got back the use of my wits I called the Hotel

Ellmore—but there was no Mrs. Harper registered there."

Gabrielle raised weighted eyelids. "It wasn't at the Ellmore that Miss Nelson was killed."

John shrugged. "Hotel rooms aren't always easy to come by. I suppose Miss Nelson was given a choice. 'Try the Ellmore, the Rothingham. Don't attempt to contact me. I'll get in touch with you when it's safe.'"

"Yes, it could have been that way, I suppose," Gabrielle agreed dully.

Watching John, listening to him, she thought suddenly, her stretched nerves rebelling and her mind turning into another channel, *I can't stand this. I mustn't do it any more,* and wondered, a little hopelessly, whether she would ever stop being obsessed by him. She had to stop, had to go on living. Why, out of a dozen men all equally personable, did one particular man put you in thrall, bind you with chains, fill your heart and your brain to the exclusion of everything and everyone else? It was like being under a spell: your judgment, your will, wilted and died, the real you ceased to exist, and you became a mere appendage, and adjunct, of someone else.

John stopped his restless pacing. He pulled a hassock the size of a bathtub close to her chair, dropped down on it. The breadth of his shoulders, his hard, lean body, the angle of his jaw, obtruded on her. His nearness was intolerable. She tried to move a little farther away, but he leaned forward so that their knees were almost touching. "Gabrielle," he said, looking directly into her eyes, "I'm going to ask you a question. You're a truthful person—and I want you to answer it truthfully. Will you?"

Gabrielle nodded without speaking. She was incapable of speech. John went on slowly: "I've been away from New York a long while—months. There was no understanding between us before I left, but—well, I suppose I took it for granted—too much so . . . Have you seen anything, heard anything—?" He put his question directly. "Do you think that Brenda is interested in some other man?"

Pain, a blinding blazing flash of it, then rage. Brenda Holmes! Why should John Muir come to her for information about Brenda Holmes, why seek her aid, assistance, in satisfying the doubt the very depth of his feeling for Brenda aroused? It was intolerable.

John was waiting for her answer. His regard was intent, demanding. She resisted the longing to strike at him, push him away from in front of her, pound at him with her fist. Instead, she reached sideways, took a cigarette from a box on a table, lit it, and said, smiling gently, "What an idiot you are, John! Brenda Holmes loves you, and no one else. Look what she did for you the other night."

John dismissed the alibi Brenda had given them with a wave of his hand. "Oh, that—yes. But she'd do that for any close friend. That's not what I mean. You're sure there's no one else?"

"I'm very sure."

The tightness went out of him. He drew a long breath and sat back, passing a hand over his eyes. When he looked at her again his eyes were clear. "I suppose I *am* a fool. But I was out of touch, and—" He turned his head. "Yes, James?" His man was standing in the doorway.

"Telephone, Mr. Muir."

John left the room. The very air of it was hateful to her; Gabrielle was instantly on her feet. She had to get away before she betrayed herself. That would be the bitterest thing of all. Thirty seconds later she was out in the coldness of the wind-swept night street hailing a cab. She was only just home when the Inspector tele-

phoned. He and District Attorney Dwyer were coming
to see her. The timbre of the Inspector's voice was
warning enough. Miss Nelson was dead. Gabrielle knew
what she had to do. She said into the mouthpiece, "When
will you be here, Inspector?" McKee said in half an
hour. It was enough, but barely. Gabrielle dropped the
instrument into its cradle and went quickly down the
hall and into her bedroom.

The Inspector and the District Attorney were punc-
tual. Hurry, and the wind, had whipped color into
Gabrielle's cheeks and her eyes were brilliant when she
admitted them, led the way into the living-room, indicated chairs, and sat down composedly in the corner of
the couch to face them. A third man, the District Attorney's stenographer, perched himself awkwardly on the
little colonial rocker next to the bookcase, notebook and
pencil ready.

Scarcely a word had so far been spoken except: "Good
evening, Miss Conant," "Good evening, Inspector." Returning her nod, District Attorney Dwyer had studied
her curiously out of round blue eyes, as though he had
never seen her before. She was struck by the change in
him. His truculence was gone. He was polite, observant,
content to remain in the background, as though the
position satisfied him.

There was no change in the Inspector. Tall and relaxed and calm, leaning forward a little in his chair, his
narrow brown gaze intent on her, he said, "You know
that Miss Nelson is dead, Miss Conant?"

"Yes." Gabrielle waved toward the evening paper on
the coffee table, lying where she had thrown it down
before going over to John's apartment.

McKee was speaking again, slowly. "If you'd care to
have your lawyer with you while you're being questioned . . ?"

"Lawyer?" Gabrielle's brows rose. "I don't believe I need one. Go right ahead, Inspector, ask me anything you want to."

"Did you kill Florence Nelson, Miss Conant?"

It was, Gabrielle thought, only what she should have expected from the police. She had been mistaken in the Inspector. He was a policeman first, last, and all the time—nothing else. "I did not."

"Then what were you doing in the Hotel Rothingham yesterday afternoon at or about the time Miss Nelson died?"

Gabrielle's eyes opened wide. She sat up sharply, staring straight ahead of her, sank back. "The Rothingham," she murmured. "The *Rothingham*." It wasn't a question, it was an affirmation.

Anxiety edged McKee's voice with impatience. "Yes, the Rothingham, Miss Conant. Florence Nelson was killed in her room in the Rothingham at between five and six o'clock yesterday afternoon. You were in the Rothingham tearoom at a quarter past five."

Very shortly after the investigation into Mark Middleton's death was reopened McKee had provided himself with excellent pictures of the people under scrutiny. A waitress in the Rothingham tearoom had identified Gabrielle from her photograph as a girl who had entered the tearoom at shortly after five o'clock. She remembered the incident clearly because Gabrielle had ordered and paid for tea and muffins, and had departed abruptly without touching her order. For the record, there would have to be a personal identification, but the Scotsman had no doubt of the result.

"Yes," Gabrielle said slowly, "I was in the Rothingham tearoom yesterday afternoon. I suppose it was about that time—although I didn't particularly notice what time it was."

She paused. Both men waited. There was a struggle

going on in her. So much was evident. To herself Gabrielle was saying, *I don't want to do this. I went to see Miss Nelson, and Glass died, and then Miss Nelson herself was killed. If I speak now, will there be more death?* She felt almost physically ill. But she and John Muir were both under suspicion and, besides, she didn't really believe— She gathered herself together.

"In the first place, Inspector, I didn't know it *was* the Rothingham I went into."

Dwyer would have spoken then, but McKee restrained him with the slightest of gestures, and Gabrielle continued, "I had been to see 'Houseboat' at the Strand. Leaving the theater and crossing the street I caught sight of Joanna Middleton on the pavement in front of me. I was surprised to see her. Alice Amory had already told me that Joanna and Claire had gone back to Stamford. I was—curious, I wondered what she was doing in that part of the city. Joanna turned into the entrance of a hotel you say was the Rothingham. I simply knew that it was a hotel, didn't know the name of it. I followed her in. But the lobby was crowded and I lost sight of her. The tearoom opens off the lobby. I thought she might be there. I went in. And then"—Gabrielle shrugged—"when there was no further sign of her, I came home."

So far Dwyer had restrained himself admirably. The girl's presence at the scene, or so near as didn't matter, of this third crime had hammered home his conviction of her guilt with such certainty that he felt he no longer needed to argue. Now she was eeling out from under their hands again with that air of grave simplicity, of childlike directness, that had McKee bemused. He had established, to his own satisfaction, that Miss Holmes and John Muir could be covering for her. Brenda Holmes *had* had cocktails with John Muir in Muir's apartment and she had arrived home at around seven o'clock—a departing maid and the cousin's testimony on that point was not to be shaken—but there was nothing, no corroboration but Brenda Holmes's word, that Gabrielle Conant had been in her apartment that night, instead of across the city on East Twelfth Street at the time Glass was killed.

McKee's reaction to Gabrielle's statement was entirely different. After the first shock of finding that she had been in the Rothingham the afternoon before, he had put her presence there down to chance—but with considerable uneasiness. It wasn't chance. Joanna Middleton—

Dwyer was already on his feet. Face faintly empurpled, he inquired with heavy and scathing courtesy, "Your phone, Miss Conant? If you don't mind?"

"Not at all. In the dining-room."

Dwyer called the Waldorf. The Middletons had checked out at noon the preceding day. He called long distance and got Joanna Middleton at her house north of Stamford. The result was astonishing. Mrs. Middleton said, "I was about to call your office, Mr. Dwyer. I read only a few moments ago of the Nelson woman's death. Gabrielle Conant was in the Hotel Rothingham yesterday afternoon at around five o'clock. I saw her on the street near the hotel, thought her manner queer, furtive. I followed her into the hotel, lost her in the lobby. But she was there, I can assure you of it."

Impasse. Two trains heading in opposite directions on the same track. Who had followed whom? McKee believed Gabrielle; Dwyer, Joanna Middleton—but even as far as Dwyer was concerned, in spite of his own personal conviction—there was a grand jury to be considered, and the situation had changed. As long as the girl was the only contestant, the only person with opportunity as well as motive, i.e., actually present in the hotel at the time Miss Nelson was killed, it had been all right to go full steam ahead. Now, with one woman's word against another's, it would be necessary to place Gabrielle Conant on the same floor, at the door, or in the vicinity of the dead woman's room, before proceeding further. Unless—

McKee had already told him about the black coat Miss Nelson was wearing when she entered the hotel, and of the disappearance of the brown coat with the hood she had worn all winter and that she had had on when she parked her car less than an hour before she fled her apartment.

The black coat had probably been supplied to Miss Nelson in transit, to alter her appearance. It was of good quality, almost but not quite new, and there was no label in it. The brown coat was not in the dead woman's apartment or at any cleaning establishment near by. The killer had probably disposed of it—but there was always a chance. Dwyer put his request silkily. "There's a coat of Miss Nelson's missing, Miss Conant. Would you mind our looking through your apartment—just to make sure?"

Gabrielle's heart skipped a beat. They weren't going to find the coat, but suppose they looked in her purse? Suppose they did? They didn't. Five minutes later she was alone in the apartment.

Back in the long narrow inner office of the Twenty-Seventh Precinct the Scotsman rolled up his sleeves and went to work. Not literally. Hands clasped behind his head, feet on the radiator, his cavernous brown gaze somnolent on a patch of night sky, he gave himself over to motionless brooding. The why and how of Glass's and Miss Nelson's deaths were all clear.

He threw both murders away, returned to the one that had activated them, made them as inevitable as ripples on the calm surface of water into which a heavy stone had been flung. Mark Middleton had died because he had given someone eighty thousand dollars—in cash. Middleton and Middleton alone knew who that someone was. McKee paraded those people one by one before his inner gaze. John Muir, the Amorys, the Middletons, Mr. and Mrs. Van Ness, the Bonds, Blake Evans.

Alice Amory was a wealthy woman. Tyrell managed some of her business. Women, gambling—and a deficit to cover? Had Middleton's eighty thousand gone to Tyrell? No sign of it. Alice Amory herself, vivacious, lively, restless, flitting hither and yon as the fancy took her—another man, and a demand for money?—no scrap of evidence there, either.

He thought about John Muir, in trouble at the time, with a five-million-dollar suit on his hands, brought jointly against him and Tritex, the company he headed. Tritex stock had fallen twenty points while the suit was pending; it had risen to a new high after the verdict, in Muir's favor and in the favor of the company, was rendered. If Muir had been temporarily short he might very easily have gone to Middleton for help. But surely a transaction of that sort would have been conducted by check, and not in currency.

Joanna Middleton, Claire, Julie Bond, Susan Van Ness? Same as Alice Amory, an indiscretion, folly, that had to be covered up with payment on the nail?—again no slightest evidence. There was no one else showing. If he was right, if the eighty thousand, in cash, was at the bottom of Mark Middleton's murder, Blake Evans could be dismissed. Evans and Mark Middleton had scarcely known each other, certainly not well enough for the older man to bestow eighty thousand dollars on the younger for friendship's sake.

Some indication of where the money had gone existed in physical form. McKee was sure of it, sure that it was for this bit of proof that someone had been searching Middleton's apartment on Central Park West when

Gabrielle unexpectedly let herself in. She had been thrust into the closet and the door locked on her because, if she had turned, she would have recognized the searcher, which again brought culpability back and tied it firmly to one of a small group of people.

McKee had gone over the apartment from end to end himself. Result—nothing. There was another way to tackle it and that was to uncover what Mark Middleton had done on the afternoon of the day he died. He had parted from Gabrielle Conant under the canopy of the Devon at around three o'clock. He had entered his own apartment at around half-past six. How had he filled the intervening hours? He had told Gabrielle he had "things to do," that he might be late for the dinner Joanna Middleton was giving, might not be able to make it at all. Things to do—what things?

The answer to that lay in those missing three hours. Detectives had been working on it, all good operators. A man of Middleton's type, big, distinguished, using canes and walking with difficulty on lower Fifth Avenue in the middle of an August afternoon, should have been easy to trace, particularly in the vicinity of the Devon. Two things mitigated against success—the time element, and the number of disabled veterans on the streets. McKee moved restlessly in his chair. The stab of discomfort was like the dull pound of an ulcerated tooth. If the attempt to fill those three hours failed, the case might never be solved.

The attempt didn't fail. At ten minutes after two that morning, first-grade detective Schomblatt brought a taxi driver into the office. The taxi driver's name was Thomas Ladd. On the afternoon of the day Mark Middleton died, Ladd identified Mark as his fare from a photograph. He had picked Mark up in front of the Devon and had driven him to a private house on East Sixty-fourth Street.

It came fast after that. The house on East Sixty-fourth Street was owned and occupied by Judge Silverbridge, and Silverbridge was the Judge who had given the verdict in John Muir's and in Tritex's favor in the suit against them.

Joseph Crewe Silverbridge had been on the District Bench for nineteen years. He was a distinguished member of the legal fraternity, noted for his knowledge of bankruptcy and patent laws. No breath of rumor had ever so much as touched his name. But there had been other judges . . . One of them was then serving a sentence for selling judicial decisions.

Todhunter was with McKee when this information came through. His face wore a look of horror. "Not Judge Silverbridge—not a man like that!" he murmured, with what for him was excessive violence.

McKee's eyes had begun to shine. He said nothing to the little detective's outburst except, "I don't know. But I'll tell you one thing. This is it. We're on the last lap. When we've resolved this we'll be over the tape."

Chapter Nineteen: THROUGH A WINDOW

AT THAT POINT Gabrielle could have given McKee valuable information. She had thought, in Joanna's sitting-room in the Waldorf, when Blake Evans had lied as to his whereabouts on the night Glass was killed, that a woman might be at the bottom of Blake's lie. She found out, by accident, that she was right. It was a glimpse only; the glimpse was sufficient, with what she already knew.

On the afternoon before, when McKee had told her over the phone that he and Dwyer were coming to see her, she had realized instantly that she had to get Miss Nelson's coat out of the apartment. As long as the woman was alive it hadn't mattered too much; Miss

Nelson knew who had killed Edward Glass. Now that she was dead and couldn't speak, possession of the coat was infinitely dangerous. There had been just time to throw it into a hatbox, take the hatbox to Grand Central, check it, and get back safely. The coat was disposed of for the moment; it couldn't stay where it was. As unclaimed baggage it might fall into the hands of the police by default, and the clerk who had checked it might easily remember her. No, she would have to destroy it for good and all.

The only place to do that with safety was in Greenfield. Early on the morning following McKee's and the District Attorney's visit, she called Susan, didn't get any answer, and sent her a telegram saying that she was coming up.

She made her plans carefully. She had received no further warning from either the District Attorney or Inspector McKee about not leaving the city—which probably meant that they had detectives watching her.

At a quarter of ten she left the apartment, carrying a suitcase and her other hatbox, walked to the corner, hailed a cab, and drove to Grand Central. In the station she made her way to the checkroom and checked both bags. The next Greenfield train wasn't until ten fifty-five. She decided to have a cup of coffee in the Admiral coffeeroom to while away the time.

The coffeeroom windows opened on a transverse corridor. Strolling along this corridor toward the entrance, she stood still at the sight of a familiar face beyond glass. Blake Evans was inside the coffee shop, seated at a table in the small inner room. There was a woman with him. Blake was in profile to her, the woman's back was turned. Blake and the woman were talking earnestly. There was an air of strain about both of them. Blake was frowningly intent on what he was saying; his companion was sitting forward, her head bent, the fingers of an ungloved hand opening and closing on the cloth in front of her. As Gabrielle watched, she pushed back her chair and rose.

The woman with Blake was his mother. Gabrielle hadn't seen her for years; she recognized her at once. After a decade of widowhood, while Blake was in college, the former Mrs. Evans had remarried and left Greenfield. She had changed very little. She was a slender, pretty woman, with small delicate features and the remains of a rose-petal skin. She had evidently married well, wore a coat of silky eastern mink and a smart hat. She and Blake went through an archway and disappeared into the main room. Half a minute later, going into the coffee shop, Gabrielle almost ran into Blake. He was alone, didn't see her, was staring ahead of him, hands thrust into his overcoat pockets, his handsome face set in stern lines.

"Blake." When she spoke his name he stood as still as though he had been shot.

Looking at him, Gabrielle was reminded of Alice's attitude when they had met unexpectedly on Ninth Street on the afternoon of the day she found Miss Nelson. Alice's response then had been almost identical with Blake's now. He was anything but pleased to see her, tried hard to conceal it. "Gabrielle—hello. What are you doing here?"

She said, "I'm going up to Greenfield. That was your mother who was with you just now, wasn't it?"

There all resemblance to Alice ceased. Blake stared down at her, his olive skin patched with whiteness. It was as though she had stumbled on some secret he was trying desperately to conceal. He put out his hand and gripped her arm. His grip was hard.

Gabrielle was amazed. What was the matter with him? "Blake!" she said sharply.

He let go of her at that. The anger in him died down.

He said tiredly, "I wish— Oh, hell, Gabrielle, have you got a minute?"

She told him she had twenty or thirty of them. Sitting beside her on a banquette in the coffeeroom he talked about his mother. He said she was married to a man whose guts he hated. "From the first moment her charm‑ing second husband disliked me as much as I disliked him, but for her sake I'd have been willing to—well, put a face on it. My delightful stepfather wouldn't have that. He resents me, is jealous of my existence. You see, he wants my mother's entire attention for himself. So"— Blake shrugged—"we have to see each other without his knowing—for fear of one of his brainstorms. I haven't been to the house for years. If he knew we saw each other regularly, he'd make her life hell."

Blake and his mother had always been deeply attached; the bitterness in him was understandable. Gabrielle said, "Was it your mother you were with the other night, the night Glass was killed, when you told the Inspector you were working late in your office?" Blake nodded. But there was more to it than that, Gabrielle thought. Blake kept eyeing her nervously, looking away, looking back. Finally, when he had paid the check and they were about to go, he said suddenly, as though the words were forced out of him, "Gabrielle, I'm going to ask you to do me a favor. Don't mention my mother to—to anyone, will you?"

Gabrielle said she wouldn't, as a matter of course. But she was astonished. Of what possible interest could the former Mrs. Evans's marital troubles with a second hus‑band be to the people she and Blake both knew? And yet there was no doubt in her mind that Blake was badly worried about something concerning his mother. The man she had married was a Judge Silverbridge—which meant nothing to Gabrielle. Nevertheless, mulling things over after she left Blake, she recalled that before her remarriage Mrs. Evans, as she was then, had lived in Greenfield, and had known Mark and Joanna and the Amorys. . . .

Crossing an arcade through the crowd she gave her shoulders an impatient shake. She was becoming obsessed with Mark's murder. Consciously and subconsciously she kept trying to relate every slightest happening to it in some fashion or another—which was absurd.

Arriving and departing passengers surging through the great central enclosure, lines at the ticket offices, knots of people around the information booth, laden redcaps; somewhere in the throng there was a detective watching her, following her footsteps. Looking neither right nor left she made her way to the checkroom. Business was brisk, which was a help. When her turn came, she proffered two checks, one for her suitcase and the other, not for the hatbox she had deposited half an hour ago, but for the one she had left there the previous afternoon. The hatbox she had brought with her that morning could sit on a shelf until she got back to New York and it was safe to redeem it.

The two hatboxes were not identical. The difference in them wasn't marked. But to a keen eye . . . Was there a detective close by? The attendant reached the low flat counter, slid her suitcase across to her, then the hatbox. Gabrielle put down a tip, picked up both hatbox and bag, and turned.

This was the time for a hand to fall on her shoulder, a voice to say, *I'll take that, please.* No one approached her. No one spoke. She made her way to Gate 24 unchallenged, through it into dense gloom and along what seemed like a mile of platform. Every step was a fearful one. If the coat was found in her possession now, it would be the end. *I put it to you, gentlemen, the accused was caught red-handed trying to destroy incriminating evidence. . . .*

The train wasn't crowded. She found a seat easily, was going to have it to herself. She swung the suitcase up onto the rack, put the hatbox under her feet. It wasn't until the train pulled out ten minutes later that she was able to draw a deep breath. The platform was sliding by and she hadn't been stopped. The knot in the pit of her stomach began to dissolve. She sat back against blue cushions and closed her eyes.

"Hi, Gabrielle . . . *Gabrielle!*"

Gabrielle stood on the Greenfield platform and turned. The train was pulling out. She had been heading for the taxi stand at the northern end. It was Tony who was calling to her. He came bounding across the graveled enclosure, in a lumber jacket and jeans, his dark head bare. In spite of the receding hairline he looked young and vigorous. He told her that they had just received her telegram. The children were sick and Susan had been at the doctor's. The medico thought that the kids might be catching something, both measles and mumps were around. They wouldn't know for twenty-four hours. "Alice wants you to stay with her and Tyrell till we know what's what. Mind?"

Gabrielle did mind, very much. Inside black leather the dead woman's coat was growing to the proportions of an old man of the sea. Was she never to get rid of it safely? At Susan's it would have been comparatively easy to dispose of—but at the Amorys' . . . It couldn't be helped.

Tony took her bags. Following him to the car and driving off, Gabrielle said the appropriate things. Of course she didn't mind. The children were the ones to be considered. It might be only a cold, the symptoms in the beginning were alike, weren't they? She hoped it was that, was glad Susan wasn't too worried, but she'd always been sensible about things like that.

At Bridge Street, instead of continuing on, Tony swung right for the shore. Ten minutes later they were at the Amorys'. The house, long, low, and old, that Alice had had restored and made over at a phenomenal cost, was set back under trees on a rise overlooking the distant Sound. Tony got Gabrielle's bags out of the back. She hated him to touch the hatbox. It was the same inside.

As they entered the hall, Alice came through the living-room doors, her hands out. "Gabrielle, darling—this is lovely. Not that I want the children to be sick, Tony, my pet, but I've asked her and asked her and she wouldn't come, and now we've got her." She rang a bell and a maid appeared. "Park, take Miss Conant's bags upstairs." She linked one arm through Gabrielle's, the other through Tony's. "It's a vile day. Come in and have a hot toddy before lunch."

In spite of her lightness, her gay tone, Alice looked tired, and she was much too thin. She had lost weight in the last few months. In the living-room, sitting before a blazing fire and sipping her drink, Gabrielle heard with a sinking of the heart that Brenda Holmes and her cousin Lucy Morrow were coming for a few days. Ever since the night of Glass's death she had felt uncomfortable with Brenda, didn't know what she must be thinking. But John was coming, too, and her spirits lifted a little. Not because he was going to be there—the less she saw of him the better for her peace of mind, if there was such a thing—but because he could help her get rid of the coat. It was his responsibility as much as hers. If it hadn't been for John, if she alone had been involved, she would have told the truth long ago, and the devil take the consequences. Even without the coat she was being accused of murder by the District Attorney—and you might as well be hung for a sheep as for a lamb. It was impossible for her to dispose of the coat here at Alice and Tyrell's, but John might be able to do it, after dark.

Tony left, and then there was lunch and the afternoon dragged on. She and Alice looked at a litter of boxer pups in the stables, and petted the horses, and at four o'clock Alice went out.

She had to go to a cocktail party. "I hate to leave you, Gabrielle. But I didn't know you were going to be here and I promised Mac Garron faithfully . . . If I'm late, make my apologies to Brenda and Lucy Morrow, will you?"

Standing at the living-room window watching the Lincoln retreat down the drive under a grape-colored sky, Gabrielle debated Miss Nelson's coat. She was alone in the house; try to get rid of it now? A gardener raking leaves near the gate, the chauffeur whistling in the quadrangle at the side, a maid passing in the hall . . . No, it was still broad daylight and too risky. And wasn't there a policeman, a detective, somewhere about? Surely there must be. Better wait until John came, she decided, or failing that, until darkness arrived.

But she couldn't stay there doing nothing. She got her own coat, tied a scarf around her head, and went for a walk. She went as far as the cliff at Highlands, stood watching waves break on the pebbly shore for a long while with a feeling of profound depression. How little men were, and how quickly they passed, and what did it all matter, anyhow? Soon she would be old and then she would be dead—unless death came before age, unless she was destined to be strapped into the electric chair with a hood over her head.

She turned her back on the water and started inland. A mist was blowing in from the sea. It began to surround her. Soon it would be solid, and darkness was coming on, the early darkness of late November. The foghorns were sounding off, distant and melancholy.

Gabrielle quickened her pace. She didn't want to get lost, not with the hatbox and its contents unprotected in her bedroom at the Amorys'. The hatbox was locked and the key was in her purse, but she felt suddenly nervous about it.

She cut across the huge parking-lot at the beach, crowded in summer, empty and desolate now, almost collided with the edge of the pavilion, and turned into Blue Mill Road. Only half a mile more. An occasional car, its headlights a bright dazzle, made her step quickly into the bushes to avoid being clipped; there was no sidewalk. Waves boomed off on her right. Whenever the fog lifted she made good time. She had rounded the point and was on the home stretch when she saw the woman, a bulky figure turning out of the Amory driveway and coming toward her. One of the maids, probably, she thought. Fog obliterated the thickset figure, rolled away, revealed the woman again, nearer this time. As they came abreast of each other the purple dusk had its way for a moment. Then the woman was gone—but in that mist-laden glimpse Gabrielle had recognized her. She was the woman Alice had been talking to in front of the bank on Ninth Street, on the day Gabrielle had met her unexpectedly in the Village, the woman Alice had pretended was a chance stranger asking where the nearest subway station was.

Alice had lied. The woman wasn't a stranger. She had come from the Amory house.

Gabrielle walked on slowly. If it had been anyone else but Alice . . . She was the frankest creature in the world. No—she only seemed to be. Seem—to appear to be true, to wear an aspect of truth and probability.

Not only the physical world around Gabrielle was dissolving, her mental world was going, too. She thought of Mark's subterfuge about the clasp of the pearl neck-lace, of Blake Evans's anxiety about his mother, his request to her not to mention his mother to anyone, and now there was this woman Alice denied having known when she *did* know her. . . .

Her elbow hit one of the Amory gateposts before she saw it. The fog had banked up in earnest. Moving through it was like swimming upright in icy water in darkness. She had to feel for the driveway with her feet. She lost it, found it, lost it again. Pin-points of light showed off on the right; she started in that direction. Her progress was slow. Unseen obstacles kept getting in her path, trees and bushes, the solid trunk of an oak. At last the house loomed up directly ahead. She wouldn't have known she had reached it except for the broken rectangle of a lighted window immediately in front of her. Hemlock branches obscured it. She pushed feathery boughs out of the way with either hand, and stood as she was without moving.

She was looking into the small room beyond the dining-room. The colored backs of books in cases, the top of a carved chair, a picture on the wall, and Tyrell Amory—but not the Tyrell she knew. The man standing in the middle of the floor was like a stranger. His hands were thrust into his pockets. One shoulder higher than the other gave him a lopsided appearance, as though he had suffered a shock. His head was bent. Even the shape of his skull seemed different, and his face, white, ravaged, was the face of someone engaged in a dreadful encounter, the outcome of which was in doubt.

Brenda Holmes was standing close to Tyrell, a few feet away. She wore a gray-green dinner gown that brought out the tones of her skin, the lights in her coiled hair. There had never been anything of the siren about Brenda; she was too sure of herself, of her beauty, for that. If anything, she lacked animation, sparkle. There was no lack of animation about her now. She was talking to Tyrell passionately, pleadingly. Her breast rose and fell with the vehemence of her words, inaudible to Gabrielle. One hand tugged at a heavy gold chain at her throat. The chain broke. So did that held pose of struggle between those two. The struggle was over. The space between them was annihilated; Brenda's arms were around Tyrell and she was clinging to him. Tyrell lowered his head still farther with a gesture of exhaustion and surrender, and laid his face against the gold of Brenda's hair.

It was then, before Gabrielle could retreat, while those two inside stood that way, completely absorbed in each other, that the curtains beyond them stirred. One of the folds of ruddy brocade masking the entrance to the dining-room moved, very slightly. Neither Tyrell nor Brenda Holmes saw the movement. Gabrielle did. The faintest flash of a thin jeweled hand; Alice was behind the curtains looking in at her husband and Brenda Holmes.

Chapter Twenty: THE BLOODY COAT

STEPPING BACK, letting the hemlock boughs swing to, and alone in blackness and the icy embrace of the fog, Gabrielle found herself shaking uncontrollably. Tyrell and Brenda loved each other. No other conclusion was possible. She fought against it, for Alice's sake. It was useless. Alice had suspected it, that was what had caused the change in her in the last few months. Now she knew. Alice and Tyrell. Their marriage was an institution; they weren't two people, they were one. . . . John also knew, or guessed. That was why he had questioned her so closely about Brenda and another man.

Gabrielle refused to make a moral judgment; only the people involved were fully aware of their own compulsions—where John was concerned she couldn't resist a throb of mingled pain and what was almost triumph. John had had no eyes for any other woman but Brenda, no other woman really existed for him. What was he going to do when he found out? What was Alice going to do? What was going to happen?

If it hadn't been for Miss Nelson's coat in her locked hatbox, Gabrielle would have walked away and not come back. She couldn't do it. She was forcèd to re-enter the house. She fumbled her way to the front door with the deepest reluctance. The hall was blessedly empty when she went in; she was out of sight, at the top of the stairs, when that orchestration began. Instruments in concert, first one and then another. Sounds first, the sound of a car outside and Alice's entrance; her second entrance, as open as the other had been secret, was followed by the small slam of the front door as the rising wind caught it. Alice to a maid: "Miss Morrow and Miss Holmes arrived, Parks?"

"Yes, Mrs. Amory. George met them. They came on the four-two."

Brenda then, even, pleasant, unperturbed: "Alice, dear —how *are* you?"

Tyrell coming into the hall from another direction and cutting in there: "Hello, old girl. I *am* glad you're home. I was worried about you. The roads are pretty bad. Have a good time at Mac Garron's?"

Gabrielle retreated. She couldn't stand any more at the moment. That, she reflected sardonically, stripping off her wet things and getting under a hot shower after she had made sure that the hatbox with the coat in it was safe—that was what people called being civilized.

The evening continued as it had begun. Gabrielle didn't know why she was so astonished. Everyone lived a secret life; the one beyond the top one was always there. You said words aloud, they were never your inward words. Even in trivial matters, if you spoke the truth as you saw it, the world would go to pieces. You said, "How are you, Mrs. Georgia? Oh, yes, of course, *do sit down and join us,*" and to yourself: *Why did I look at the woman? She's a most horrible bore; now we'll be stuck with her for ages!*

That was the way it was that night. It was as though the scene in the little room beyond the dining-room had never taken place. The complete absence of reaction on anyone's part was subtly terrible. An outcry, accusations, sobs, screams, even blows, would have been preferable.

Alice pretended that she knew nothing, had seen nothing, and the pretense was so excellent that if it had been possible Gabrielle would have been deceived.

Dinner, and then a bridge game afterward, with Alice and Brenda as partners against Tyrell and Lucy Morrow—Gabrielle didn't play. During the game Lucy Morrow felt cold and her maid brought her a jacket. More illumination: the woman Gabrielle had seen earlier, the woman Alice had been talking to on Ninth Street, was Lucy Morrow's maid. Brenda lived with Lucy . . . The depths to which Alice had had to descend, Gabrielle thought sadly. She had evidently bought or tried to buy information about Tyrell and Brenda from Lucy Morrow's maid. It was horrible.

John didn't come. He phoned that he was going to have to remain on in town on business. By half-past ten they were all in bed, or at least in their rooms. Gabrielle fell asleep thinking of Alice and Tyrell, Tyrell and Brenda, Brenda and John, and of the dead woman's coat, and how she was to get rid of it. She woke to the sound of foghorns and the whiteness of mist banked against her windows. Susan called at ten o'clock; there was nothing the matter with the children but a bad cold. If Gabrielle wasn't afraid of catching one . . .?

Gabrielle emphatically wasn't. Tony drove over at around eleven, and over Alice's protestations and to her own infinite relief, she was out of the house before lunch.

That afternoon she found the letter, but not at once.

After she got to Susan's, Gabrielle's one idea was to dispose of Miss Nelson's coat. If it hadn't been for John Muir, if John hadn't been involved, she would have confided in Susan and Tony, enlisted their help. As things were, she couldn't, and the task she had set herself wasn't as easy of accomplishment as she had hoped. The day continued to be wretched, cold and damp, with intermittent fog and a wind off the sea. It confined them indoors. Tony was at work in his studio in the garden, Gabrielle with Susan before the fire in the living-room; it was unexpectedly difficult for Gabrielle to get away by herself.

She had made up her mind what to do with the coat. To burn heavy cloth in that weather would not only be impracticable, it would be literally a signal fire to the detective she couldn't see, but who she was convinced was somewhere in the obscurity beyond the windows. Now and again she went to one, probing the half-seen gardens, the road in front of the house. She saw a bakery truck, the two Misses Whitraub, perambulating pedestrians in all weathers, an occasional car flitting past, some linemen busy on a pole at the head of Evergreen Avenue branching off to the south—nothing and no one suspicious.

At around two o'clock, when she said she thought she'd stroll around outside and get a breath of air, Susan went with her. At a little after three when she announced her intention of walking in to the post office, Tony said he'd drive her. It began to look as though she would have to wait until night, and then, shortly after four, her chance came. Susan was busy with the children in the nursery, giving them their baths, and Tony was in the village getting meat for dinner.

Gabrielle didn't waste any time. Into her room and

out of it again by the door opening on the side veranda; she wore a tweed suit and carried the brown coat,
plaid side out, over her arm. The house was between her
and the road. The place for which she was making was
a pine wood over the hill to the north. She moved
quietly but with an affectation of nonchalance, in case
eyes were watching her. Once inside the wood, a wood
in which she and Susan had played as children and
which in spite of its new growth she could still chart
accurately, she felt confident that she could throw off
pursuit. The path to the pine wood ran past Tony's
studio, down into a gulley, across the brook, and over a
rise to another long dip filled with twenty acres of
green shielding branches.

There was still plenty of light left. The fog wasn't
as thick as it had been yesterday evening at Alice and
Tyrell's. Alice and Tyrell. A wave of sick distaste hit
her. She switched her thoughts hastily and walked on.
This was the danger spot. She was out in the clear now,
in the middle of what was the croquet lawn in summer.
Grass underfoot, dry and brittle, a small whirl of faded
leaves; if she was under observation this was where she
would be seen.

She paused near a leafless snowball bush at the far
side. Opening her purse, she took out a cigarette and
turned, as though idly studying the weather—and her
heart stood still. High up, to the south, above mist, a
gigantic bird poised in mid-air was facing in her direction. It was a telephone man, at the top of a pole, sil-
houetted against the dark sky. Only it wasn't a telephone man. The flash of a pair of glasses, the intent
attitude . . . The man was a detective. She was convinced
of it.

The distant figure was swinging rapidly down. He
disappeared from view. The detective was some distance
away. There was a lot of ground between them; if she

ran she could easily lose him. She turned, started on at a headlong pace—and collided with Tony, coming out of the studio.

"Gabrielle! What in the world—" Tony righted her, laughing. "Where are you off to in such a rush?" His smile faded as he looked into her face.

She had to get away. She said quickly, "I think there's a detective pretending to be a telephone man watching me, Tony. If he comes this way, keep him, will you? Tell him—oh, I don't care what you tell him." Caution made her add hastily, "I'm sick and tired of the police, sick and tired—let them worry for a while. All I want is a couple of hours of peace. I *won't* be constantly molested and spied on, I simply won't!"

Tony grinned at her. In the mist, with shadow filling his eye sockets, he looked vaguely like a skull. . . . Was his gaze on the coat over her arm? It didn't appear to be—and he seemed to understand. "Okay," he said, "take yourself off, honey. I'll cover for you, but be sure and be back for dinner, I got a swell roast of beef." He was looking past her, toward the road. "Quick," he said, "someone's coming around the corner of the house," and started forward.

Gabrielle didn't linger. Pausing for breath behind the garage she heard Tony say loudly in answer to a murmured query, "Miss Conant? Who the hell are you?" And then, not quite so loudly: "No, I haven't seen her, I don't know where she is. All I know is that she didn't come this way."

She was safe, but by what a narrow margin. Gabrielle filled her lungs with air and resumed her interrupted journey.

She was right about the telephone men. Two of them were detectives. There were more detectives in the Amory grounds, and outside Joanna Middleton's house in North Stamford. In New York, at four o'clock that afternoon, McKee sat gazing through the window of his office at blurred rooftops with distaste and uneasiness. The weather was the same in the city as it was in Greenfield. Fog blanketed the entire East Coast. Fog . . . He knew that Gabrielle had left the Amorys' and was with her cousin, Susan Van Ness. She was in no more danger there than anywhere else, perhaps less. . . . He took his glance from the afternoon, already darkening down, and turned back to the woman primly upright in the chair beyond his desk.

The woman was Mrs. Pendleton, Mark Middleton's ex-housekeeper. Mrs. Pendleton had very little to add to her previous statement, but there was one new thing. She hadn't seen Mark Middleton's visitor, the visitor who had killed him. She said that when she left the apartment Mr. Middleton was alone in his study. She *had* seen the pearls.

She was very positive about it. "Yes, sir. The box, a green-leather box, was on his desk, beside the telephone. It was open. I noticed the pearls laying in it particular, they were so pretty, kind of glowed."

The Scotsman drew a starfish on the pad on his desk, put eyes on it, and a slobbering mouth; he had been right. The pearls were in Mark Middleton's possession when he died.

Mrs. Pendleton said, "I thought maybe the necklace was for Miss Conant, a nice young lady . . ."

A nice young lady. Would she stay nice, could he keep her nice? McKee wondered, after Mrs. Pendleton had gone. He thought of Florence Nelson's face in that room in the Rothingham when they lifted her from the floor. Almost, then, he regretted not having let Dwyer take Gabrielle Conant into protective custody—for questioning. But phrase it ever so finely it would still have been an arrest, and the stigma would stick, unless the case were speedily resolved.

The fog thickened over the rooftops. McKee went on doodling. The starfish grew three extra tentacles. John Muir owned fifty-one percent of the stock of Tritex, the company he headed, Alice Amory owned, or had owned, a sizeable block of shares, so did Joanna Middleton. . . .

The door opened. Siebold stuck his head in. "Car's downstairs, Inspector."

With the movement of a man escaping from a trap the Scotsman was on his feet and flinging into his coat. Consequently he was not in the office three-quarters of an hour later when the message came through from Detective Bernstein in Greenfield that they had temporarily lost contact with Gabrielle Conant.

In that escape from surveillance to which she was helped by Tony, Gabrielle felt nothing but a vast relief. John had failed to turn up, and she had to get rid of Miss Nelson's coat, unaided, by herself. Thanks to Tony, it was almost done. She hadn't been pursued, stopped. Silence and the fog, bare black branches beaded with moisture—and just ahead the green wall of the pines, waving a little in the faint wind. The air was raw but not really cold. The path she was following ended abruptly at the spreading green paws of an enormous white pine. It was a specious ending. Gabrielle lifted boughs aside, and the path was there again in the brown gloom that was almost night, but less perceptible now, the slightest of depressions on deep layers of dried needles that were resilient and slippery underfoot.

Even at midday with a brilliant sun it was dim in the pine woods; now it was all but dark. She had had the forethought to bring a flashlight with her. She took the flashlight from her purse, switched it on. Dry interlacing branches from which the needles had fallen impeded her progress. They snapped with tiny explosions as she pushed them aside. Occasionally she paused uncertainly between familiar landmarks, the blasted chestnut, the fallen oak. It was for the pool in the hollow that she was making. The little pool was in the very middle of the wood that stretched from the back of Susan and Tony's land as far as the state road. The ground around the latter was soft, would be easy to dig. Scatter dead leaves and pine needles over it and it would look as though the surface had never been touched.

She went past the prostrate trunk of the oak where she and Susan and Tod Derringer, dead on an island in the Pacific, had played as children. How huge the pine forest had seemed then! In reality, even with its new growth, it wasn't very big. But it would do. People seldom came here nowadays. . . . She continued to forge forward in an unreal world, magic and silent and still, here and there going around instead of through clumps of withered brambles. No use coming out of this looking as though she had been in the wars.

The deep gloom—scarcely a wisp of daylight penetrated through the roof of green—forced her to keep her torch on continuously. The pool at last, a mere cupful of water surrounded by a few clumps of coarse grass—but Gabrielle was dismayed. The pine forest had been sliced off. Twenty feet beyond the western edge of the pond the trees stopped abruptly. Beyond thinning pine boughs light played mistily on a stretch of blasted stumps extending almost to the state road.

She stood still irresolutely. Go back and bury the coat near the oak? No. An overwhelming desire to get rid of it decided her. Nobody would ever think of looking here. She threw the coat to the ground, knelt, and began to work. She had been afraid to bring a trowel with her; she used a piece of wood from a dead branch, and her hands. The ground was soft, frost hadn't penetrated here. Fit the coat into the hole and see how much deeper she would have to go.

Gabrielle picked it up. She had already looked in the pockets. They were empty. But as she doubled the coat unceremoniously into a bundle she felt a slight thickening under folds of the cloth. Straightening the coat out, she put a hand into first one pocket and then the other. There was a rip in the right pocket, a large rip, at the side. Had something fallen through the rip and down into the lining?

Something had. Gabrielle undid loose stitching at the bottom of the hem and pulled out a piece of paper. It was a single sheet of notepaper, part of a letter—there was no salutation and the sentences at top and bottom were incomplete. It was written in pencil. Gabrielle held the torch close and read the indifferently formed characters.

Not bad here but I miss you and wish you could be here too. The job is a snap. When it's finished maybe we can get somewhere, maybe go south together. That's what I'd like. I've got my rheumatism again because of the damp and being inside so much. You've always wanted to see Flori—

That was all. There was more writing on the other side, not consecutive, and equally unimportant as far as specific information went. It didn't matter. The information was there in another shape. She reversed the sheet, her eyes on the heading. The paper was a fine bond. At the top was engraved: *William Glouster, Sound View, Rorotan, Connecticut.*

Crouched at the edge of the little pool, oblivious of the stealing coldness, the silence and brown gloom, Gabrielle stared fixedly at her find. She knew the house from which the notepaper had come. It was five miles to the south, this side of Rorotan, a huge ugly Victorian house all turrets and battlements and bay windows, on a point swinging out into the Sound. She knew the

Glousters who lived there, had met them at the Hunt
Club. William Glouster, a great oak of a man with a
military precision about him, was prominent in local
affairs. He would have made an excellent drill sergeant,
if he hadn't been a very wealthy man. His wife, Dorinda,
was almost as tall as he was, a large bosomy woman with
a booming voice, a managing air, and a loud laugh.

The sheet of paper, she hadn't the slightest doubt of
it, was a letter, or part of a letter, from the round man,
the "Bert" of the photograph, to Florence Nelson. Other-
wise, why should it be in Miss Nelson's pocket? And
Miss Nelson had spoken of a trip—and a trip was mentioned here. It was almost impossible to connect the
Glousters with anything criminal—and yet it was their
stationery and the paper was fresh, the writing unsmudged.
It hadn't been written very long ago. . . .

Gabrielle's head went up. Behind her, in the direction
from which she had come, there was a small sharp crack.
It was the sound of breaking wood. She swiveled, a cold
feeling in the pit of her stomach. Her vulnerability was
frightful. She was in the middle of a circle of light surrounded by intense gloom and walled in by trees and
the edge of the pool. Had she been followed? Was
someone watching her from the path along which she
could see no more than a few feet? She switched off the
torch, listened intently. The thudding of her heart was
the only thing she could hear in the stillness.

Nothing happened. There was no further noise. She
forgot her fear then, wholly absorbed by the tremendous
import of her discovery. With Miss Nelson's death the
only link with the round man had been severed. Now
she held in her fingers an almost certain lead to his
whereabouts. The Glousters might be harboring the
round man innocently, he mightn't be with them now,
might have gone elsewhere. There was only one thing
to do. Talk to the Glousters first, make sure she was

right—and then go to the police.

Three-quarters of an hour later she was at the gates of Sound View, a name that was typical of the sound and factual Glousters, under a dark sky faintly powdered with stars.

Chapter Twenty-One: FOUR DEAD, ONE TO GO

GABRIELLE WOULD HAVE ARRIVED at her destination sooner, only that there was no taxi available in Greenfield and she had had to take the bus. Before boarding it in front of the library she had phoned Susan that she had run into a girl from the office in town, and was going to have a cocktail with her, and not to wait dinner. So that was all right.

She walked between the gateposts and up a driveway banked with shrubs below leafless maples—she couldn't see them but she knew they were there—with an almost buoyant step. What were the Glousters going to tell her? Was the round man an acquaintance, a friend, an employee? The letters had spoken of a job. As she recalled the Glousters, they were always having jobs done, new electric gadgets installed, gardens remade, trees felled and groves of different ones planted; they did everything in a large way. The little gatehouse was lightless and dark when she went past. So the round man didn't live there. In the main house then.

The drive twisted and turned on itself, ending in a huge graveled sweep below a vast terrace distantly visible from the road below. Gabrielle rounded the final bend, emerged into the open, and stood still, staring blankly. The mist had gone. It was very dark. There was no moon and the stars were dim and few, but you could see. The bulk of the house, massive, towering, ivy-hung, faced her loweringly, blocked against the faintly paler tones of sky. It was completely black. There wasn't a light anywhere. The Glousters were not, as they would have said, "in residence." The place was deserted, closed up. There was no one there.

Gabrille's bright hopes fell to the ground. Despair touched her with a shadowy finger. There was never to be an end to the inner darkness in which she moved—never. She had dreamed, audaciously, of herself delivering the round man into the hands of the police. What nonsense! Her journey had been in vain. She had come on a fool's errand. Behind the house waves crashed gently on the shore, mocking her delusions of grandeur.

Aimlessly, without expectation, she wandered across a stretch of dried grass toward the side of the house. The Glousters weren't people to live in obscurity. If they had been at home every window would have blazed. The glass of a conservatory—it was that sort of place—the faintest of dark glimmers, more windows above, long irregular rows of them, blank, eyeless; the whole ugly gigantic structure was empty, untenanted.

There was nothing to do but go away. About to turn, Gabrielle caught her breath. There was a light! It flashed on suddenly. She couldn't see the source of the light, only the reflection of it, a pale handful of refracted glow high upon the glossy leaves of a tall larch, growing close to the end of a cupolaed wing. The light was on in an upper story. It hadn't been there a second before. The house wasn't empty. There was someone inside.

Without pausing for thought, Gabrielle launched herself in the direction from which the light was coming, her eyes on the golden shimmer of glossy leaves, afraid to lose that beam. She had covered perhaps fifty feet of ground when she came to a sharp halt. The sound of her footsteps on a cement path was what brought her to her senses. In the stillness immediately surrounding the house, above the wash of the waves, they positively rang, a warning tocsin that said, *You are being invaded.*

There is an intruder here.

Where she stood under trees the darkness was intense. She was alone in it, surrounded by it on every side. She might as well have been at the bottom of the sea. No one knew she had come here. Glass had died, and Miss Nelson had died, because they had come too close to a murderer. . . . With the utmost caution, fear a hollow trembling again in the pit of her stomach, Gabrielle stepped backward—and was seized.

In that instant of overwhelming terror, as still as a snared bird, thoughts rocketed across the surface of her mind like shooting stars: *I was seen in the wood. . . . I was followed here. I walked straight into a wide-open trap. . . .* There were pictures, too, the picture of Glass's face, pressed against the beige rug of Miss Nelson's dinette. . . .

The arms gripping her, the hands binding her own arms to her sides, loosened a little, as though her invisible captor had received a shock. Gabrielle tried to pull herself free. "Let me go!" she cried in a strangled voice.

The gripping hands and arms fell away, and she was free. An indrawn breath, a voice out of darkness said, "Gabrielle!" in a tone of astonishment.

Swaying, dizzy, Gabrielle found her feet under her, stood erect. History was repeating itself. All this had happened before, not long ago. The voice was John Muir's. In just such a fashion on the night she was decoyed to the Jordon's on the lower West Side, John Muir had reached out and pulled her in under scaffolding.

And when they had both withdrawn and were a dozen yards off, in the lee of a clump of birches beyond the larch, almost the same colloquy as had taken place then was repeated. "John—what are you doing here?" "What are *you* doing here, Gabrielle?" She told him, quickly, about finding the letter. Exultation ran along her veins revivingly when he spoke. She was right. The round man was in the house. John said that Pete Basil had tracked him here earlier in the day. Pete had gone for help, leaving John to keep watch. John had done better than simply watch. He had managed to get a window open, and had already entered the house on an exploratory trip, interrupted by Gabrielle's arrival. "I heard someone and came out to see . . ." He was going back in again.

Gabrielle said firmly, "I'm going in with you."

John didn't like it. In the end, when she said she didn't want to go alone through the dark grounds, that she would be scared to death, he agreed. "At that, you'll probably be safer inside."

He took her hand, guided her. Amazing experience, utterly divorced from normality, eerie and strange and yet with a certain juvenile element about it reminiscent of childish games, of stealing up on an implacable enemy with a stick that was a sword, of being lost in an impenetrable forest that was a field of waving wheat, because the actual procedure, if illegal, was simple enough. Inside the border of laurel and rhododendron and dwarf pines that masked the base of the house, John went first over the sill of a low window, leaned out, helped her up, and stood her on her feet on the thickness of carpeting in darkness. He had warned her against making the slightest noise. He closed the window behind him. Gabrielle didn't hear it come down, heard only the tiniest click as he locked it. He took her hand again, opened a door, led her a few yards in complete blackness. "Wait a second." His voice at her ear was only just audible. He left her. There was a faint rustle of curtains being pulled to, then John switched on a torch. Gabrielle looked around in that whisper of light.

They were in a room that was half sitting-room, half study. A huge, uncluttered desk, glass-fronted bookcases filled with rows of books that looked as though they were never touched, a filing-cabinet, two large handsomely upholstered wing chairs at either side of an empty fireplace, tables, lamps, hunting prints on the walls; Mr. Glouster's passion for order, regimentation, evinced itself in neatly framed placards above the bookcases announcing their contents. *Shelf A, Dickens; Shelf B, Belles Lettres; Shelf C, Balzac, Daudet* . . . There was something pathetic, touching in those carefully lettered guides to culture. Did the Glousters know what was going on, that their house was being used as a hiding-place by a criminal?

John was a dark shape at the door listening for sounds beyond it. There were none. He came over to her, said, keeping his voice low, "I'm going, Gabrielle. Lock the door behind me, and don't open it under any circumstance, no matter what happens, no matter who speaks to you, until I come back."

"No matter who speaks to you"—the phrase was shocking in its baldness. John didn't elaborate. The collar of his ulster was turned up. His hat, down over his forehead, put a black band across his eyes. In dimness above torchlight, his face, fine-drawn but composed, was unreadable. He was like the captain of a ship, going about larger concerns with only a fragment of attention to spare for a chance passenger unexpectedly thrust upon him.

He watched her, waiting for her assent. Gabrielle hesitated. She didn't want to be left alone, neither had she any desire to go creeping around the house at John's heels, fearful of what the next step might disclose. And she would only be an encumbrance to him. . . . She nodded. "Don't worry. I'll stay here. I'm not particularly brave."

"And you won't open the door to anyone until I come to get you?" He was insistent. She said no, and then he was gone, as silently as a feather drifting. Gabrielle locked the door behind him and went and sat down in one of the wing chairs in front of the hearth. Darkness was a cloak around her shoulders, a vast cloak that covered not only her but the whole room. The windows were curtained. There was no reason why she shouldn't keep her torch on. She pressed the button, looking aimlessly about at shapes in the dim half-light, dim except for a single spot of brilliance that moved jerkily. The dancing circle touching now books in one of the bookcases, now the edge of a hunting print, the leg of a chair, disconcerted her with those broken glimpses. Her hand was shaking. She held the torch steady on her knee. The door was locked, the windows were locked, she was in no danger, nothing could touch her, get at her here. But what about John?

She told herself that John knew what he was doing. He had already explored the house, at least partially. And if it came to a personal encounter, the round man, soft and pudgy with flesh, would have no chance against John's six feet of bone and muscle, his hard fitness.

The room was cold. Sitting stiffly erect, her feet flat on the floor, Gabrielle discovered with horror that she was going to sneeze. The round man might be in a nearby room; a sneeze could be fatal. She loosened her hold on the torch, dropped it into her lap, and grabbed for her purse. Twisting the catch she snatched at a handkerchief, and stopped the sneeze, just in time.

Her purse had fallen to the floor, spilling things broadcast. Among them was the green-leather box with Mark's pearls in it. The box had sprung open. The pearls lay on the carpet, a coil of pale bubbles glowing softly with their own light. She picked up the box, started to reach for the pearls, and desisted. The satin bed on which the stones had lain had come loose from its moorings. One end of it was up in the air. If she hadn't found the round man's letter in Miss Nelson's coat earlier it mightn't have occurred to her to look further. She did look. There was something between the satin and the green leather. It was a slip of paper.

Gabrielle drew the slip of paper out. There was type-writing on it, three or four lines. It was a note addressed to Mark. It said: *Mark—Thanks for the leg up. I was temporarily short and needed cash and the eighty thousand was a Godsend, helped me out of a tight spot. I'll have it back to you in a couple of months, if that's okay. Thanks again, old man. This will serve as a receipt.* The name signed to the note in ink, in a handwriting she knew, was John Muir's.

Gabrielle sat motionless, staring down at the slip of paper that was a receipt as though it were a poised cobra about to strike. About to strike? It had already struck. The poison was racing through her veins.

So that was where Mark's eighty thousand dollars in cash had gone—to John Muir. The Inspector had said that when they found that out they would know who had killed Mark. Well, that was clear now. How clever John had been, how very clever. She didn't feel anything at all, except perhaps admiration at his cleverness. It was as though a nerve controlling her emotional system had been cut, severed. But her brain was working; it clicked on mechanically, a deadly little machine tabulating facts.

The round man was John's accomplice, too. On the day that she had first seen him he had come to Mark's apartment to get the money, had carried it to John Muir. Pete Basil, John's investigator, hadn't discovered the round man's whereabouts. And most emphatically Pete Basil hadn't gone for the police. Oh no, no, indeed. John had known where the round man was all the time. And now he was going to kill him, as he had killed those others, before she, before anyone else, saw him, talked to him. That was why John had left her shut up here.

She ought, she thought detachedly, to do something about it. But what? If she left the house, she could get out through one of the windows. By the time she got to the police it would be too late. . . . If the round man was warned he might be able to save himself. She had already brought about two deaths by her interference. She might be able to save one life.

Gabrielle left the pearls lying where they were. She got up, put the slip of paper into her pocket, walked to the door, opened it, and listened. Not a sound. She switched on her torch. If she came on John before she found the round man she would pretend fright. *I got uneasy. I couldn't stay in that room.* Meanwhile, use caution. The moving spot of light swept the great empty spaces of a cavernous hall with a staircase off on the right. Try the lower floor first. The light that she had seen from outside had come from the back of the house. There was a door at the back of the hall. With the unswerving gait of a somnambulist she went to this door, opened it on a passage lined with wall cabinets and another staircase ascending into blackness at the left. On the wall beside the dark mouth of the stairs, neatly lettered in dark red, was the legend: *Staircase 3.*

Gabrielle smiled. An amusing glimpse came back to her, of William Glouster at a Hunt Club ball holding up numbered cards in a game that was being played. Glouster had been an expert accountant before he made his money and someone had remarked that he had a passion for numbers.

Numbers. 1, 2, 3—Mark and Edward Glass and Florence Nelson. The round man would make four. Perhaps there would be five. Perhaps John intended to kill her later, when he had disposed of the round man. . . . No tremor shook her. She was as cold as a stone and as completely unfeeling. The passage she was in ended in an enormous kitchen. Darkness, silence, nothing, except that the huge range, the great Monel metal sink, the vast cupboards, the tables and counters and stools had an air of waiting for something. A groan, perhaps, and the thud of a falling body. Would a shot herald it? Or would it be a blow with a knife, a club?

She really must find the round man. She went through another door at random and was in a transverse corridor at the rear of the house. Ah, light at last. A white-shaded bulb in the high ceiling shone down on mustard-colored walls, on a floor covered with brown and white linoleum. The corridor was empty. The only break in it was a doorway some twenty feet to her right in the opposite wall. Lettering on plaster beside it said: *Staircase 4*.

Gabrielle moved toward the door slowly. Not a sound anywhere; yes, there was. It was the sound of surf on the beach below, louder now, but still muted by the walls. The door to Staircase 4 was a little open. Doors, Gabrielle thought dispassionately, were interesting. There had been Miss Nelson's front door, with a dead man beyond it, and Miss Nelson's kitchen door, with John Muir coming through. What was behind the door of Staircase 4? Find out.

She went toward it, quietly. It was better not to make any noise because noise would be a warning and she wanted to avoid that until the last possible moment. John Muir's hands, hands she knew so well, were quick, and strong. They had gripped her roughly, pinning her arms to her sides, only a short while ago. Odd that there wasn't even loathing in her. There was nothing whatever but emptiness, negation, the same emptiness that filled those silent spaces through which she moved.

She was at the door of Staircase 4. It was open a foot, enough to let her through without disturbing it further. She slipped through the opening sideways, stood still.

She was on a small square landing at the top of a flight of stone stairs going down steeply into blackness. The air was colder and felt damp, smelled of dampness. Light, very faint, was coming from somewhere out of the abyss below. It was a good distance away. She couldn't locate its source. Moving forward a little, but not too far—she had herself become a part of the darkness—she looked over the railing, and knew then what the place was. It was a boathouse. Two immense doors in the east wall opened on the Sound. They were closed. Inside of them and far down, a cement platform surrounded a great square filled with black water.

A launch upside-down on struts occupied part of the runway at the back. The one opposite the staircase was empty. She couldn't see the runway beneath the staircase, stepped closer to the railing. The light was coming from a lantern near the launch, an electric lantern, on a squat base. She caught back an involuntary cry at what it revealed.

The round man was there, looking up at her, looking straight into her eyes. His own eyes, without glasses— he must have removed them—were fastened immovably on hers. The whites glittered faintly in the dim light. He was lying at ease in the bottom of a rowboat tethered to a stanchion, his head pillowed on the seat. He saw her, of course, he couldn't help but see her, and he didn't look away, didn't blink or make the slightest movement. He didn't move because he was dead.

No, the round man didn't move, but something else down there did. Blackness and the dark water and the smell of damp and the dead man in the rowboat, all immobile, lifeless; and then that stir. It had color to it, took on shape. What she was looking at was a blue shimmer on the snub nose of a revolver, pistol. The weapon was coming out from under the turn of the stairs. It was pointing upward. The hand that held the gun was John Muir's.

An infinitesimal fraction of time too small for the brain to measure held horror like a great suspended bubble. In that freezing instant of silence between lap and lap of water the bubble burst. The silence was smashed to pieces by the shrill clamor of a bell.

Gabrielle heard just the beginning of it. As the edge of the wave of sound touched her ears the gun in John Muir's hand jerked upward. Fire spat at the muzzle. A gigantic fist hit Gabrielle between the shoulders. Before her body struck the first few downward steps consciousness was gone.

Chapter Twenty-Two: CONFESSIONS BY TWO

"YES, TODHUNTER?"

McKee looked up from the desk in William Glouster's study, in the room in which John Muir had left Gabrielle Conant when she first entered the house more than nine hours earlier. It was almost three o'clock in the morning. The house wasn't, as it had been then, in darkness. It blazed with lights, and the halls and corridors were full of men, state troopers soldierly in uniform and the detectives McKee had brought with him on that final assault.

The ringing of the bell that had clanged in Gabrielle's ears before her body went pitching down the cement steps in the boathouse had been set off by the opening of the boathouse doors before the nose of a police launch. The doors were still open. The indicator in the bell box in the kitchen stood frozen at Staircase 4.

Todhunter said to McKee, "We've got them all here, the Van Nesses and the Amorys and Miss Holmes, and the Middletons and Bond. Do you want to talk to them now, Inspector?"

McKee nodded. "I think so. I'd like to finish up to-night. How is Miss Conant?"

"Not too bad," Todhunter said, with the first vestige of cheerfulness. "No bones broken, no concussion—the doctor says that what she needs is rest."

"Saving the medical gentleman's favor," McKee said dryly, expelling smoke from the bottom of his lungs, "rest is precisely what she doesn't need, right now. What she's got to have is the truth. I know she's pretty well knocked out—but she'll be better for it later on."

Gabrielle had talked to him when she was first revived. Eyes blank and fixed, the shining pupils, enormously enlarged by the sedative she had been given, she had told him, in a monotonous voice that neither rose nor fell but continued on one dead level, everything that had happened, as she knew it, from the beginning.

The only thing that might have helped, if they had known it earlier, was Florence Nelson's coat and the letter inside the lining pointing to the whereabouts of the round man. And even that—he doubted whether it would have made any real difference in the end. The round man, Bertrand Oliver, was doomed from the moment Mark Middleton's death was called murder.

"Have them bring Miss Conant, Todhunter, and then bring the others."

"Yes, Inspector." The little detective went mournfully on his errand. The windup of a case always distressed him.

Chairs from other rooms were carried in. Presently William Glouster's study was full. The Inspector behind the desk, a stenographer at a table, detectives at the door; Gabrielle sat in the wing chair to the left of the fireplace, the chair from which she had risen when she read the slip of paper concealed in the jewel box, risen like a sleepwalker, and gone to what was, for her, very nearly the end of time.

A bandaged temple and wrist, a strapped shoulder, strapped ribs; the drug she had been given dulled physical pain. She sat almost as though she were still asleep, except that she was too erect, her face as empty as a slate that had been wiped clean; her exhausted eyes, concealed by fringes of dark lash, fastened on hands clasped in her lap, as though she had been posed that way for a portrait and instructed not to move.

No one spoke to her, nor did she speak herself. There was no talking whatever; that had been done when they were first brought to the house, with sound and fury. Indignation, anger, expostulations—they had been told, coldly, that Bertrand Oliver was dead and that the case was nearing an end, and that was all.

Facing Gabrielle and the Scotsman were Joanna and Claire Middleton, Claire very young and frightened, the Amorys, Susan and Tony, and Philip Bond. It was amazing, Gabrielle thought apathetically, how like their usual selves they were, in spite of the hour and the circumstances. What mysteries men and women were, even those you knew best. There was no closeness, no truth, no real contact between one human being and another. She, for instance, saw Joanna out of her own eyes, and everything that she herself was, that she had been from the moment she entered the world—no, further back than that; everything her ancestors had been, had seen, and thought and felt—shaped her vision.

Where was John Muir? Not in custody; the Inspector was talking. He startled her distantly when he said that no arrest had yet been made, that before the perpetrator was taken into custody and charged with the deaths, by violence, of Mark Middleton, Edward Glass, Florence Nelson, and Bertrand Oliver, it would be necessary to get certain details clear, for the record.

He began talking about Mark, put Mark in his study in the apartment on Central Park West shortly before he died. "Seated," McKee said, "much as I am now, with this"—the tip of a delicately blunted forefinger touched the green-leather box holding the pearls—"on his desk in front of him."

The frost-bound stillness was broken by a tiny gasp. Gabrielle raised her lashes. It came from Susan. McKee didn't look at her; he was looking at Tony. "I believe you told Miss Conant, Mr. Van Ness, that Mark Middleton gave you these pearls in front of the Hotel Devon at around three o'clock on the afternoon of the day he was killed. Would you care to change your statement?"

Tony had collapsed in his chair. The air seemed to have gone out of him. His body looked flat, one-dimensional. His throat working convulsively, he moistened his lips and finally spoke. "I didn't kill him—Mark. No matter what you say—I didn't! You can't fasten it on me! He was dead when I went in. I swear it. . . ."

He continued to pour out words. They gushed from him like water from a faucet. He had been in the Devon, near the cloakroom, within a few yards of Gabrielle and Mark, when Mark showed Gabrielle the pearls. He had heard Mark say that the clasp had to be fixed. He had gone to the Devon to ask Mark for a loan, knew Gabrielle wouldn't like it, and didn't want to approach Mark while she was with him. They left the hotel together. Mark put Gabrielle into a cab alone, but before he could get to him, Mark had climbed into another cab and driven off. Tony said he had to have money. That evening he had gone to Mark's apartment. As he rounded the turn from the elevator and stepped into the transverse corridor he had had a fleeting impression that someone had just moved from Mark's door. He didn't think anything of it, then. Mark's door wasn't quite closed. He tapped, didn't get any answer, walked in, and found Mark dead, as he thought, on the study floor.

The pearls were on the desk. The lid of the box was up. He was horrified. He was also desperate, and he had had a lot to drink. He had snatched up the pearls and gone. The next thing he knew he was in the street. He proceeded with the tale he had already told Gabrielle. He had been mad, it was a mad thing to have done. He knew it. . . . His voice dribbled off incoherently.

McKee made absolutely no comment on his story, except: "You say you had an impression of movement in the corridor outside Mr. Middleton's door when you first entered it. Can you elaborate on that, Mr. Van Ness?"

Tony couldn't. He shrugged heavily. "I don't know. It was just an idea. Maybe I imagined it. But the door was open and I—when I thought about it afterward, I thought that maybe whoever killed Mark heard me coming and dashed in the other direction, toward the stairs, without stopping to pull the door closed properly."

The silence throbbed. Mr. McKee let it go on for a moment. Then he settled back in his chair. "I think you all know that whoever borrowed, or instigated the borrowing, of eighty thousand dollars, in cash, from Mark Middleton, killed him."

"Whoever borrowed eighty thousand dollars in cash" —Gabrielle examined a fingernail broken to the quick. . . . The Inspector knew to whom the money had gone. Why was he beating about the bush? It was stupid of him. His voice went on and on, tiresomely. He said that once the missing money had come to light, the police had turned their attention to who, among Mark's friends, needed money at the time Mark had converted his securities into cash. Mr. Muir and Mr. Muir's firm, Tritex, Incorporated, leaped to the eye. Mr. Muir and Tritex, Incorporated, were being sued for five million dollars by Crosby and Sons on charges that the defendants had conspired to copy the Crosby system of production and design and other knowledge, and to compel certain manufacturers to sever their connection with the Crosby company and to destroy the Crosby company's source of supply. With this suit pending, McKee said, the stock of Tritex had fallen sharply.

A pause; McKee was looking at Alice.

"I believe you had large holdings in Mr. Muir's company back in June, when this happened, Mrs. Amory?"

Alice stared at him stonily. "No."

"No?" McKee's brows rose. "Then how do you account for the fact that your broker sold a large block of Tritex shares in July, a transaction on which you received a handsome profit, as the shares had risen sharply after the suit was decided in favor of Tritex?"

Alice looked steadily at the Inspector, looked away. Her lips opened, and closed. They were blue around the edges of blurred lipstick. She wasn't going to answer. She stared at space.

McKee didn't attempt to force an answer from her. His attention was already directed elsewhere. "And you, Mrs. Middleton," he said, "I believe you held and still hold stock in Tritex?" Joanna said calmly, "That's correct, Inspector," and nothing more. She was encased in a shell of composure it would have taken a sledge hammer to smash.

The Inspector didn't use one. He abandoned both women, went on musingly: "The break in this case came when we found out what Mark Middleton did on the afternoon of the day he died. Before that, we knew simply this, that the man Miss Conant called the round man, and whose name was Bertrand Oliver, called at Mark Middleton's apartment on June the twenty-fifth and in all probability took the eighty thousand dollars in cash away with him in his briefcase, and that a little more than some eight weeks later, Mr. Middleton caught sight of Oliver in the lobby of the Devon and showed strong anger. We didn't know why. We didn't know where Mr. Middleton went that afternoon, or what he did in the hours immediately preceding his death. Then we found out. After taking leave of Miss Conant in front of the Devon, he drove to the house of Judge Silverbridge on East Sixty-fourth Street."

A stir ran through the room.

"Yes," McKee said, interpreting it, "Judge Silverbridge was the judge who gave the verdict in John Muir's and Tritex's favor in the suit against them. If the verdict had gone the other way, if it had been adverse, Tritex couldn't have weathered the blow. John Muir's personal fortune would have been wiped out and the investors in Tritex would have lost heavily."

The Scotsman looked thoughtfully over the faces turned on him. "Our next discovery was that on that afternoon, the afternoon Mark Middleton saw him, Judge Silverbridge had a stroke. Returning home a few minutes after Mark Middleton left the house, the Judge's wife found Judge Silverbridge in a state of collapse on the library floor."

McKee made some sort of signal to a detective near the door. The door opened and John Muir came in. Gabrielle dragged herself up from seas of weariness that threatened to engulf her. Why did she have to be there, to see, to listen?

"Mr. Muir, I have here this receipt." The Inspector read the note to Mark from John aloud, explained where it had been found. "Undoubtedly," he said, "Mark Middleton meant the eighty thousand dollars he expected to receive from you, Mr. Muir, as a wed-

ding present for Miss Conant. He put this note into
the box with the pearls, beneath the cushion on which
the pearls lay, probably meaning to surprise her. He
intended to give her this wedding gift when they
lunched that day in the Devon. What he learned while
he was waiting for Miss Conant there made it impossible, which was why he invented an excuse for
keeping the box containing the pearls, and the receipt,
in his possession—until he had done what he intended
to do, and which he carried out, in part."

Cold, cold as ice, John's voice. "Inspector, I did not
write that receipt. I did not receive eighty thousand
dollars from Mark Middleton. That is not my signature."

"You're claiming that somebody else borrowed the
eighty thousand from Mark Middleton, in your name,
and forged your signature?"

"Yes."

"Thank you, Mr. Muir." McKee turned back to the
others.

"Late this afternoon I drove up to see Judge Silverbridge at his home in Dutchess County. The Judge is
an invalid, has never recovered from the shock of what
happened when Mark Middleton went to see him last
August. I saw the Judge, talked to him. The Judge
talked to me.

"Bertrand Oliver, Miss Conant's 'round man,' the
man who was killed here tonight, was a protégé, a sort
of henchman, of the Judge's. Becoming interested in
Oliver as a boy, the Judge put him through school and
later found him jobs, using him often himself in a confidential capacity. When Mark Middleton was waiting
for Miss Conant in the lobby of the Devon, he saw
Bertrand Oliver there. Oliver wasn't alone. Judge Silverbridge was with him, was just parting from him.

"Mark Middleton didn't know who Oliver's companion was then, and, as far as Oliver went, he simply knew he was the messenger who had carried away the eighty thousand dollars destined for Mr. Muir. No, Mark Middleton had no idea who Oliver's companion was. Two men standing near Middleton enlightened him. Speaking in a confidential voice, one man said to the other, 'There's Judge Silverbridge—and his bagman, Oliver. You'd never think, would you, that Silverbridge was on the take? But I guess there's no doubt of it.'

"Mark Middleton was thunderstruck. He realized instantly that he had been made the butt, the victim, of a conspiracy to defraud, that the eighty thousand dollars in cash John Muir had borrowed was the Judge's *pourboire,* his payment, for the decision against Crosby and Sons and in favor of John Muir and Tritex. When he went to see the Judge, Mark Middleton accused him of having taken a bribe of eighty thousand dollars in return for favors received, told him he was going to expose him and everyone who had been a party to the transaction."

The distant sea boomed, wind beat at the walls; inside the crowded room, except for the Inspector's voice, there wasn't the slightest sound.

He said, "Had Mark Middleton been able to carry out his intention, the decision in favor of Tritex would have been reversed, and the Judge and anyone and everyone involved brought to trial and sentenced to long prison terms." McKee shrugged. "Mark Middleton wasn't able to carry out what he intended to do. Back in his apartment, he called, not Mr. Muir, who he thought was in South America, but the man who had asked for the eighty thousand dollars on Mr. Muir's behalf, in Mr. Muir's name. That man is Tyrell Amory."

Gabrielle sat very still. The house was rocking like a

ship. Someone was talking. It was Tyrell. Tyrell was saying in a loud empty voice, "Yes, I did it. Yes . . ."

Gabrielle didn't look at him. The Inspector was finishing up. He said that Judge Silverbridge was entirely innocent. The Judge had reached the decision in favor of John Muir and Tritex on the merits of the case. Unfortunately, there was a leak, and his decision had become known in advance. Tyrell Amory was in trouble. Without Mrs. Amory's knowledge he had invested a large sum of his wife's money, more than half of what she had, in Tritex. When the Crosby company had filed suit, the stock had fallen heavily. A favorable verdict could send it soaring. Tyrell Amory was approached and offered a favorable verdict—price, eighty thousand dollars, in cash.

Tyrell had no money, but Mark Middleton had. Mark was generous, open-handed, had come to the assistance of his friends on other occasions. Tyrell had gone to Mark, representing that John Muir, with whom he was in constant touch, was temporarily short of cash with which to bolster his own stock by quiet buying, a perfectly legal procedure. This was the easier to do because John was in South America and not expected to return for some time. The receipt, purportedly forwarded via Tyrell by John to Mark, was a forgery.

All had gone well. Tyrell had managed to unload his wife's shares at a profit and reinvest them as she had originally directed. In addition, by selling shares of his own that he had bought when Tritex was low, he was ready to pay Mark back, when Mark saw Judge Silverbridge and Oliver in the Devon, heard the comment of the man near him, and put two and two together. The truth had a way of leaking out. It wasn't the first transaction of that sort that had been negotiated. It had happened twice before.

As he talked, McKee had been scribbling absently on

a piece of paper in front of him. He laid the pencil
aside. Everything he had said, done, throwing suspicion
now here, now there, laboring certain points, dwelling
on them, had been for one purpose. He didn't know
whether or not he was going to be successful in what
he was attempting. No use waiting any longer—put it
to the test. He raised his eyes, and looked, not at Tyrell
Amory, but at the woman on Tyrell's left.

"Miss Holmes," he said, "you were the one who went
to Tyrell Amory with a legal verdict for sale. I charge
you with the murders of Mark Middleton, Edward
Glass, Florence Nelson, and Bertrand Oliver."

The silence was complete. It was like the intense stillness after a tremendous flash of lightning and before
the advent of thunder, Gabrielle thought dazedly. A
sound broke it. Brenda Holmes laughed.

It was a quiet laugh, a little ripple of amusement.
There was something blood-chilling in its composure,
in the way her beautiful face didn't change, the way her
skin held its bloom, her blue eyes their light. She said
in a languid voice, "Some of your deductions are correct, Inspector. Not all. You've been arguing with in-
sufficient knowledge. Your conclusion is wrong. I didn't
kill anyone. The man you want, the man who killed
Mark, and that private detective, and the Nelson woman,
is Blake Evans."

Gabrielle wrestled with stupefaction. Brenda's voice
stopped. There was another sound then; it was the opening of the door. Blake Evans stood in the opening, between two big men. His clothes were in disorder, dis-
array, as though he had been in some sort of melée, but
his handsome face was just as it always was, attractive,
debonair, faintly smiling. It was a white smile. There
was a glittering quality to it. Blake didn't glance at
Brenda, who had turned sharply. He was looking at
McKee. He said, slowly, in what would have been an

indifferent tone except for the whip of savagery in it, "You were right, Inspector. I was wrong. You thought Miss Holmes would talk. I didn't. I acknowledge my mistake. I'm quite willing to talk now."

"John!" Brenda Holmes's cry was almost a scream. She was up and out of her chair, was across to where John stood, an elbow propped on one of the bookcases, had flung herself against him, her arms wound tightly around his neck. "John," she cried frantically, "don't listen. It isn't true that I . . ."

She must have known it was futile, useless, that she was already lost. The ensuing five minutes were frightful. Claire Middleton sobbing wildly, Joanna trying to quiet her, Tyrell speaking, and then the Inspector. Brenda Holmes and Blake Evans were both charged with murder, repeated four times, and removed.

Tyrell was taken away, too. Alice went with him, a new, a different Alice, subdued, stern, but with the veil of despair gone from her. Tyrell wasn't in love with Brenda Holmes. He never had been. The bond between them had been hateful to him. When Alice, and Gabrielle, had seen them together in the little room beyond the dining-room the night before, Brenda was pleading with Tyrell to remain silent, for all their sakes. Tyrell had had no hand in murder. The others had managed to persuade him that Bertrand Oliver was the real culprit.

Tyrell had wanted to go to the police. That was why Oliver had been killed that night; they were afraid of Tyrell, of what he might do. It was Blake Evans who had sent Gabrielle crashing down Staircase 4 in the boathouse, Blake Evans at whom John had fired. Evans had killed Oliver earlier, when he first entered the house. He had gone upstairs to collect Oliver's clothing so that there should be no trace of him left.

The Glousters had gone abroad the previous May.

Oliver was there without their knowledge. They had never heard of him. Brenda knew the Glousters, knew the house would be empty and an admirable hiding-place. Oliver had lived there quietly from August on, pretending to be cataloguing the Glousters' library to the few local people he encountered.

While Blake Evans was upstairs, John had found Oliver dead in a boat ready on the black water in the boathouse. The plan had been to take Oliver out into the Sound in the rowboat, dump him overboard in deep water so well weighted down that it would be a long while before his body broke the surface, by which time he would have become unrecognizable.

Some of this Gabrielle learned then, some of it later on. Other things were made plain, too, but not there. The house gradually emptied. Gabrielle, McKee, and John were among the last to go, in John's car. They drove through the first tinges of gray light to an all-night coffee shop near the shore, over John's objections. "She ought to be in bed." The Inspector didn't agree. "Miss Conant's too keyed up to sleep and I imagine there are things she wants to know. No, Muir, I think she'd better have it all cleared up now."

Over coffee at a white table at the back of the clean little shop bright with chromium and enamel and blazing lights, while the dawn struggled into being beyond the curtained windows, the Scotsman talked.

The affair between Brenda Holmes and Blake Evans had been going on for years. They couldn't afford to marry. It was one of those poisonous relationships that had ruined them both, breaking down moral fibers that were never strong.

Blake Evans was Judge Silverbridge's stepson. The Judge disliked and distrusted him; he couldn't, for his wife's sake, forbid him the house. Evans had taken advantage of his position twice before, selling secretly, in advance, decisions the Judge had already made and that needn't have been bought at all.

Evans had made a full confession, determined that Brenda, who at the last would have betrayed him to save herself, should be equally implicated—the affair between them had by that time worn thin.

Bertrand Oliver had been a tool, snatching at a chance to make a little gravy on the side; he got five thousand for his work, which had consisted of delivering Mark's money to Evans and changing the large bills into smaller ones. Tyrell had been a dupe throughout. After that interview with Judge Silverbridge, in whose protestations of noncomplicity he didn't believe, Mark had phoned to Tyrell, Tyrell had phoned to Blake Evans, and Evans had gone to the apartment on Central Park West and had killed Mark with Mark's own gun.

"I imagine," McKee said, "that Mark had it in readiness in case of trouble. He wasn't quick enough . . ."

At any rate, Mark was dead and his death was pronounced suicide—a verdict which Tyrell accepted—and for a while it must have seemed to Brenda Holmes and Evans that they were sitting pretty. McKee stirred his coffee. "Miss Conant was the only threat. I wasn't in the city, and her protestations that his death was murder got nowhere. But there was one fly in the ointment—a very large fly. The receipt for the eighty thousand dollars, signed with John Muir's name, had vanished. It was not among Mark's papers, which Tyrell Amory, as a close friend and under the pretense of helping Philip Bond, went through very carefully indeed."

John interrupted there. "If nothing had happened, Inspector, if Mark had lived, weren't they afraid Mark and I would have gotten together and the truth about the loan would have come out?"

McKee said, "They argued, correctly, I think, that Mark was not the sort of man to remind you of benefits received; not knowing it, you couldn't mention it to him. In addition, Mark was going to be in the West for a long while. . . . Incidentally, Miss Conant," the Inspector remarked to Gabrielle, "it was Tyrell Amory who shoved you into the closet in Mark's apartment when you surprised him making a last desperate search for the forged receipt."

With it missing, John had come home from South America. They were afraid of him, of what he might do if his suspicions were aroused. His suspicions would be aroused if he met Gabrielle, and heard her story—which was why the attempt had been made on her life on the subway platform on the afternoon of the day of John's return, by Evans.

The attempt was unsuccessful. John and Gabrielle met at Tyrell's birthday party that evening. It was Brenda who had opened the door while they were together in Tyrell's study. John had seen her hand on the knob and, although she had slipped away by the time he got to the door, he recognized her perfume when he joined her in the living-room. Brenda had heard John planning to meet Gabrielle later on, hence the second attempt at murder that same night.

It was Evans who had called Gabrielle in a disguised voice, directing her to go Jordon's on the lower West Side. As McKee had surmised, there was to have been a pretended pursuit of the round man and at the end of it death for Gabrielle, in an obscure spot in New Jersey. When and if her body was eventually discovered her death would have been called self-destruction, brought on by despondency over Mark's suicide. John's presence, outside the restaurant—he had been seen by Evans—had stymied the second attempt.

McKee said that it *was* Alice Gabrielle had seen in a cab on Sixth Avenue that night. While Evans was busy about his abortive adventure in crime, Brenda had summoned Tyrell to a conference in her cousin's flat on Washington Square. Alice had followed Tyrell, had watched him go in, and had returned home convinced that he was Brenda's lover.

The attempts on Gabrielle's reason, planned by Brenda Holmes and carried out by Evans—he had had keys made for her apartment from the one in Susan's possession—had been made in an effort to convince John that she wasn't sane, that her allegations concerning Mark's death were fancies of a sick mind. Everything that had been done to her had been done by them together or separately, as opportunity offered.

Again the pair met failure. Then had come the planting of three of Mark's bills, still unchanged and in Brenda's hands but too hot to handle, in order to throw active suspicion on Gabrielle. There, however, McKee said, Evans had run into heavy weather.

Glass was in Gabrielle's apartment, doing his little job of examining her desk for Joanna, who was becoming restive and wanted results, when Evans came in, planted the bills in the lamp base, and set the fire that brought about their discovery. From that moment on Glass abandoned Gabrielle and devoted his entire attention to Blake Evans.

Gabrielle's call to John Muir asking him to meet her at Miss Nelson's had been overheard by Brenda when she arrived at his door earlier that evening for cocktails. At that point McKee digressed.

"You, too, misfired that evening, didn't you, Mr. Muir?"

John nodded. "Yes. I suppose you searched my rooms and found the dictaphone? I was convinced all along, as Alice was convinced, that Brenda and Tyrell were lovers as well as companions in crime. I asked the Amorys and Brenda for cocktails, meant to get Alice into another room and leave Brenda and Tyrell alone. I thought they would seize the opportunity to talk things over and I would have final proof. It didn't come off. Tyrell didn't turn up, and I had to go out."

At any rate, McKee said, Florence Nelson, Bertrand Oliver's girl friend, of whose existence neither Brenda Holmes nor Evans had had the slightest suspicion until she was tracked down by Gabrielle, was a pistol pointed at their heads. Gabrielle and John were going to see her. It was nip and tuck there. The meeting couldn't be permitted to take place. Evans went over to Miss Nelson's apartment. She was out. Time was growing short. When she came back he rang her bell, was admitted, represented himself as a friend of Oliver's and told her Oliver was in danger, that the police were on his trail and that they were coming to the apartment to question her. Instant flight was the only thing that would save her and the man she loved.

Miss Nelson had no real idea of what was going on. Oliver hadn't confided in her. She simply knew that he had been engaged in an undertaking that, if not criminal, was on the shady side of the law. Evans impressed on her Oliver's danger should his whereabouts become known, and sent her out of the apartment by way of the fire stairs. He gave her the names of several hotels to try, instructing her not to attempt to contact either him or Oliver, that he would get in touch with her later. Meanwhile she was to remain hidden. Terrified, she did as she was told, wearing a coat she had bought at a thrift shop on her way home that afternoon, a detail which had hampered them in their search for her.

She was safely gone and Evans himself was about to leave—he hadn't many minutes to spare—when Glass, who had followed him to the apartment, admitted himself with the aid of a skeleton key, a handy little tool of his trade he kept by him, and walked into the living-room. "Glass demanded money for his knowledge of the planting of the bills, Evans pretended to agree, diverted his attention and"—McKee shrugged—"just as later, when the chase got too hot, he went to the Hotel Rothingham and eliminated Miss Nelson."

The Scotsman lit a cigarette. "When you saw him with his mother in the coffeeroom the other morning, Miss Conant, Evans was persuading her to give him an alibi covering the time of Florence Nelson's death. You recall his saying earlier that he was in his office, when he wasn't?" Gabrielle nodded stiffly. McKee gave her a veiled glance with worry in it, and continued. "It was in Mrs. Middleton's room in the Waldorf that I first became definitely suspicious of Evans. It was obvious that Claire Middleton was jealous of him, thought he was in love with another woman—you, Miss Conant. Joanna Middleton shared her daughter's suspicions. Joanna was actually following Blake Evans, whom she had tracked from his office, when he entered the Rothingham on the afternoon Miss Nelson was killed. Mrs. Middleton lost Evans but saw you."

McKee said that to kill Florence Nelson was a mistake. Oliver was a poor weak creature, and a perfect tool, but there were limits, and he had a genuine affection for the woman. He was living in isolation in the Glousters' house on the shore but sooner or later he would find out. . . . Another obstacle reared itself menacingly. Tyrell Amory was getting restive. They had managed to convince him, because he wanted to be convinced, that Oliver had killed both Glass and Miss Nelson. Amory wanted to make a clean breast of things, and turn Oliver over to the police. "So"—the Scotsman shrugged—"you know what happened tonight."

Gabrielle nodded. It was all clear, and terrible.

Widening light, iron-gray beyond the curtains; in the bright little shop it was still night. The counter, the

tables and chairs, the salt and pepper shakers, the sugar
bowl, John, the Inspector, were all curiously insubstan-
tial. The real world was the permanent twilight of those
scenes the Inspector had unrolled. Gabrielle was back
in them, must live there always, she thought; she, and
she alone, was responsible for three of the lives that
had been taken. She said so in a low voice, her eyes on
the paper napkin she was fingering. "If I hadn't gone
on insisting that Mark's death was murder, if I had let
it go—those others wouldn't have died."

John had been sitting back, following the Inspector
closely and asking an occasional question, as engrossed
as though she weren't there. When she spoke he leaned
forward and took her hands. "No, Gabrielle," he said,
"you had nothing to do with it. I was the one they were
afraid of. If it hadn't been for me, none of it would
have happened."

He was right, in part, Gabrielle thought drearily, but
a shared responsibility was no help, no panacea. She
knew at last that John had never loved Brenda Holmes,
that he had simply pretended to do so in order to be
able to be with her continuously, watch her closely. She
also knew that he had warned her against marrying
Mark because he was convinced that Mark was still in
thrall to Brenda, in spite of disillusionment. He had
probably stumbled on some hint of her relationship
with Blake Evans. Now Brenda was no longer a barrier.
But what might have been between John and herself,
in another existence, had become impossible with the
weight of those three lives that had been taken dragging
them down. There had been only one albatross. She,
at least, could never endure those three gray ghosts who
would always be with her, in every room, in every chair,
at every table, in corners and in passageways, under the
sun and under the stars, mournful and implacable and
eternally persistent.

The Inspector spoke then. He said crisply, smiling a little, "I don't like to disabuse your minds, but I must. If you, Miss Conant, had never raised your voice, and if you, Mr. Muir, had never come home, if you had re- mained in South America indefinitely, the result would have been the same in the end."

They stared at him, startled, while he told them of Mark's call to him, over his own private wire, made within seconds of Mark's death. He wasn't in New York. Detective Todhunter had taken the call. He told them of Todhunter's conviction that Mark had been killed. He said, "Once we started to investigate, Miss Nelson and Bertrand Oliver were as doomed as though they were already dead and in their graves. They had to be eliminated. As for Glass, he brought his death on him- self. You two retarded us more than you helped; you had nothing to do with what actually transpired. That was foreordained from the moment that the shot that killed Mark was fired. However—credit where credit is due. You did help us tonight, Mr. Muir. We had lost sight of Miss Conant, we didn't lose sight of you. When you followed Tyrell Amory to the Glousters' in his vain attempt to see Oliver tonight, vain because he got no answer and couldn't get into the house, we followed you."

Gabrielle continued to stare at McKee, but without any longer seeing him. The relief was so tremendous that it was almost like pain. A heavy stone rolled away from her heart, unsealing it. She was not responsible. John was not responsible. They were free, unchained, relieved of the frightful burden of guilt.

A horn sounded outside. The Scotsman was on his feet. "I'll leave you now. Later . . ."

Gabrielle didn't hear the rest of what he said. The counterman was in some hidden recess. China rattled and water gushed. She and John were alone. His hands

tightened on hers. His grip was firm, gentle, healing:
They looked at each other. There was no need of words.
The night was gone and it was morning, a gray November morning with an icy wind out of the north. It was a
wind such as had almost blown Gabrielle down when
she had thought that it was Brenda Holmes John loved.
Let it cry now as it would, it was powerless against that
inner warmth that was like wine. Nothing divided John
and her now. Nothing . . .

Coming in, the counterman was astonished at the
order he received. The tall man—athletic type, with
plenty of dough, you could see that—said to him affably,
"Let's have another cup of coffee." And the pretty girl,
who had looked so down and who was now on the up
and up, said over her shoulder, although she had had
no chow, ". . . and let's have another piece of pie," and
her eyes promptly filled with tears.

Half a minute later the two of them were going
through the door, the guy's arm around the girl. The
counterman looked at the twenty-dollar bill in front of
him, then after them. They were getting into the Cadillac convertible out front. He put the bill in his pocket,
reached under the shelf, opened a bottle of beer, and
toasted them. "Here's luck." Drinking heartily, he
watched the car recede around the turn.

www.ingramcontent.com/pod-product-compliance
Lightning Source LLC
Chambersburg PA
CBHW030306200626
46816CB00002BA/780